Colin Bateman was born in Northern Ireland in 1962. For many years he was the deputy editor of the *County Down Spectator*. He received a Northern Ireland Press Award for his weekly satirical column, and a Journalist's Fellowship to Oxford University. His first novel, *Divorcing Jack*, won the Betty Trask Prize.

Divorcing Jack

'A joy from start to finish . . . Witty, fast-paced and throbbing with menace, *Divorcing Jack* reads like *The Thirty-Nine Steps* rewritten for the '90s by Roddy Doyle'   *Time Out*

'As sharp as a pint of snakebite ... Richly paranoid and very funny, and it manages to say more about the Troubles in 280 vivid pages than reams of earnest reportage ever could'
                                                          Sunday Times

Cycle of Violence

'Fast-paced, very black and very funny: Roddy Doyle meets Carl Hiaasen'   *Independent on Sunday*

'Terrific, mordant wit and a fine sense of the ridiculous ... the writing is great'   *Evening Standard*

Of Wee Sweetie Mice and Men

'Fast, furious, riotously funny and at the end, never a dry eye in the house'   *Mail on Sunday*

'If Roddy Doyle was as good as people say, he would probably write novels like this'   *Arena*

Empire State

'Bateman on epic form in gloriously over-the-top saga'
                                                          Daily Telegraph

'A hugely enjoyable novel ... blessed with a beautiful sense of irony ... It's like Carl Hiaasen, Tom Wolfe, and Roddy Doyle at their best'   *The Herald*

BY THE SAME AUTHOR

Divorcing Jack
Cycle of Violence
Of Wee Sweetie Mice and Men
Empire State
Divorcing Jack (screenplay)

COLIN BATEMAN

Maid of the Mist

HarperCollins*Publishers*

HarperCollins*Publishers*
77–85 Fulham Palace Road,
Hammersmith, London W6 8JB

www.**fire**and**water**.com

This paperback edition 1999
1 3 5 7 9 8 6 4 2

First published in Great Britain by
HarperCollins*Publishers* 1999

ISBN 0 00 649803 5

Set in Aldus

Printed and bound in Great Britain by
Caledonian International Book Manufacturing Ltd, Glasgow

For Andrea and Matthew

PROLOGUE

———◆———

Death came to the village set on the banks of the great Niagara. It arrived with the autumn and liked it, so it stayed on into winter.

The Indians prayed and they made offerings to appease the great God Hinum, but the deaths continued. The witch doctors were summoned. They put on their masks and rolled their bones and after many hours cried in one voice: 'A great sacrifice must be made!' Although in Indian.

And so it was that on the eve of her marriage to Sahonwadi, the beautiful princess Lelewala, daughter of Chief Eagle Eye and Najaka, agreed, eventually, to sacrifice herself.

Her betrothed, Sahonwadi, bravest of the braves, labouring over his wedding canoe on the edge of the village, was not told.

Lelewala, her heart heavy, could not even say farewell to him.

But he saw her setting out into the current in her canoe. He raced into the village and only then discovered the awful truth. She looked back and saw him climb into another canoe and paddle after her. She screamed at him to stay, but he would not. He was in love.

He was strong and soon drew level with her. But it was too late. They were in the grip of the great Niagara. Even as the river sucked them over the edge of the Falls he reached out to her and she to him and their fingers almost, almost touched.

And then they were gone.

1

The Artist Formerly Known as Pongo was off his head on coke
again. He lolled in the rear of the white Cadillac as it embarked on
its third trawl through the backstreets of Niagara Falls, occasionally
breaking into backing vocals on one of his own songs as it rattled
out of the speakers, but soon trailing off, bored. It had been a
quiet and unsuccessful night, and his driver, 'Uneasy' Rawlins,
was hoping it would stay that way. His eyes flitted occasionally to
the sad wreck in the back and not for the first time he regretted
the fact that there were no weekends in rock'n'roll. He was still
waiting for his day off. Even God rested on the Sabbath, although
he probably didn't have an album to finish.

'Here,' Pongo yelled from the back, 'stop here! This is the place.
I can *smell* it.'

Rawlins muttered to himself as he pulled the car off the road
into the car park of a rundown-looking diner. They'd exhausted
the regular bars already. Now they were reduced to diners. As a
last resort it would be the brothels. Rawlins would do the paperwork, credit cards and confidentiality agreements, Pongo the screwing. It was satisfactory for neither of them. In the bars he couldn't
drink because he was driving, in the brothels he couldn't screw
because he was married and loved his wife. At least in Texas Slims
he could maybe get something to eat while he checked the place
out.

Rawlins, as per usual, parked the Cadillac far enough from the
main window to ensure that everyone inside had a good view of
it. While Pongo set about organizing another line, Rawlins hurried
across the car park.

It was a little after midnight. There were a dozen customers in
the place. On first look, none of them appeared to be in the required
range. Four fat bikers squeezed into a single booth. Three elderly
black women at separate tables. A young guy asleep beside some

3

school textbooks. Another booth with two couples, holding hands, laughing. Rawlins took a seat and ordered a coffee, glanced back at the Cadillac, then added a hamburger to the order.

As the waitress finished writing, she nodded through the window at the car. 'Who's the bigshot?' she said.

Rawlins's eyes narrowed. *Maybe.*.. she was stick-thin; she was chewing gum; her hair was short and dark; her complexion pale; the only make-up she wore was some badly applied eyeliner.

'Can't say, miss.'

She looked back to the vehicle, then turned and passed the order through to the kitchen. She returned a moment later with his coffee. 'Somebody famous?' she asked. Rawlins gave a little nod. 'Like, *rilly* famous, or just *slightly* famous . . . ?'

He shrugged. 'Depends, miss . . . y'know, on what kind of music you like.'

'Music? Hey, is he a . . . I like all types . . . gimme a clue? Is he, like, on MTV or something?'

Rawlins nodded again. 'All the time.'

'Jeez.'

Not that he was, not for a few years, but people presume, once you get that household name.

Her eyes were wide now, the starry look he'd seen a thousand times. She wasn't far off being hooked. A cute kid. Working late in a diner to keep her in cheap clothes or to pay school fees. Smart enough to serve hamburgers, not smart enough to ask herself why the hell a rock'n'roll superstar needed to trawl second-rate diners for dates. *Dates.* Jesus, that was the word Pongo used. It was quaint and old-fashioned and totally inappropriate. He shook his head. He shouldn't even bother. Say there was no one suitable. Throw her back in the river.

'How's that burger doin'?' Rawlins asked.

'Few minutes. Go on, who is he?'

'He doesn't like to cause a fuss. Hates crowds.'

She crept closer. 'Won't say a word,' she whispered.

'Look, miss, I really . . .'

'Please!'

She virtually squealed it. The bikers looked round. Rawlins summoned a pained expression. Hell, it was what he was paid for. Part of it, anyhow. 'Shhhh now . . .' he said, all cute and folksy,

4

'what did I say? Hates a fuss. OK, if I tell you, you won't shout and scream?'

'I promise!'

'OK. *OK*. A clue. OK?'

'OK.'

'His last album was called *Sincerity*.'

Her brow furrowed. She glanced out at the car. 'Michael Jackson?'

Rawlins shook his head, grinned over the rim of his coffee cup.

'Bon Jovi? Bruce . . . ? Michael Bolton?'

He kept shaking. He set the cup down. *Here we go*. He began to sing, his voice poor, the volume low, but the chorus virtually a national treasure: '*I got the ice/You got the heat/I got the groove/You got the meat . . .*'

'Pongo!'

'Shhhh! Jesus, girl . . . I told you to keep it . . .'

'*Pongo!* At our diner!' She slipped into the seat opposite him and pressed her face to the window. 'He's in there? God!' She put her soft white hand on his arm. 'Could I meet him?'

'Absolutely not.'

'Oh please, please . . . just for one minute . . . please. Just let me say hello. Get his autograph. I have all his records. Please. I'm his biggest fan! Please!'

Rawlins rolled his eyes. 'Well . . .'

'Please!'

'He really doesn't like . . .'

'Please!'

He hunched forward conspiratorially. 'I tell you what. You bring me the burger. If it's good I'll go out and have a word with him. If, and I mean if, he says it's OK, I'll bring you out to see him, OK?'

'Oh God . . . would you!' She was half laughing, half crying. 'Oh God.'

'What's your name, miss?'

'Katharine, Katharine Stewart.'

'How old are you, Katharine?'

'Uh . . . fift . . . seventeen.'

'OK, I'll see what I can do. The burger?'

'Comin' right up! God, I can't believe I'm going to meet Pongo.'

He stuck a finger out at her, cute folksy to stern uncle. 'One thing, Katharine. You must never refer to him as Pongo. If you have to use a name at all, you call him The Artist, OK?'

'The Artist? What's the . . . ?'

'Just do as I say, OK?'

'OK!' She slipped out of the seat and hurried towards the kitchen. 'God,' she whispered dreamily, 'I'm going to meet Pongo.'

Katharine had her top off and Pongo's cock in her mouth.

As he drove Rawlins had one eye on the road, one on the mirror. She was stoned, of course. A couple of lines of the finest Colombian did that to most of the little ones; if they'd used drugs before, and most of them had, they certainly weren't of such quality. Usually they didn't take much persuasion. Katharine certainly hadn't, which was a good thing as Pongo was well beyond using his communication skills. He'd barely grunted at her awed *hi*, merely sat her down, pulled down his zip and shaken his penis at her like it was the polite way of saying hello. And there she was, working away at it like it was an honour to be asked. Rawlins shook his head. Maybe it was.

He mouthed at Pongo in the mirror. 'Home?'

Pongo shook his head and thumbed out the door.

Rawlins nodded. Back to the diner within thirty minutes and just a bad taste in her mouth to remember him by. Not even an autograph. Usually they didn't remember until they were out of the car. Other times he signed with the disappearing ink he had shipped in from a joke shop in Brooklyn.

There was a low groan from the rear. Then the customary awkward silence. Pongo was looking out of the window, bored, not even bothering to zip himself up. The girl was deciding whether it was love or lust: swallow or spit. She decided on love. She looked up at him, still star-struck.

'Gee,' Katharine said, sitting back, wiping her lips, 'I sucked Pongo's cock!'

Pongo's head rolled towards her. His eyes were bloodshot, his nostrils flared. 'I'm not fucking . . . *Pongo* any more!'

She giggled, not sure if he was serious or acting. Rawlins had seen his one movie effort, *Dance Little Sister*, and wasn't sure either. She squeezed his knee, then moved to rest her head on it with the undoubted intention of looking lovingly up into his eyes. Except, she said: 'You'll always be Pongo to me,' as she brought her face down.

Pongo screamed: 'I'm not fucking Pongo!' and brought his knee up, catching her under the chin, ramming her jaw closed and forcing her teeth into her tongue. She leapt backwards, hitting the passenger door with force.

The door shot open. Rawlins yelled as the girl disappeared. He turned, could see just her legs on the back seat. She hung precariously out of the door, her head just a couple of inches off the road. Pongo just looked at her, a half-vacant grin on his lips.

Rawlins slammed on the brakes, but knew immediately it was the wrong action. The girl's legs bounced off the seat and out. As the wheels locked her head crashed off the asphalt with a sickening thud. Pongo's head rebounded off the front passenger headrest. He sat back as the car came to a halt, peering forward to check his face for damage in the driver's mirror.

'What the fuck you doing, man?' Pongo shouted, hand to his nose. There was a drop of blood on his hand. Just one.

Rawlins looked to his mirror, just in time to see a Coca-Cola delivery truck round the bend and crush the rest of the poor little waitress to pulp.

'Oh shit,' Rawlins said.

'Rawlins, shit! Get back in the fuckin' car!'

He ignored Pongo. His legs were jelly, but he walked, walked like a zombie towards her, the crushed little girl. His fault. *His* fault. She was just some dumb waitress working late because she needed the money. Dammit, he knew she wasn't as old as she'd said. She didn't look no more than thirteen. *Thirteen*. And he'd killed her as surely as if he'd thrown her out of the Caddy himself.

Pongo was out of the car now, yelling after his driver. He stamped his silk-slippered feet. Rawlins was walking up to the bitch like he could do something about it and with every step Pongo's career was disappearing down the plughole.

Pongo turned back to the vehicle. The driver's door was open, and Godfuckit if Rawlins hadn't taken the keys as well. Pongo knew for sure he was fucked now. He climbed into the back and scrambled around locating every stash he could remember, then he walked to the side of the road and opened them up to the wind. *Fuck it.*

He turned and looked back up towards where the body lay. He sniggered. At least she'd died happy. And he sniggered again, because the Coke lorry driver had been stupid enough to stop too; he wasn't laughing at that, but at the sign in huge letters on the side of his truck: COKE ADDS LIFE. Not in this fucking case it doesn't.

The Coke man and Rawlins were standing together, a little to the side of the body, and looking up at the windscreen. Pongo giggled. They were examining the damage, they didn't care about the young thing squished across the road. Talking insurance.

As Pongo started to walk towards them, with every intention of offering the Coke man cash to drive on, a police car pulled up. Maybe the Coke man had CB'd them. Maybe they were just passing; whatever, that plan was out the window. Pongo was still about a hundred yards off – cocaine certainly wasn't speed, he felt like he was walking uphill through snow, and in a sense he was – and he could see that there was just one cop. He'd joined Rawlins and the driver in looking up at the windscreen.

Whatever happened to compassion? He would write a song about the death of compassion.

Still, if even the cop was primarily interested in the damage to the vehicle, maybe he could be bought off too. Be more expensive. As much as a million, but shit, the Old Cripple could stump up that much, no problem.

The cop didn't even turn as he drew level. Pongo gave a little smile: it was undoubtedly a tragic accident, but there was no reason why he shouldn't also enjoy the look of shocked recognition when the cop did finally realize whose presence he was in. The Artist Formerly Known as Pongo. He would probably ask for an autograph, and then pretend not to be disappointed when he scrawled 'The Artist'.

Rawlins, the Coke driver, the cop: their eyes, their heads, were moving in tandem, mesmerized by the beat of the windscreen wipers. Pongo followed their gaze and for a bored moment didn't realize what he was seeing.

And then he saw what they saw, and he screamed. Caught in the blades, moving left, right, left right, was the little girl's nose.

2

When Inspector Frank Corrigan called his grandfather to tell him he was going to settle in Niagara Falls, his grandfather shouted: 'What the hell do you want to live in Africa for?' down the line, his voice so strong and caustic that he sounded like he was guldering in the next room, not three thousand miles away in Ireland.

This was way before Lela, of course. This was in the Nicola period, which started about six months after he arrived in town, transferred up after getting shot in both legs dealing with a bank job in Toronto. There's no need to go into *that* too much beyond saying that it was not a good time for him. He was depressed. He drank. He went and wrote something stupid: his signature on the marriage licence, and *that* was the start of the Nicola period.

Of course it didn't seem stupid at the time. It seemed wise and adult and romantic and the way it was meant to be, right up to the point where he was living alone in the darkest, dingiest apartment on Garner Road. Nicola had nailed him for some pretty good alimony, but they still got on OK. She gave him unlimited access to his daughter at weekends. All four of them – that's her new guy, Born Again Bobby, as well – even got together for dinner sometimes. Not too often, as Bobby didn't drink and Corrigan most certainly did. The table chat would invariably get heated, then plain angry, with Nicola somewhere in the middle trying to act as peacemaker even though she knew she should throw Corrigan out for doing it to her again.

That's where he was, causing trouble, cradling the child, drinking a beer, half-watching Canada *vs* Team USA in the final of the Ice Hockey World Cup, the night Maynard Dunn, crewman on the *Maid of the Mist* and occasional drinking partner, called, all excited. Maynard's big voice boomed, 'Hey, Corrigan, we just pulled a woman from the water . . .'

And then the line went dead and there was little Aimie grinning up with her finger on the button. 'Aw for Jesus . . .'

Corrigan bundled her on to the ground and stared at the phone – Bobby smirking at him the whole time – waiting for Maynard to call back, but guessing he wouldn't because he'd be pissed at Corrigan hanging up on him. Nicola eventually got him the phone book, but by the time he tracked Maynard down it was too late; there was no reply.

Bobby was pretending to watch the hockey but the supercilious smirk remained in place and Corrigan had a sudden urge to slap his fat face. He could think of better ways of spending a Saturday night than looking at something blue and bloated, though looking at Bobby wasn't that much less repellent and besides, he'd probably get more interesting conversation out of the corpse.

Bobby was stressed out because he was a manager up at the Sir Adam Beck Generating Stations. He wasn't personally responsible for sucking out the 54 million litres that came from the Niagara River every minute to light up Ontario, but he acted like he was. Bobby was personally responsible for good relations with the employees, and right now the unions were out on strike. There had been threats and accusations and some bastard had released 1.8 million litres of raw sewage into the river just to further muddy the whole situation.

No wonder they're on strike, you big fat balloon, you're an overbearing, self-righteous, judgemental bastard. And my wife chose you instead of me.

Corrigan said he had to go. There was no big campaign to make him stay; even Aimie just gave him a bored *You'll be back* stare and went to sit on Bobby's knee. This annoyed Corrigan as much as it pleased Bobby, but he said nothing. He tousled her hair on the way past and when the door was closed behind them he surprised Nicola with a kiss on the lips from which she extracted herself just milli-seconds into *lingering*. This gave him a nice, warm, if very slightly bitter feeling as he stepped down on to the drive and then looked up at her on the porch.

'Sorry,' he said, with a little shrug of his shoulders. He meant for being argumentative, but she thought he meant for the kiss.

She gave him a little smile. 'That's OK,' she said softly. They looked at each other for a few more moments, then he turned to the car and she shouted after him: 'Are you OK to drive?'

He looked back up. 'Do you want to drive me?'

She smiled and shook her head. He leant against the car. 'So how's it really going with Moses the Lawgiver?' he asked.

The smile faded. 'Don't start, Corrigan.'

'I'm not starting anything. You look like you've lost weight.'

'What're you saying, he *made* me lose weight?'

'No! Just an observation. An unconnected observation. You look good.'

'Thanks, Corrigan.'

'What'd he do, lock you in a cupboard and feed you through a straw?'

'Corrigan . . .'

Corrigan scuffed a foot on the grass. 'I don't like the way he's moving in on Aimie,' he said quietly. 'Does he ever hit her?'

'No!'

'I mean, does he chastise her when she's bad? I'll bet he doesn't, and that's why she likes him and doesn't like me.'

'Corrigan, she *loves* you. You're her father, you'll always be her father.'

'And you were my wife, and you said you'd always be my wife.'

'I thought there was a body up at the Falls.'

Corrigan nodded. 'Well at least she isn't going to run out on me,' he said, and climbed into the car. He regretted it immediately. He rolled the window down and smiled weakly up at her. She hugged herself and managed to return the smile.

'You'll drop by tomorrow.'

'What?'

'The house. There's people coming to see the house.'

'I'll do my best.'

'It's your house, Frank.'

'I know. I'll do my best.'

'Don't do your best, Frank. Just do it.'

He nodded once, but it was neither a nay nor a yeah.

3

'You look like you've been to see the Fat Man,' Maynard said cheerily, turning from the group of crewmen he was chatting to as Corrigan approached.

Corrigan rolled his eyes. 'He's got some sort of sinister hold over her. He's brainwashed her. Drugged her. Subjected her to weird sexual practices. You know it. I saw her reading the fuckin' Bible for godsake. I don't want my daughter exposed to that kind of environment.'

Maynard laughed. 'Still, rather a fat Christian than a loser like you.'

Corrigan managed a little sneer and changed the subject. 'So,' he said, 'tell me about the stiff.'

'A stiff? Who said anything about a stiff? The woman's alive.'

'Oh,' said Corrigan.

The first woman to go over the Horseshoe Falls – as opposed to the smaller, less impressive American Falls a stone's throw down the river (although it would have to be a pretty small stone and a really strong arm) – and ignoring for the moment the legend of Lelewala, was Annie Edson Taylor, a sixty-three-year-old schoolteacher from Bay City, Michigan, who on 24 October 1901 stuffed some pillows into a metal-hooped barrel and climbed in. Her assistants sealed the top of the barrel then pumped in what they believed would be enough air for a week, using a common bicycle pump, before towing her out into the river.

At just after 4 p.m. the barrel went over the edge and instantly disappeared into the curtain of falling water. Seventeen minutes later it floated out from behind the Falls and got dragged ashore. Out staggered Annie Taylor, somewhat delirious but utterly triumphant, convinced that not only fame awaited her, but also fortune. She died in the poorhouse.

At least old mad Annie had had a barrel. *This* woman, whoever she was, if she'd gone over without one and survived, could be worth a fortune in the right hands. The only other person who'd gone over without protection was a seven-year-old boy called Roger Woodward, who'd been swept over after falling out of a boat. It was 1960 and values were different; he was written about all over the world and probably hadn't made a cent.

Corrigan was thinking films. TV. A book. Several books. Newspaper serialization. Why not? Everyone else does it. Befriend her. Sign her up. Shit, he was going to arrest her anyway; get her to write it all down then flog off her statement to the networks. Corrigan tutted, shook his head. Were things really that bad?

Yes they were.

A damp friggin' apartment.

A permanent hangover.

Life's a bitch, then you die.

He looked at his watch. A little after 11 p.m. Maynard had phoned at 10.20. It was a wet, miserable Saturday night and most of the country was watching the hockey. There'd only be skeleton crews on most of the Toronto or Buffalo TV stations. Maybe he'd just ask for her autograph and inquire how she managed to hold her breath for so long.

They rode the lift to the *Maid of the Mist* dock in silence. The Falls illuminations had been switched off at eleven so there was nothing to see, but the sound was thunderous. Corrigan loved it. Loved the power of it. Sometimes he thought he didn't genuinely like Maynard at all, he just liked the excuse to come down here and see him and *feel* the Falls. Since he'd come to Niagara, Corrigan'd been out on the boat nearly two hundred times. Sometimes pressed in with three hundred Japanese tourists, them all decked out in the identical little blue macs they got free to keep the spray off, sometimes with just Maynard, late at night, cruising into the mist.

Maynard punched him on the arm and nodded forward. Corrigan explained about Aimie cutting off the call. Maynard shrugged. 'So what's the crack?' Corrigan asked.

Maynard stopped, looked towards the Falls. 'We pulled a woman from the water. She's alive. Wasn't even wearing a fucking lifejacket.'

'A suicide?'

'Who gives a fuck? She went over. She survived. We got a call from a tourist up on the Parkway, says he's seen a body in the water, just as the lights were being switched off. That's all we need, night like this and Canada one up in the second quarter, but hell ... we get the *Maid* out there and spend fifteen minutes cruising up and down. Finally we see her, floating face down, and drag her in. Thought we just had another floater, but then she coughs up half the river and there she is good as new. Pretty beat up, but good as new.'

'So what'd she say?'

'Nothing. But get this: she's wearing a Native American dress.'

'She's a fuckin' Indian?'

'A Native American.'

'Uhuh. I'm Irish. You're American. She's a fuckin' Indian. That's all we need, an Indian protest. It'll be the friggin' environment. Or they'll be pissed off about not getting a casino on the reservation.'

Maynard shrugged. The rain was growing steadily heavier. Corrigan shivered again. Maynard spent half his life in the Falls' mist; dampness was second nature.

'So,' Corrigan said, 'she's in hospital.'

Maynard shook his head. 'I got Annie Spitz to take her. Keep her away from the vultures, y'know? Gave her a call, explained my situation, within five minutes she was down here, lawyer in tow, signed the Indian ...'

'That's Native American to you ...'

'... on the spot despite the fact that she was staring at a fuckin' wall the whole time, and now she has her own room down at Turner. *You* know that place.'

The Turner Women's Refuge. Through police work, of course. *But also.* Nicola had sought refuge there. Once. They'd been rowing for two days solid and she'd needed the break. To the best of his knowledge there were no refuges for men who needed a break from their wives, except for those that served beer. He'd sat outside in his car, but he hadn't gone in, and after a couple of days she'd come home and they were all smiles again. And then she'd filed.

'Yeah, I know it. Easier to get into fucking Fort Knox.' Corrigan's radio crackled. He said: 'Excuse me,' and turned away. Maynard lit a cigarette and listened in.

'You better come down, Frank.'

It was Mark Stirling, down at the station, sounding breathless.

'Tell me why.'

'Just come down, Frank.'

'Mark, stop being so fucking cryptic.'

'Trust me, you'll love this.'

'Trust me, I'm busy.'

'OK, your loss. I'll handle it myself.'

'Handle what yourself?'

'If you're not interested, it doesn't matter.'

'Mark.'

'Frank.'

'At least give me a clue.'

'I'd give you one, Frank, but I'm not much of a singer.'

'What the fuck is that supposed to mean?'

'I'm being cryptic. Come and see, Frank, you won't regret it.'

He cut the line.

4

Turner House was a three-storey building on Stanley Road. Year round it was a safe harbour for some eight to ten women. That night eight to ten women stared Corrigan down as he was admitted through a side door, then searched. There were jokes to be made about a woman patting him down, jokes about pistols and being pleased to see him, but it wasn't the time or the place so he kept his mouth shut and sucked some more on the breath fresheners he'd found in the glove compartment.

Off to the left he could see a dining table littered with plates and maybe a dozen bottles of wine. 'Celebrating?' Corrigan asked.

'Divorce came through,' said his searcher, a bulky woman with tattoos on her tattoos, who then led him down the hall to a small, cluttered office. 'Wait here,' she said.

Corrigan took a seat. There were piles of folders on the desk, others spilled out of a filing cabinet behind it. One wall was entirely dominated by Polaroids of women. One half of the wall showed them with their black eyes and busted noses and swollen lips; in the other half they were smiling, confident, glasses raised, sisters together. He lifted the cover of the top file on the desk and . . .

'I wouldn't, if I were you.'

He sat back. 'Sorry, just . . .'

'Just leave it alone.'

Annie Spitz was tall, maybe six foot, too thin for her height. She'd a pair of spectacles perched halfway down a slightly bent nose, at the top of which was a thin scar where it had once been split. She wore a man's dinner jacket over a white open-necked shirt and black jeans. He'd seen her talking to the hookers on Ferry Street three or four times and reckoned she was either a pimp or a social worker.

Corrigan stood and extended a hand. 'I'm Frank Corrigan . . .'

'I know who you are.'

'Maynard, of course . . .'

'Maynard, of course. But also – *I know who you are.*' She looked at him over the top of her glasses, patting as she did the pile of folders. She let it hang in the air.

'We're divorced now,' Corrigan felt compelled to say.

'I know,' said Annie.

He glanced at the wall. He felt like there were three hundred bitter women looking at him. Eventually he said: 'Do you mind if I smoke?'

She shook her head. Then she pushed a heavy glass ashtray across the table. 'Do you know that ninety per cent of battered women smoke?' she said.

'Before, during or after?'

'Are you trying to be funny?'

'No. I'm genuinely interested.'

Annie drummed her fingers on the table. 'OK. You're here to see the swimmer.'

Corrigan nodded. 'How's she doing?'

'She's pretty shaken up. She's in her room.'

'Has she said anything?'

'Sure.'

Corrigan leant forward. 'And?'

'And how much?'

'And how much what?'

'How much are you paying?'

'I thought I showed you my badge. Police business.'

She nodded and repeated the question.

Corrigan tutted. 'You'll be looking for a donation to Turner House. How much are you thinking of?'

'Twenty-five.'

'That shouldn't be a problem.'

'Per cent of whatever you make on the story.'

'Whatever *I* make? Lady, I . . .'

'And I wasn't born yesterday. Anyone survives going over the Falls, it's a licence to print money. We're a women's refuge. We need money to survive. *She* will need money to survive. I'm sure we can come to some arrangement.'

Corrigan smiled. 'I suppose it's not unheard of for a few dollars to be offered for my co-operation. The question is, how would you ever know what I make from the story?'

'Because I have the best lawyers and accountants in the state, because I've had all their wives in here at one time or another. They can't afford not to work for me. Do we have a deal?'

She led him up two flights of stairs.

Nicola had been seven months pregnant. He'd come home and found her in bed with Born Again Bobby. Seven months pregnant, and he had a bigger stomach than she did. And she could never explain it, certainly not while he sat staring at the TV, while she walked round and round him, trying to say something, but not saying anything; as Bobby languidly pulled himself into his circus-tent trousers and sauntered out the door like he'd just fucked a $10 whore. Even later, when things had quieted down, she couldn't say how or why Bobby had talked her into bed, although she muttered a lot about hormones.

The whore moans. He'd thought it, but hadn't said it.

When they reached the top floor Annie led Corrigan to the end of a narrow corridor. She produced a key and slipped it into the lock, and, guessing what he was thinking, said: 'For her own protection. There are bars on the window too. They're supposed to stop you lot getting in, but if you're prepared to go over the Falls, jumping out a window isn't going to faze you.'

They stepped into the room. The light was already on. On a single bed opposite the window a woman lay with her back to them. She'd thrown off her bedclothes, exposing tawny skin. A dress was draped over the back of a chair, water dripping from it on to the floor. It looked suitably *native*.

'You asleep, honey?' Annie said quietly. There was no response. 'Poor dear,' she said after a few moments.

Corrigan wasn't impressed. 'Can't you poke her, or something?'

Annie glowered at him. 'Sure. Why don't I just go up and punch her?'

He stepped back. He took hold of the door handle. 'Is it my imagination,' he said, 'or is there a bit of a draught in here?'

'Don't you . . .'

He slammed the door.

The Indian came rearing up out of the bed, naked.

Later, analysing it, he thought his jaw hung down like a fool because she was the most beautiful woman he had ever seen.

5

While Annie hurried her into a nightie and Corrigan looked diplomatically half-away, the words just flowed from her. As she spoke her long black hair danced about her shoulders the way long black hair had danced about shoulders back in primeval times, around the campfire with wolves howling in the background, and warriors and stuff. With the nightie in place she stood and stepped towards him, brushing Annie off as she tried to restrain her. She stared into his eyes and he stared helplessly back.

Her words were tough yet lyrical, guttural but somehow poetic, all aided and abetted by rapid hand movements and little spastic jerks of her head. There was an anger about her, a pleading intensity that threatened to overwhelm him. He wanted to grab her, hug her to him, whisper words of reassurance, but he stood stiff and awkward and embarrassed as the tears began to cascade down her cheeks. She turned from him, disappointment etched on her face like broken stick bridges over a flooded land, and turned her imploring eyes on Annie, who stared back, bewildered. Then she threw up her hands in frustration and sank slowly to her knees.

Annie knelt by her side and put a consoling arm around her. She looked hopefully up at Corrigan and gave a little shrug.

'Have you any idea what the fuck that was all about?' Corrigan asked after a few moments. 'What language?'

Annie shook her head.

The woman – girl, whatever, he reckoned she was pretty young, early twenties maybe – was shivering in Annie's arms, looking at Corrigan and whispering something simpler now, just the single word, over and over.

'It sounds like *sahon. . . waddy . . .*' Annie said, '. . . *sadhon. . . wadi . . . ?*'

The girl looked at her, as if there might be the beginnings of some communication, then pointed suddenly at Corrigan.

She yelled, 'Sahonwadi? Sahonwadi!'

Corrigan raised his palms to her. 'What can I do . . . ? Sahon . . . wadi . . .' he said.

She started to try and raise herself, but her legs had been sucked by the great Niagara and would no longer work for her. Annie tried to help, but her own legs were too long for her to manoeuvre comfortably with such a weight in her arms. They began to splay like a baby giraffe's. Corrigan shot out a hand to help.

The girl cowered back. Annie and Corrigan exchanged glances.

'I guess,' Annie said quietly, 'a refuge is a refuge in any language.'

Downstairs, Corrigan said he was going to the casino.

Annie said: 'Well, that's helpful.'

'I know someone might understand all that crap. And maybe recognize this.'

He held up the girl's dress. It looked black, with the water, but was probably a dark blue. It was elaborately embroidered with light blue, white and pink beads in the shape of a tree. At the front it was buttoned by a series of silver brooches, each around six inches across. Besides feeling damp, the dress smelt *old*. Corrigan suspected that it was either a tribal heirloom, or something that'd been salvaged from a '70s disco.

'Not tonight,' Annie said. 'She's been through enough.'

Corrigan pulled his collar up. 'Just remember, the longer we wait, the quicker it becomes old news, the less money we make for the shelter.'

'If I thought for one moment you were interested in making money for the shelter, Inspector,' Annie said, folding her arms across her chest, 'I'd welcome you back tonight with open arms. As it is, I think you're wasting your time. I've seen cases like this before; women from ethnic backgrounds often revert to their native language when in trauma. You come back tomorrow, I guarantee she'll be speaking perfect English.'

Corrigan stepped out into the rain.

Annie said: 'Well, good luck anyway.'

'Thanks.' It was nice. He stopped, nodded back. 'Incidentally, the scar on your nose. Did a man do that by any chance?'

There was a sharp intake of breath and her face reddened. 'What scar?' she said.

6

Pongo shivered. He cried. He lay on the bed. He stood in the corner. He pummelled his head against the cell door. The police officer with the little Hitler moustache, the one who'd arrested him and hit him with his nightstick when he'd started screaming uncontrollably at the little girl's nose and wouldn't shut up, came in to the cell and started taping up the glass panel in the door.

'What're you doing?' Pongo sobbed.

'Fuck up and sing us a song,' Officer Mark Stirling said.

Pongo sat on the bed and started singing.

The girl's nose, left, right, left, right, left, right.

Or was it right, left, right, left, right, left?

His life was over.

The cop was right. In the squad car he'd said: prison and fucked up the arse by an enormous black man. A beautiful boy was a prized asset in priz. He'd be singing one notch higher by Friday.

He couldn't control his knees. They were popping up and down like he'd been whacked with a reflex hammer. He needed Colombian.

'FBI,' he said again.

'What the fuck is this fixation with the FBI?' Stirling asked again.

'FBI,' Pongo said.

Barry Lightfoot was a member of Egg Scramblers Synonymous (*Synonymous with what? Shit work, man, shit work*) Corrigan knew from his early mornings at the Clifton Diner. Like most short-order cooks, he had another job as well, working overnight as a slot technician at Casino Niagara, the new gambling emporium overlooking the Falls.

Corrigan arrived at a little after 1 a.m., dank and tired, and hurried to the elevator. He rode to the second floor, ignoring the atrium waterfalls and the babble of the high and low rollers. He found Lightfoot, with some difficulty, wedged behind a slot machine; there were fifty one-armed bandits in this particular bank of machines, all but one being played. A low roller, shorts, Hawaiian shirt, three chins, was waiting for Lightfoot to finish repairing his machine. Corrigan tapped him on the shoulder and said: 'Police.'

The guy went to find another machine. Corrigan loved the power of that word. There were others too. *Lawyer, heroin, terrorist* and *hippopotamus* usually got them moving too. Lightfoot didn't look impressed; he watched the gambler depart, then glanced at the ceiling. Corrigan followed his gaze. Video cameras.

'Thanks,' Lightfoot said. Like all of the employees, he was not only immaculately turned out but had also undergone a lengthy indoctrination in customer relations. Rule number one was not to piss them off. His smile remained in place, but his eyes told another story.

'You're working long hours, my friend,' Corrigan said.

Lightfoot turned back to his slot. 'You sound like the Lone Ranger.'

'What do you do, go direct from here to the scramblers?' Corrigan asked.

'I'm working,' Lightfoot hissed in response, 'I've three warnings over my head. Now what the fuck do you want?'

Corrigan produced the dress from inside his coat. He'd half dried it on the car heater on the way over. 'Do you recognize this?' he asked. 'It belongs to one of your people.'

Lightfoot snorted. He barely glanced at it. '*My people.* You mean a slot technician?'

'You know what I mean. She's in some kind of trouble; problem is we can't communicate with her. She's talking ... Native American.'

'Corrigan, I'm not into all that crap. You want to talk to someone, you go down to the basement, ask for Tarriha. Maybe he'll help you.'

'Tarriha. OK. Tarriha. What's that, an old Indian name?'

'Sure,' Lightfoot said, 'means Valet Parking.'

* * *

He found Tarriha in the underground parking bay, jumping from a Merc like a teenager, but his face looked old enough to have spat on Custer at the Little Big Horn.

'Lemme see,' he said when Corrigan told him about the dress. He took hold of it, pressed it against his nose and breathed in. Then he unfolded it and examined the beadwork and the embroidery.

'I'm trying to identify the girl who was wearing it.'

Tarriha's lip curled up. He handed the dress back. 'She dead?'

Corrigan shook his head. 'Can you tell me anything about it?'

Tarriha shrugged. 'Maybe.'

Corrigan took out his wallet and removed a twenty-dollar note. He folded it in half and flicked it back and forth across his fingers.

Tarriha's lip curled further, exposing yellow teeth. 'You insulting me? I am Tarriha, of the people of the hill, of the Tuscorora Iroquois. I earn more than that for parking one fucking Merc, and you're asking me to betray my nation.'

'I'm asking you about this dress. It's no big deal.'

'For twenty bucks you're damn right it's no big deal. Forty bucks and I'll tell you all about it.'

Corrigan gave him another twenty. He didn't mind. They had a fund for this sort of thing. The only problem would be asking for a receipt later. Tarriha crumpled the notes and pushed them into the back pocket of his casino uniform. 'Iroquois dress. You know Iroquois?'

'Sure,' Corrigan replied weakly.

'Iroquois League has six tribes. Mowhawk, Onondagas, Cayugas, Oneidas, the Senecas and Tuscororas. This is Tuscorora.'

'Made on a reservation?'

'Our reservation dresses come from Taiwan. We ain't made them like *this* for fucking ever. Hundred years, two hundred, more.'

'You speak, uh, *Tuscorora*?' Corrigan asked.

Tarriha's eyes narrowed ever so slightly. 'I might,' he said.

When the cab pulled up at Turner House, the whole building was in darkness.

'Ah,' said Tarriha, 'women's refuge. Figures.'

Security lights came on as they approached the front door. Corrigan rang the bell and after what seemed about three hours an eye appeared at a peephole. He shouted his name and said he needed to see Annie.

A couple of days after that, with Tarriha shifting his weight from one foot to another, a hand opening and closing in each of his uniform's trouser pockets as if he was trying to make space for an expected influx of cash, Annie unbolted the door. She was bleary-eyed; she wore a pink dressing gown that was too short in the sleeves, which made her look even taller. Behind her Corrigan could see two other women, each of them strategically placed – one by the telephone and one a little to the right of the door so that she had a clear view of Corrigan and Tarriha, and could shoot either or both of them dead with the shotgun she held confidently to her shoulder.

'I thought I told you to come back tomorrow,' Annie said, looking suspiciously at Tarriha.

'You told me to come back tonight if I was really interested in helping the refuge. And I am.'

'Uhuh.'

'C'mon, Annie. It's better to find out what's wrong now. Maybe she has a kid somewhere, did you think of that? Alone, afraid.'

'I can blow his fucking head off from here,' the shotgun woman growled.

Annie shook her head. She even managed a smile. 'OK, *Corrigan*, maybe you have a point. We'll wake her, your friend . . .'

'Tarriha,' said Corrigan, 'of the Tuscorora Iroquois . . .'

'. . . can have five minutes, at least to establish if she wants to talk, OK?'

She stepped back from the door. As they crossed the hall the shotgun remained trained on them. Tarriha growled, '*Five minutes*,' under his breath. They'd agreed $60 an hour for his translations, irrespective of how long they took. They had an even bigger fund for this kind of thing.

For the second time that night Corrigan was led up the stairs to the locked and barred room. This time Annie knocked softly on the door after unlocking it, then slowly opened it. She lay in the same position as before; her back was exposed; the nightie was draped over a chair.

Annie stepped into the room, followed by Corrigan and Tarriha, and for a few seconds all three of them gazed at the tranquil form lying half-naked on the bed.

Then Tarriha rammed his foot down on the wooden floor, barked like a dog and yelled something in what Corrigan presumed was Tuscorora.

7

Corrigan hurried up the steps into the station. He checked with the desk to see what was happening. There'd been a minor fracas at the casino – there was a convention of flower arrangers or something equally pointless in town that week and it was always the innocuous ones that were the most trouble, like they'd something to prove – and a couple of drunk drivers, but nothing of note, nothing to justify Stirling getting all mysterious.

'Where's Stirling?' Corrigan asked.

'Downstairs with a prisoner.'

'Anyone special?'

'Depends on your musical taste.'

'What's that supposed to mean?'

'I don't know, sir. Officer Stirling instructed me to say that if you asked. I have no idea who it is. Came in with a blanket over his head.'

'OK. All right.'

Corrigan got himself a coffee and went down to the cells. There was a chalkboard at the end of the corridor which showed that two of them were occupied. One by someone called Bernard Rawlins. The other by ?

?

A question mark in cell two.

A question mark, at the very least, over Mark Stirling's next promotion.

Corrigan shook his head and checked cell one. Black guy in a chauffeur's uniform sitting on the edge of the bed.

He opened the door. The guy stood up quickly. He looked scared.

'That's OK,' Corrigan said, 'sit down. You want a coffee?'

Rawlins shook his head.

'What've you done?' Corrigan asked.

Rawlins looked to the far wall, but meaning the other side. 'I done nothing.'

'Next door, huh?'

Rawlins nodded. He sat down, slowly. 'I done nothing,' he said again.

Corrigan pulled the door closed behind him. He peered through the next window. Or tried to. There was tape over the glass. *Fuck.* Corrigan banged on the door. After a few moments it opened a fraction and Stirling peered out. He was grinning.

'Mark. What the fuck are you playing at?'

Stirling peered behind him, then opened the door a fraction more and slipped out. He was that skinny. He pulled the door closed behind him and said: 'You'd never guess.'

'Mark, I don't intend to fucking guess. Just tell me.'

'No, guess.'

'Mark . . .'

'Go on, go on, go on . . . who do we have in there?'

Corrigan rolled his eyes. 'President Keneally. Harrison Ford. The Lindberg baby. How the fuck do I know?'

'Not even close. OK. Three-second clue.' Stirling pulled the door open. Corrigan looked in. Good-looking boy, tear-stained, white jumpsuit, long hair, shivering, nose bleeding, eyes bulging . . . door closed. 'Easy now?'

Corrigan shook his head. He took another sip of his coffee then set it down on the floor. 'Mark, just tell me who it is, before I put *you* in a fucking cell.'

'You really don't know?'

'I really don't know.'

Stirling looked incredulous. 'It's Pongo,' he said.

'Who the fuck is *Pongo*?'

'You're serious?'

'I'm serious.'

'The singer.'

Corrigan shook his head. 'Sorry, lost me.'

'He's *huge*.' Stirling started to sing something, jutting his head forward at the same time, egging Corrigan on to remember it.

'Sorry. Although I hope he sings it better than that. OK, Mark, you've had your fun, now what is the singer Pongo doing in one of my cells, and why all the fucking mystery?'

It was a name given with a child's mix of venom and jest, a soubriquet spat from a split lip after a playground collision at an exclusive private boarding school nestling in the Green Mountains in Vermont. *Pongo*. Ali was thirteen and one of the few students of non-European extraction attending the school and therefore subject to more accidental collisions than most. He couldn't remember now the name of the boy who had delivered it: only the fact that it had mystified him. *Pongo*. He had thought at first that it was a reference to body odour, but dismissed that; if anything, he washed excessively. Soon everyone was calling him Pongo, even the Old Cripple. In fact it wasn't for another six months that he discovered Pongo was from *101 Dalmatians*. And another month after that to establish the connection: spots. His pus-puffed face was a testament to a losing battle with puberty and what were Dalmatians famous for but their spots? He had hated it for a long time, long after puberty had departed and left in its wake a near perfect complexion, and a boy blossomed into youth and not inconsiderable beauty.

He had never really understood what the Old Cripple did for a living, but one day a car came to the school and he was forced to pack his bags and depart with barely an hour's notice. His father was relocating to New York. It meant a change of friends, and a change of name. He was no longer Ali, he was someone else. There had been two or three names since. It was the nature of the Old Cripple's business and he had to accept it. The only thing of lasting value he brought with him from Vermont was Pongo.

A lonely teenager in New York turned to the only thing he had any love for: rock'n'roll. He taught himself guitar, began to compose songs. He bought a drum-machine, then a portastudio – the Old Cripple was, of course, extremely wealthy, despite, or possibly because of his sudden geographical shifts – and recorded a demo in his bedroom. He thought it was pretty cool. Sent it to Warner Brothers. A photo as well. They *hated* the demo, but loved the photo.

So out they came to the current mansion to take a good look at him. Then they closeted themselves away with his father, who knew how to drive a hard bargain. Within a month he was in a real recording studio, he had a producer, a team of songwriters, a stylist, a PR woman, a single, a video and a guest appearance in a top teenage soap opera.

It was the start of Pongo mania.

Twelve number-one singles, hit albums in every country in the Western world.

He sang of teenage love. He swivelled his exquisite hips. The music they chose for him was an odd hybrid of Motown and gangsta rap, with the gangsta removed. Music critics dismissed it as cop-rock: horns, soul and respect for the law. But it came at the right time. Gangster violence was not only tearing up the cities, but the farmlands as well. Music was harsh and tuneless and every second word was *Mothafucka*. This was sweet and wholesome and a mother would be proud to buy it for her children, and she wouldn't mind getting Pongo into bed either.

He was *huge*. For five years he was the number-one-selling recording artist in the United States. If he wore it, it was fashion, if he drank it, it was cool. He said no to drugs, safe sex wasn't even on the agenda. There was no sex at all. During his five years at the very pinnacle of the profession, teenage pregnancies fell by 15 per cent.

And then one day something dreadful happened.

He grew up.

Stirling had a big smile on his face now. He patted Corrigan's arm. 'Frank, Frank. Somedays, somedays the light just shines on you. There was me thinking, god damn this town's been quiet for too fucking long. You know how quiet it's been . . .'

'I know how quiet it's been.'

'Then, there I am driving back to base and there's a fucking accident beside the river. Coke lorry runs over a little girl, fifteen years old. Kills her. Squashes her.'

'That's nothing to laugh about, Mark.'

'No. Of course it isn't.' The smile hadn't slipped any. 'But the joke is, Frank, the fucking joke is – she fell out of Pongo's car. He was fucking her in the back seat and she fell out.'

'He tell you this?'

'No – he's too fucking out of it. His driver did. *He's* scared shitless. I check the car out, what do I find? A fucking pound of coke. A pound, Frank. Sitting there in a fucking cookie jar.'

'OK, Mark. Very good. I await the punchline.'

The grin slipped a little. 'OK, maybe it's not a joke. Maybe it's more like your black comedy. Frank, c'mon, a genuine pop star, the kids love him, their folks love him too, he's as clean as Santa Claus – and we can tie him into the death of a little girl and with enough coke to keep half of Toronto happy. They'll destroy him.'

'And that's your idea of a funny?'

'No, Frank, I'm not thinking of *him*, I'm thinking of *us*. The whole fucking world will descend on us. TV. Radio. Newspapers. One thing they like at headquarters is good publicity. We're talking promotion, big promotion. We're talking the front of *Police Review*. We're talking *celebrity*. The guys that nailed Pongo.'

'And that's why all the cloak and dagger?'

'That's why all the cloak and dagger. We control this, it'll be the making of us.'

'Mark?'

'What?'

'What about the girl?'

'Like I say, squashed.'

'Her name, Mark, her name. What about her parents?'

'Katharine. Katharine Stewart. She's in the morgue. I haven't contacted her parents yet, Frank. I wanted to run this past you first.'

'Run *what* past me?'

'The interviews.'

'Jesus Christ, Mark. There's a dead girl out there and all you can think about is interviews.'

'I can't do anything about the dead girl, Frank. But I can do something about Mister Celebrity cokehead in there.' He slapped his hand against the cell door. His face had coloured a bit and he was looking at Corrigan as if *he* was the crazy one. 'I arrested him, why shouldn't I benefit from it? You can be fucking sure somebody will; why shouldn't it be me? Or us? Look, I'm cutting you in and all you can do is piss on it. I thought you'd be up for it.'

Corrigan sighed. 'Look, Mark, I'm not trying to piss on it. I just

. . . fuck, get a statement from him first, OK. One step at a time, OK?'

'But we can keep it under wraps?'

'We'll keep it under wraps for a while. Sure. It's the middle of the night. See what he has to say.'

'He keeps asking for the FBI.'

'He knows he's in Canada?'

Stirling nodded. 'Sure. Keeps saying we're too small.'

Stirling stepped out of the way as Corrigan moved to the cell door, then pushed it wide with his foot. He stood in the entrance shaking his head at the forlorn figure inside, the Artist Formerly Known as Pongo.

8

Corrigan suspected that someone, somewhere, was doing a rain dance. It was a little after 5.30 a.m. and it had been pouring since shortly after he was born. *It never rains but it pours.* The psycho Indian over the Falls, and Pongo in the cells. Neither of them talking. Well, one of them ranting in an ancient language, the other hugging his knees and repeating *FBI, FBI* for hours on end.

He needed to get cleaned up. There would be camera crews and photographers there in the morning. Hundreds of them. They'd decided to keep the Pongo thing quiet, but word would have leaked out. It was bound to.

He reached his apartment building and tramped unhappily up the stairs. He unlocked the front door and stepped in, kicking some bills out of the way in the process. It was perfectly dry inside, but it *felt* damp. His intake of alcohol was now just a sour brain-aching memory. He stripped off his clothes and left them lying in a heap at his feet. In the bathroom he used his elderly electric shaver, then razored the rest of the growth off under the shower. The hot water relaxed him almost to the point of a standing sleep. When finally he staggered out, Corrigan stood for several moments examining his ghostly reflection in the mirror, then sprayed shaving foam under his arms.

He burst out laughing and returned to the shower to wash it off. And suddenly he wasn't laughing any more. It was the sort of stupid thing he might have done before, but the joy of it would have been walking into the bedroom and showing Nicola; they both would have roared with laughter. But now there was no one: there was a pile of wet clothes and the faintly musty smell of a lonely life.

He dressed, and was heading out of the door when he noticed the red eye winking on the answerphone. He tutted and hurried across. There were three messages: the first from a reporter called

Madeline Hume from Channel 4 in Buffalo; her voice was warm, with a hint of flirtation, which he thought was pretty depressing in a complete stranger on a friggin' answerphone, saying she'd heard about the Native American woman who'd gone over the Falls.

Can we talk? Of course we can, we can talk about how you managed to get my unlisted number. He glanced at his watch and wondered how much Sitting Bull had managed to wring out of the swimmer.

The old Indian had insisted on being left alone with her. He had also insisted on a bottle of whisky and cigarettes, and then he'd locked the door. Neither Annie nor Corrigan thought it was a great idea, but the girl, although she looked confused, had remained silent while Tarriha spoke, and she did seem calmer. In the end they decided to take the chance. Annie, naturally, insisted on her putting the nightie back on before they left.

Annie and Corrigan sat on the stairs at the end of the hall. Corrigan smoked. Annie coughed. It was a true partnership. Every twenty minutes Corrigan knocked on the door and asked how much longer they'd be, but all he got in response was something guttural from Tarriha that he would probably have found quite offensive if he'd understood it. Finally he'd whacked his fist against the door in frustration.

'Hey Corrigan,' Tarriha said, remaining behind the locked door, 'this story, it don't come in one straight line. It comes in knots, man, know what I mean? I gotta untie, I gotta straighten, I'm earning my money, Corrigan.'

Corrigan tutted. 'C'mon. Give me something. Do you even know her name?'

There was silence for several moments, then Tarriha said slowly: 'Lelewala.'

Can we talk? Sure, we can talk, we can talk about Lelewala. It's a hit and myth affair.

The myth: an Indian princess who sacrificed herself by rowing over the Falls to appease the Gods who had loosed a terrible evil among her people.

The rumour: a story made up by white men to attract more tourists.

The hard-sell: t-shirts, mugs, umbrellas, sweaters, all bearing her likeness.

The second message was from Nicola. She was crying. 'Corrigan, are you there? Can we talk?'

Yeah, sure, you've had a blow-up with Born Again Bob and you want to cry on my shoulder. Except you divorced my shoulder. And my head, and my heart.

The third message was from Nicola as well; the information panel above the tape said it had been recorded at 4.15 a.m., two hours after her first. She sounded calmer, but somehow sadder. He could just hear Bob's dull monotone in the background. If Bob had started at, say, midnight, it would probably take him another three weeks to read her the whole Bible.

Nicola my dear, you've made your bed, and now you're going to have to lie in it with that big fucking whale.

At a little after seven he met Stirling at the Clifton Diner. They ate eggs and bacon while Stirling hummed and hawed over a press statement he'd typed up about the illustrious Pongo. By rights it should have gone through headquarters, but Corrigan didn't mind his partner having his little moment in the public eye. He'd probably shuffle into the photographs himself. There'd been half a dozen reporters outside the station. All of them for the swimmer. Evidently the station wasn't as leaky as he'd thought.

Although the summer rush to the Falls was over and business was now winding down for the winter, the diner was as busy as ever. As usual there was a convention in town. Horticulturalists, this time. Here to network and see the Falls. But it took five minutes to see the Falls and you couldn't work all the time. So they were filling up on a big breakfast and getting ready to hit the casino. Corrigan had half expected them to be little old lady florists here for a winter break, but they were big guys, tough and sharp and bejewelled. It was just like any other business, he supposed; say it with flowers, sure, then nail them on the percentages.

His phone rang. 'If it's Letterman,' Stirling said, 'tell him to join the queue.'

Corrigan rolled his eyes. 'What?' he said.

'Corrigan? It's Annie Spitz.'

'Annie. What's happening? Has Kissinger emerged yet?'

'I think you better come down.'

She sounded stressed. 'What's the matter, what's wrong? Is it
. . . Lelewala?' He surprised himself by using the name so easily.

'Just get down here,' Annie said plainly, then put the phone
down.

9

Corrigan was searched then ushered down the hall to Annie's cluttered office. She nodded grimly as he took a seat.

'By my calculations,' Corrigan said dryly, 'yer man upstairs has cost the Canadian taxpayer somewhere in the region of $500 already. I hope to God you have good news for me.'

Annie sighed. 'Corrigan, I don't normally do this, in fact I *never* do this, but as we seem to be working together . . . I should tell you that your ex-wife is upstairs.'

'*She* speaks *Tuscorora*?'

'She came in a couple of hours ago. I'm afraid she's been assaulted.'

His first reaction was involuntary: his face reddened and he said: 'It wasn't me.'

Annie's look was initially confused, and then sympathetic. She had first thought of him as arrogant and self-possessed, but this confirmed her later assessment of him as merely insecure. She could see the pulse throbbing on the side of his head, the fingernail going to his lips, the eyes settling on nothing, nowhere. She wondered which way he would go. Prior to her work at Turner Annie had worked as a probation officer and she reckoned there were two classic reactions to this type of situation: those who would rush immediately to console the injured party, and those who would first seek revenge on the perpetrator. Those who sought revenge first, she found, generally didn't love their wives at all, but were merely re-enforcing property rights; those who consoled their wives were generally in love. Those who did neither were rare. And usually unbalanced.

'Is she badly hurt?'

'Her face is pretty banged up. It'll heal. She asked for you.'

Corrigan nodded. His eyes flitted to the pictures of the battered

36

women on the wall. 'I loved her more than anything,' he said slowly, 'and she broke my heart.'

'That's sad, Corrigan.'

'Yeah.' And then his eyes jolted suddenly back towards Annie. 'Jesus Christ – Aimie. My daughter, is she . . .'

Annie raised a placatory hand. 'She's OK. We've a play area out back; she's with the other kids.'

Corrigan let out a sigh of relief. He pushed his chair back and stood. 'I should go and talk to Nicola.'

Annie shook her head. 'Can't do that, Corrigan.'

'Why the fu . . .'

'He broke her jaw.'

'Oh.'

'We have a surgeon on permanent stand-by. We could do a heart transplant upstairs if we had to. Her jaw's all wired up.'

The fingernail returned to his lips. When he spoke his voice was slightly strangled, although it wasn't the question she expected.

'How did she ask for me then?'

'Pen and paper.'

'She called me twice last night. Looking for help.'

'You refused?'

'I was *here*, for godsake.'

'Ironic.'

'Where is she?'

'I'll show you.'

Corrigan sighed loudly. 'Can't you just tell me? I'm not a fucking child.'

'I know what you are, Corrigan. You're a man. And that's why we're so fucking busy.'

She had panda eyes. So swollen that the tears had to go on an uphill journey before they could flood down her cheeks. He hugged her gently while Annie hovered in the doorway.

When they parted Annie said: 'Do you want me to leave you alone?'

Corrigan nodded, but she stayed where she was. For a moment they didn't understand, then it dawned on Nicola and she nodded.

37

Annie left, but the door remained ajar and her footsteps sounded down the hall, although not very far down the hall.

'Oh God,' Corrigan said, looking at her face.

She lifted a notepad from beside the bed and scrawled quickly, *Am I that bad?*

'No! *No.*' Her eyes remained fixed on him. 'Well, yes,' he added. 'What happened?'

Aimie saw you kiss me through the window. She told Bobby. He wasn't impressed.

'So it's my fault.'

No!

'I'm going to throw that fucker in the river.'

No.

'Nick, he's going inside for this.'

No.

'You're just going to let him get away with it?'

She shrugged.

'Has he done anything like this before?'

She shrugged again.

'Why do you stay with him?'

I love him.

'But you call me when you're in trouble.'

I love you too, Corrigan.

10

His face was red and his heart was drumming. He kept saying to himself: leave it, let it be, it's not your business any more. Police business, sure, but not *your* police business. But the pedal was to the board and before he really knew it he was outside the Sir Adam Beck Generating Station. There were about thirty pickets standing with placards by the entrance, and two cops keeping a lazy eye on them. They straightened up as he approached and he chatted to them for a few moments, like he was just there to check up on them, then drove on through to the administration block.

He arrived at the front desk and asked to see the wife beater.

'Wife . . .' said the receptionist, looking at first down a list of employees as if it might be a position within the company. Something down among the generators, something oily. Then she looked up and said: 'Oh.' She was a matronly woman with a tight black perm and lipstick on her teeth.

'Bobby Doyle.'

'Why, Mr Doyle isn't married.'

'*My* wife, missus.'

'Oh, well, I don't . . .'

'Just tell him I'm here. Frank Corrigan.'

'And what company are you with, Mr Corrigan . . . ?'

'The Royal Shakespeare.'

She looked at him blankly for several moments, then lifted the phone. 'Mister Bobby? There's a Mr Corrigan from Royal Shakespeare to see you.' She gave a little giggle to whatever the response was then nodded and replaced the receiver. 'Go on up. The elevator's on the left. Second floor.'

Bobby sat behind an expansive desk, in an expansive office, with expansive views. He had an expansive girth and an expansive mouth and the way he sat, with his head tilted down, his chins seemed to cover a wide expanse of his chest. This was the man Nicola regularly climbed on top of to make love. At least that was the way Corrigan figured it. He couldn't imagine Bobby on top at all. The poor woman would die. Bob waved Corrigan into a chair and said, 'To what do I owe the pleasure?' Corrigan crossed the floor and took the seat, all the time trying not to picture Bob naked and rippling and screwing his wife.

'You broke my wife's jaw,' he said.

Bob closed a folder, sat back, put his hands behind his head and smiled. 'I broke your ex-wife's jaw.'

'I don't believe you're smiling. I really don't believe that.'

Bob opened a drawer and took out a cigar. He lit up and blew smoke across the desk towards Corrigan. 'I'm smiling because I'm fascinated, fascinated by what you plan to do about it. You try to steal *my* woman, and you come here to complain about *my* behaviour.'

'I gave her a peck on the cheek. You broke her fucking jaw, for God's sake.'

'You're right. For God's sake I did. And now she knows not to do it again.'

'I thought you were supposed to be a Christian?'

'I am.'

'What is it, some obscure branch of the Presbyterians, the "if thy wife offends thee beat her fucking brains in" branch?'

'There's no need for profanity, Corrigan.'

'There fucking well is. Lots of fucking profanity.'

Christians. He'd had enough of them back home in Ireland. Fighting with each other. Killing each other. All in the name of love. And now here was Big Fat Bob crowing over breaking his wife's jaw.

Corrigan removed his pistol from its holster.

'You needn't think you're going to scare me with that,' Bobby said. But suddenly he didn't sound quite so bullish.

'We've just got these,' Corrigan said, rubbing his hand down the barrel. 'Upgrades. Used to be .38-calibre service revolvers. This is a .40-calibre semi-automatic Glock pistol. It can do a lot of damage.'

He let it sit for a few moments, then smiled. Bobby didn't like the smile. He swallowed. He'd gone a little pale. He was remembering. One of the workers had gone postal with a gun five years before. Wounded fourteen. He looked at Corrigan, at his pale face and his red eyes, and wondered.

'You're pretty sure I'm not going to shoot you,' Corrigan said, keeping his eye on the gun. 'It would be pointless. Nicky's not dead, she doesn't want to press charges. Why lose my job, go to prison over a woman who betrayed me? But then you're thinking, what's to stop him claiming he was attacked? That someone angry enough to break a woman's jaw isn't going to go peacefully when a cop comes to arrest him. He's a cop, for godsake, he can make it look like there was a struggle. Are you thinking that, or am I reading you wrong?'

Bobby just looked at him. He wasn't thinking *anything*. His sweat glands were, though. It was a cool room, but there were suddenly puddles under his arms. They *dripped*.

Corrigan turned the gun slowly until it was pointing at Big Fat Bob. 'The thing is, *Bobby*, I'm from Belfast. I was a cop there for five years. You ever hear of the Falls Road? I was stationed there. Toughest beat in Europe. We shot terrorists for breakfast. Do you understand what I'm saying? Once it gets in your blood, it stays in your blood. I could shoot you dead, right now, and not even think about it, because I'd get away with it. Back home, we did it all the time, because they were never going to end up in court. They were killers, but the law protected them. So we had to get rid of them our own way. Do you understand what I'm saying?'

Bobby nodded slowly.

'On the other hand,' Corrigan continued, 'this is Niagara Falls. It's a nice and peaceful land. There's really no need for a gun.' He set it down on the desk. Bobby's eyes flitted to the weapon, then back to Corrigan. 'I carry it with me all the time, but it isn't always loaded. Depends how I feel in the mornings. One morning I'll load it all up, just in case. Others, I'll empty it. Keep it empty. You can feel too secure with a gun; sometimes it's good not to carry that responsibility around with you. That *possibility*. Do you understand what I'm saying?'

Bobby nodded again.

'Thing is,' Corrigan said, 'I just can't remember whether I loaded it this morning or not.'

Bobby swallowed. Suddenly he knew what was coming.

Corrigan lifted his gun. He aimed at Bobby's chest. His finger slipped on to the trigger.

'You *know* it's not loaded,' Corrigan said.

Bobby nodded. But he was thinking of his last words.

'You *know* I wouldn't shoot you even if it was.'

Bobby nodded. He tried to picture the Lord, but he could only picture the gun.

'But I want you to swear to me that you'll never lay a finger on her again. Because if you do, I'll come and find you and I *will* shoot you. Do you swear that?'

Bobby nodded.

'Say it.'

'I swear I won't lay a finger on her.'

'That's better. Now just remember it.'

Corrigan pushed his chair back and stood. He looked down at Bobby and said: 'You need an ashtray.'

Bobby followed his gaze and saw that the forgotten cigar clamped tightly in his hand had burnt clear down to the tip, burning his fingers in the process, and he hadn't even noticed. Now he did. Now he felt the pain. He gave a little yelp and let go of it, pushing back in his chair and cupping his burned fingers protectively in his other hand as the glowing remnants of the cigar peppered the paperwork on his desk.

Corrigan turned to the door. He still had the gun in his hand. When he reached it Bobby called after him. 'Corrigan – I'm sorry.'

'Don't apologize to me, Bobby. Apologize to her.'

Bobby nodded.

Corrigan opened the door.

'Just one thing,' Bobby said. 'Was it loaded?'

Corrigan looked at him. He raised the gun.

He pointed it.

He pulled the trigger.

11

Corrigan had just parked outside Turner House when a car door slammed behind him and a young woman in a black trouser suit and high-heeled ankle boots came clip-clipping up to him.

'Inspector Corrigan, isn't it?' she said, her head jutting forward and her smile small and slightly self-conscious, which made him think maybe she wasn't sure about her teeth. She looked to be roughly his age. She had red hair, cut short. Her nose was slightly turned up, as if it had been thumped repeatedly by a small person. 'Madeline Hume, Channel 4. I left a message for you. You didn't get it?'

'I got it. Ignored it.'

'Oh. You gave the story to someone else.'

'I didn't give the story to anyone. It's not mine to give.'

He continued to walk towards Turner House. She followed after him. 'Why not?' she said to his back. 'She's being held here at your request.'

Before he rang the bell he said: 'Because I have a few loose ends to tie up.'

'Maybe I can help.'

'I doubt it.'

He rang. In the three weeks before it was answered she said: 'Are you being deliberately nasty, or have I done something to annoy you?'

'Deliberately nasty.'

'The woman's in there, isn't she? The one who went over the Falls?'

Corrigan nodded wearily.

'They wouldn't let me in to talk to her.'

The door opened. Annie Spitz nodded out at him, then rolled her eyes at Madeline Hume. 'I thought I told you to fuck off!' she barked.

Madeline turned to Corrigan. 'Sisters,' she said, 'always stick together.'

Corrigan was as surprised by Annie's venom as Annie herself evidently was. She blushed and waved her hand in front of her face. 'God, I'm sorry,' she said hurriedly, 'it's been pandemonium this morning.'

'Annie,' Corrigan said, peering forward to see if the big woman with the shotgun had him in her sights, 'tell me Tarriha's finished with her. Tell me I don't owe him any more money.'

'Who's Tarriha?' said Madeline.

'Tarriha,' said Annie, 'is not only finished, but gone. Split.'

'Oh for Jesus . . . what about Lelewala?'

'Who's Lelewala?' said Madeline.

'Lelewala's gone too. She wouldn't stay. What could I do? Before you ask, Nicola's gone too. Took Aimie. Must be the cooking.'

'Nicola . . . ?' began Madeline.

'Jesus, Annie, I thought this was a secure house . . .'

'Hey, c'mon, it's secure for those who want to be secure. It's not a prison.'

Corrigan tutted. Annie glared. 'Did they say anything? Did they give any indication of where they were going?'

'Who?' Annie said, exasperated. 'Which one? They weren't moving collectively.'

'*Any* one.'

'Nicola's gone home. Said someone . . .'

'That fat bastard . . .'

'Listen to me . . . she said someone was coming to look at the house. At least, she *wrote* someone was coming to look at the house.'

Corrigan threw up his hands and blew out some air. 'OK. *OK*. Lelewala. *Did* she revert to English?'

'I don't know. She didn't say anything. She just ran out.'

Corrigan let out a deep sigh and leaned his head against the door frame.

'Could one of you tell me what's going on round here?' Madeline asked, looking from one to the other.

'Too much,' Corrigan said, 'and not enough.'

12

Corrigan let Madeline take him for coffee. He didn't know why. It just seemed like the least stressful option. It was a dingy café in downtown Niagara. Half a dozen tables. Packets of salt stolen from McDonald's sat in little cups. It saw maybe five or six tourists a year. There was a yellowing *Maid of the Mist* t-shirt for sale behind the counter.

'So,' he said half-heartedly, 'you operate out of Buffalo.'

'Channel 4. About a year. New owner brought in a fresh news team when he took over. I'm from Albany. You?'

'Niagara,' said Corrigan.

She looked doubtfully at him. 'Tell me about the woman,' she said.

'I could tell you,' Corrigan said, 'but then I'd have to kiss you.'

'*Kiss* me?'

'*Kill* you.'

'You said *kiss* me.'

'I did not.'

'You certainly did.'

'You may have wanted me to say kiss you. But I did not. Why would I want to kiss you?'

'You tell me.'

They looked at each other. Corrigan resisted a smile. Her face reddened. 'I'm sorry if I misheard,' she said.

She had a nice face. She was friendly. He lit a cigarette.

'If it's a question of money,' Madeline said, 'I'm sure we could sort something out.'

'Are you trying to bribe me?'

She smiled. 'I was thinking more in terms of paying for the coffee.' She reached over and took one of his cigarettes. She lit it, blew smoke in his direction.

The waitress stumped across with a glass ashtray and cracked it down on the table.

The ashtray said Budweiser across it. The waitress said nothing.

'I know a Native American went over the Falls,' Madeline said, 'and that there must be a reason for it, but every reporter in the state is on to it by now. The longer we leave it, the less valuable it becomes.'

Corrigan nodded. 'So meet my terms.'

'What *are* your terms?'

'Coffee *and* a danish.'

'I don't think that will be a problem.'

'And a five-hundred-dollar donation to Turner House.'

'What's got you so keen on Turner House?'

'They do a good job.'

'Who's Nicola?'

He took a sip of coffee. 'You ask a lot of questions.'

'Actually, I think that's my first. Or second.'

His mobile rang. He said, 'Excuse me,' and turned away.

It was Stirling. 'You better come in, Frank.' His voice sounded a little strained.

'What's the problem?'

'Pongo's the problem.'

'What's Pong . . .' He stopped. He looked at Madeline, then turned slightly to one side. 'What's happened? You get him talking yet?'

'Yes sir, I did.'

'So?'

'I think you better come down.'

There was silence for several moments, then Corrigan said: 'I'll be right there.' He clicked off, then stood suddenly, the chair squeaking on the dark linoleum floor. 'I'm sorry,' he said, 'but I have to go.'

'What's . . . ?'

'Police business.' He turned for the door. Madeline pushed her chair back and hurried after him.

'What about the girl?' she said.

'What girl?' He opened the door and stepped out on to the sidewalk.

'The girl that went over the Falls.'

'Sorry. You know as much as I do.'

'No I don't.'

He stopped. 'No, in fact you don't. I'm sorry. There's nothing much I can tell you. She's run away. I'll have to track her down. If you can do it, be my guest. Then give me a call.'

He smiled and turned away.

She tutted. He walked back to his car and opened it up. He started the engine. There was a tap on the window.

It was Madeline. 'Inspector?'

He rolled the window down. 'What?'

'Could you lend me a couple of bucks for the coffee?'

'What?'

'I came out without my purse. I'm sorry.'

He rolled his eyes.

'Sorry,' she said. 'You can arrest me if you want.'

He smiled. He checked his wallet. He'd given his smaller notes to Tarriha. There was just a single hundred-dollar note. He took it out and made a show of examining it. She smiled and plucked it out of his fingers. 'Thanks,' she said and hurried back to the café.

'I'll wait here for the change,' he called after her.

She didn't respond. He looked at her bum as she walked. It was nice and small. When he raised his eyes a little higher he realized that she was standing in the door of the café looking at him looking at her bum. He looked away.

A minute later she hurried back to the car. He rolled the window down again to collect the change. But she ignored him and walked round to the other side and slipped into the passenger seat. 'She looked like she'd never seen a hundred before,' Madeline said breezily, then looked expectantly at Corrigan. 'The least you could do,' she said, 'is give me a lift back to my car.' She handed the change to him. He started to count it.

'Don't you trust me?' she said.

'No,' said Corrigan. He took out five dollars and handed it back to her. She looked confused. 'What's that for?'

'A taxi.' He reached across her and pushed the door open again. 'I told you, I'm in a hurry.'

She nodded. Then she pulled the door closed again and said: 'Who's Tarriha?'

'What?'

'Annie Spitz mentioned Tarriha. What's he, another Indian?'

'That's Native American.'

'Native American. Is that what he is?' Corrigan nodded. 'What was he doing? He her lawyer?'

'Translating,' Corrigan said.

Her brow crinkled. 'Translating what?'

'What do you think?'

'Do you know where he lives?'

'I could tell you if I knew you better, but at the moment I have my reservations.' He smiled.

'You *can* trust me,' she said. She smiled winningly, but not winningly enough. Corrigan shook his head. Another time, another place. 'Ask around,' he said. 'You're the reporter.'

She looked at him. The smile had become a scowl. 'OK,' she said, 'I get the message.' She crumpled the five dollars in her hand and dropped it into his lap. 'I'll survive,' she said, and got out of the car.

13

Pongo looked up. He was a pitiful sight. 'I want you to understand,' Corrigan said, 'that I have no idea who you are, and I haven't a fucking clue what your songs are like. On that basis, shall we proceed?'

Corrigan pulled out a chair and set it down in front of him. He straddled it. Stirling remained at the door. There were tears on Pongo's face and snot above his top lip. His eyes were poisoned rabbit red and his gums were bleeding. He was one step down from miserable, coke-miserable, or lack-of-coke-miserable. Diet Coke. 'I wanna make a deal,' he said.

'A record deal?' Stirling said from the door.

Pongo buried his face in his hands. His shoulders started to shake.

Corrigan reached forward and slowly eased the hands away from Pongo's face. 'Son, there's a little girl has died. She fell out of your car. And you had an awful lot of drugs in that car. Do you mind telling me what kind of a deal you had in mind?'

'I can't tell you. They'll kill me.'

'Of course you can.'

'I can't!' Pongo sat back on the bed and wiped something green and stringy away from under his nose with the sleeve of his white jumpsuit. 'And even if I did, they'd kill you. So what's the point?'

Stirling rolled his eyes. 'Just tell him,' Stirling said. 'You told me.'

Corrigan sighed. 'Son, do you want me to call your lawyer?'

Pongo sprang forwards. 'God-fuck *no*. He's part of it.'

'Part of what?'

'Can't you get me the FBI? *Please?*'

'Son, we are not getting the FBI for you. This is Canada.'

'K-A-N-A-D-A,' Stirling said from the door.

Pongo shook his head against his hands. Then his eyes appeared above his fingers. 'I can't go to prison,' he whispered, 'they'll kill me.'

'I didn't say they'd kill you,' Stirling said, 'I said they'd *fuck* you.'

'You don't understand!'

Corrigan shook his head. 'Plainly not,' he said. He turned for the door.

'Wait!'

He stopped.

'Can we make a deal? To keep me out of prison. To let me stay here. I like this cell. It's good.'

'It doesn't work like that, son.'

'C'mon!' He was having trouble catching his breath.

'Just take it easy, son.'

He took a deep gulp of air and then let it slowly out. 'You mean,' he said, 'if I offered you something big, so incredibly big it was bigger than the biggest thing you ever thought of, you couldn't cut me a deal?'

Stirling clicked his tongue. 'If it was bigger than the biggest thing we ever thought of, sure we could cut you a deal. If it was that big.'

'Mark . . .' Corrigan said.

Stirling stepped forward and slipped into Corrigan's vacated seat. 'Hey . . . c'mon, Pongo, don't spoil the show, tell him about the convention.'

Pongo snorted up. It wasn't pleasant. 'I didn't mean to kill the girl,' he said, his voice weak and high, 'it was an accident. I really didn't. But I can't go to prison. I can't. I have such plans, big plans. I wanna write a proper album. Proper songs. Songs that mean something. I don't want to be the fucking corporate entertainment at my father's convention.'

Corrigan leaned back against the door and folded his arms. 'Who's your father?'

'The Old Cripple.'

'The Old Cripple?'

'The Old Cripple.'

'Who the fuck's *the Old Cripple*?' Corrigan said.

'He's a superhero for the disabled,' Stirling said. Then said: 'Tell him.'

Pongo shook his head despairingly at Stirling. 'That's why I need the FBI! If he hasn't heard of . . .'

'Son . . .' Corrigan began.

'I know! No FBI. OK, OK!' Pongo's nose cracked audibly as he wiped it on his sleeve again. He tried to steady his breathing again. 'My father,' Pongo said. 'The Old Cripple. Everyone knows him as the Old Cripple. He's running a convention in town right now. Horticultural convention.'

'Town hasn't smelt so good in years,' Corrigan said.

'Except, it isn't flowers they're conventing about.'

'Conventing?' said Stirling.

'What is it, son?'

'It's drugs. *Drugs*. A drug convention.'

'Like medical and pharmaceutical?' said Corrigan.

'Like heroin and cocaine and acid and Ecstasy and every fucking drug in the world.'

'Oh, right. I see.' Corrigan looked at Stirling.

'He's serious,' Stirling said.

'Uhuh.'

'I swear to God. Every major drug baron in the world is here. They're carving up the world. Signing deals. I swear to God. They do it every year. Different location.'

'I think,' Corrigan said, 'we might have noticed.'

'I'm telling you the truth. I swear. I mean, I mean . . . Jesus . . . it's not the sort of thing you make up . . .'

'Unless you're coked up and facing murder one.'

'For fuck . . . I mean . . . c'mon . . . c'mon . . . I can prove it . . . I mean, I can name names, I can do that. Get a pen, get a pen . . . get paper . . . get paper . . .'

He was starting to lose the thread.

Corrigan sighed. They'd have to get a statement out of him one way or another; perhaps giving him paper would get him started. They'd have to contact his people, his father, whoever he was, maybe his record company, get him a lawyer. Before dinner there'd be a suit from New York or LA organizing bail.

Stirling got him paper. 'What're you playing at, Mark?' Corrigan asked as he hurried back.

'I think it's brilliant,' said Stirling. 'He's fucking deranged.'

He made a great show of putting the paper down and brandishing a pen. 'Right then,' he said, 'there you go. Get some of those names down; we'll soon get this convention sorted out, then we'll see what we can do about these charges.' He stopped and scratched his head. 'Of course, if they really were international drug dealers, they wouldn't be staying here under their real names, would they?' He winked across at Corrigan.

'Of course not!' Pongo exclaimed. 'But they're here. Here! Right here! Shit, shit ... OK... the names ... the names ... I'll give you some names. You check them out, you check them out and then tell me whether I'm crazy. I know you think I'm crazy, but I'm not crazy. You'll see.'

He sniffed up hard, then bent suddenly to the paper and started to scribble. Stirling looked across at Corrigan and winked. 'How many names you reckon you'll have for us, Pongo?'

Pongo didn't look up. 'Don't know. Maybe twenty, thirty.'

'Not a very big convention, then.'

'Shit, man, those are only the names I can remember! There's a hundred and fifty of them *at least*.'

'Tell me,' Corrigan said, 'do you see drug barons everywhere you look?'

'Yes!' He continued to scribble furiously. 'I just want to make my music. I don't want to go to gaol. I give you this, you let me go, OK?'

Stirling nodded thoughtfully. 'We can't just cut you one like that, Pongo, we have to check this out.'

Pongo's face sagged a little and he stopped writing. 'I can wait here while you check it out, can't I? I like it here. It's safe. I didn't mean to kill the girl.'

'We'll see what we can do.'

Corrigan opened the cell door, allowing Stirling, smirking, through first. Just as it was closing Pongo said: 'Be careful.'

Corrigan paused a moment. 'Why?' he asked.

For a moment Pongo's face assumed a seriousness Corrigan had not noticed before; his voice was deeper and his gaze steady. 'Don't underestimate the importance of this convention to the people involved. It can only take place in conditions of utmost secrecy. People have been bought off. People have disappeared. If you try checking this on a police computer, you will disappear as well.'

Corrigan nodded. 'Well if we can't check it,' he asked, 'how can we possibly know if you're telling the truth?'

Pongo nodded thoughtfully. 'You'll just have to trust me,' he said.

Corrigan closed the door. He kept his silence as they walked along the corridor, waiting for Stirling to justify calling him in like that. But when they got to the stairs they just paused for a moment, looked at each other, then burst into laughter.

14

They had coffee and they had biscuits. It was noon and Stirling was *still* perfecting his press statement. Corrigan felt sorry for Pongo. Sorry for anyone who could get into that state. His career, whatever it had been, was clearly over. Once the media got hold of him, they wouldn't let go. He almost felt inclined to go out and buy a Pongo CD to see what all the fuss would be about.

Almost.

Drug convention in Niagara. He couldn't even remember the last time they'd had a drugs bust in the town. There hadn't yet been any evidence of crack cocaine, though just a couple of hundred miles across the border it had reached epidemic proportions. Coke wasn't really a Niagara kind of a thing either. Which, he supposed, made it the perfect place to have a drugs convention.

Like most police forces they turned a blind eye to the odd bit of dope, but whatever few dealers there were had enough sense to keep their heads down. He was partial to the odd joint himself. Just to relax. To take some of the pain out of his shot legs. To lie back on the deck of the *Maid of the Mist* with Maynard and enjoy the Falls and talk shit. He never actually bought it, of course. He had an understanding with Maynard. Corrigan buys the drinks, Maynard supplies the draw. It wasn't even a regular occurrence. Once a month, tops.

He looked across at Stirling, mouthing the words of his laboriously written statement. He waved the cigarette box at him. Stirling declined.

'Whatever way you look at it,' Corrigan said, 'you have to give Pongo full marks for imagination. A convention of drug dealers masquerading as horticulturalists. Ironic or what?'

'Ironic drug dealers,' said Stirling. 'Now there's a first.'

Corrigan had a sheet of paper before him as well. Pongo's list of international drug dealers. He crossed to the computer that sat on a desk by the window and switched it on. It gave him immediate access to a huge data bank of information on criminal activity in Canada and the United States. It was rarely used.

Stirling, watching, said: 'What're you doing?'

Corrigan smiled, a little self-consciously. 'Just running a few of Pongo's names through, see if they check out. He gets his drugs from somewhere, we might get a bust out of this as well.'

He started to type.

'Frank?'

'Mmmmm?'

'What if it's not all bullshit? What if he's right?' Stirling had put his pen down and was looking thoughtful. 'I mean, obviously he's wrong, but *if*, if he was right, and you type those names in, what if we disappear, like he said?'

Corrigan laughed. 'I thought it was only cokeheads got para-noid?' He turned back to his typing. He'd finished the first name. His finger moved to the send button. It hovered.

He looked across at Stirling.

'Just a thought,' Stirling said.

Corrigan sat back. 'You know,' he said, 'if you think about it, drug barons must have conventions. They must do. It stands to reason.'

Stirling shrugged. 'Suppose so. They have to make deals, just like any other business. Find out what's new. I don't think there's like a *Drug Dealers' Quarterly* or anything, is there?'

Corrigan snorted. His finger reached for the button again.

'Y'know,' Stirling said, 'if you want, we could check it out our-selves. Pretty easily. Just take a walk down to the Skylon Brock, ask a few questions.'

'You're serious?'

'Partly.'

Corrigan sat back from the screen. 'I suppose we can't do any-thing with Pongo until he settles himself a bit. We can't let the press see him like that or they'll tear him to shreds.'

'That's not our responsibility.'

'I know, but it's only fair.'

'What's fair got to do with it? We're police.'

'So what will we do? He doesn't even want us to phone his lawyer.'

'I don't know. I suppose we *could* walk down there, get some proper coffee, have a look round.'

Corrigan pulled at a lip. 'As long as we don't tell anyone.'

Stirling smiled. 'God, who could we tell?'

Corrigan erased the name from the computer screen. He could check them out later.

They took a walk along the river. It was bitingly cold.

'Must be difficult,' Corrigan said, 'being that young, having all that money. Women throwing themselves at you.'

'I could live with it.'

'Could you?'

'For a couple of weeks anyway. Then I'd go home.'

They arrived at the Skylon and pushed through the doors into reception. It was busy. There was a sign saying: SKYLON WELCOMES INTERNATIONAL HORTICULTURAL CONVENTIONEERS. There were four or five carts full of flowers, and behind them babes in various national costumes giving out samples to conventioneers.

Corrigan didn't know what he was looking for. He had attended a thousand conventions. Niagara was that kind of a town. Conventions turned up every conceivable type of person. If you were looking for someone suspicious or studious or creepy or high-flying or nerdy or anything, you'd find them. There were guys who prompted a nudge from Stirling, guys who looked like drug dealers, kind of smooth and bejewelled, but they might as well have been flower dealers into daffodils.

Corrigan accepted a complimentary red rose off a girl in a red skirt and red t-shirt. 'So,' he asked her, 'much crack cocaine available today?'

She smiled and said something in Spanish and moved on. Corrigan shrugged at Stirling. They approached the desk.

The receptionist – her name was Connie; it said so on her badge – smiled up at him. 'Inspector Corrigan,' she said, 'good morning.'

He nodded and said: 'So, how's the convention going?'

'Just fine, thank you.'

'You have a programme, something like that? List of guests?'

'Sure thing. There any problem, sir?'

Corrigan smiled. 'No trouble. Except with weeds.' He winked.

She handed him a programme.

'Most of them staying here?' She nodded. 'Usual, high-spirited crowd?'

'Yeah, I guess. Most of them are just so *sweet*.'

Corrigan passed the programme to Stirling, who began to flick through it. There wasn't a lot of detail. Layouts of the hotel and the casino next door. A list of the seminars and their locations. Titles like: 'Floral Marketing in the Digital Age', 'Preserving as Fresh: Cryogenics in the Greenhouse', 'The Future's Bright, the Future's Tulip: from the Bulb Fields of Holland'.

'There can't be that much to say about fucking flowers,' Stirling observed.

They walked next door to the casino, then took the elevator to the top floor where all the high rollers hung out.

'Thing is,' Stirling said, 'if there are drug dealers, they're not going to walk around with syringes hanging out of their pockets. They're going to look like businessmen. Like him.'

There was a clean-cut guy in a grey suit reading a convention programme. He was middle-aged, he had wire glasses. He had a little yellow convention badge. Corrigan looked at Stirling, Stirling shrugged, they walked across. They identified themselves.

He blinked up at them, his face pink, his smile cagey. 'Yes, officers, what can I do for you?'

'You have any identification, sir?' Stirling said.

'Certainly.' He produced a leather wallet. He offered his driving licence. 'I done anything wrong?'

'No, sir,' said Corrigan, 'just routine.'

'Walter J. Golden,' Stirling said.

'That's me,' said Walter.

'Texas,' said Stirling.

'Lone Star state,' said Walter.

'So,' said Stirling, 'I gotta lotta weeds at the bottom of my garden. What you recommend?'

Walter looked at him, confused for a moment. 'Well,' he said.

'Don't you know?' Stirling asked.

'Well, I'd be thinking you need to talk to a gardener.'

'You mean you really don't know? What kind of a horticulturalist doesn't know how to . . .'

'The kind lives in a five-million-dollar penthouse apartment in

Dallas.' He was a bit red about the gills now. 'The kind imports five million tulips from Amsterdam every month and distributes them throughout the country, but who doesn't have any goddamn weeds in his garden because he doesn't have any goddamn garden. *Honestly.*' Walter zipped the licence out of Stirling's hand. 'Now if I can be of any further assistance, don't hesitate to ask.' He turned, pressing the licence back into his wallet, and in a few moments had disappeared back into the throng.

'Well?' said Corrigan.

'Well?' said Stirling.

'*Have* you got weeds at the bottom of your garden?'

Stirling shook his head. 'I haven't got a garden either. Walter and I have so much in common.'

'What do you think?' Corrigan asked.

Stirling shrugged. 'Tulips from Amsterdam. Amsterdam being the drugs capital of Europe, of course. Laxest laws on the continent. You know they can smoke dope in public? They have dope cafés. You can order it off a menu. And hookers who sit in windows showing their . . .'

'I take your point,' Corrigan said.

15

Stirling returned to the station; Corrigan went looking for Barry Lightfoot. He had to tour the building three times before he spotted him. Lightfoot saw Corrigan about the same time and ducked down behind a machine. He peeked around the corner only when he was sure Corrigan had missed him, but he hadn't, he was standing staring at him peeking around the corner. 'Do you ever sleep, Barry?' Corrigan asked.

Barry shook his head. 'What you want now, man?'

'I'm trying to track Tarriha down. I owe him some money.'

'You're *chasing* Tarriha to give him money? Man, you got your life back to front.'

'You know where to find him?'

Lightfoot's eyes flitted up to the security cameras. Then he pointed along the rows of gaming machines. Just for show. 'Reservation, across the border,' Lightfoot said. Corrigan gave him a *look*. 'OK, and he rents a room on Bridge Street too. But most of the time you can find him in Whiskey Nick's. On Drummond.'

'What's he do there?'

'Drinks,' said Lightfoot.

'Figures.' Corrigan smiled. 'I thought he might have another job.'

'No,' said Lightfoot, 'menial employment, drinks too much. He's pretty much your stereotypical Indian.'

'Cheers,' Corrigan said, 'I owe you one.' He turned to leave, then stopped and said: 'Incidentally, you haven't come across any international drug dealers on your travels, have you?'

'What?' said Lightfoot.

Corrigan shook his head. 'Nothing,' he said.

Madeline Hume was just trying the door of Tarriha's room in a collapsing boarding house on Bridge Street when Corrigan appeared at the end of the corridor. She looked round suddenly and said: 'Oh.'

'It's probably locked,' Corrigan said. 'Most people do these days.'

'I wasn't . . .' Madeline began. 'In case he didn't hear me.'

'Uhuh,' said Corrigan.

She was wearing black ski pants and a sky-blue denim jacket over a white t-shirt. Her hair was damp and there was a love bite on her neck. She stood back from the door and looked at Corrigan expectantly.

'What?' said Corrigan.

'Aren't you going to kick it in?'

'Uhm. Why?'

'That's what you do.'

'Oh. Right.' He lined up in front of it. Raised his foot. Then he dropped it again and held a finger up. 'Oh. No. I just remembered. It's not what we do. That's what they do across the border.'

Her lip curled up. 'What are you, a *Mountie*?'

'Nope,' said Corrigan, trying the door himself, 'failed the exam. Besides, red isn't my colour.'

She tutted and withdrew a card from her purse. She slipped it under the door. 'There,' she said.

Corrigan smiled. 'I'm going to Whiskey Nick's, if you care to join me.' She looked puzzled. 'It's a bar.'

She smiled hesitantly. 'You're inviting me out for a drink?'

'No,' Corrigan replied, 'I'm inviting you across to meet Tarriha. He drinks in Whiskey Nick's.'

'Oh.' She smiled hesitantly. 'What's brought on this new spirit of co-operation?'

'Pity,' said Corrigan and turned for the stairs. She couldn't see the smile on his face. He couldn't see the steam coming out of her ears, but he could picture it.

They drove to Whiskey Nick's in silence. Apart from Madeline drumming her fingers on the dash. Apart from Madeline humming along to some country and western on the radio. Apart from the rain beating against the windscreen. He'd been to Whiskey Nick's before, a few times, by himself. It was just a local bar, maybe a little less sophisticated than most, and most were pretty unsophisticated. He couldn't remember much about it, except that there was no one called Nick involved in the business.

Eventually Madeline said: 'You were talking about your wife, weren't you?'

'What?' said Corrigan.

'Back at the women's refuge. You were talking about your wife.'

'Jesus. You mull things over, don't you?'

She shrugged. 'Her jaw was broken. By a fat guy. But you haven't arrested him, because he's still out there. She's gone back to him, hasn't she?'

'Here's Whiskey Nick's,' said Corrigan, pulling the car into the side of the road.

'It makes me *so* angry,' Madeline said. 'No wonder you're distracted.'

'I seem distracted?'

'I bet you'd shoot him if you could get hold of him.'

'I already did.'

She waited for him to smile, so he did. 'You must still love her.'

'Now there's a case of putting two and two together and getting six.'

'And he broke her jaw. God. What an animal. Can I do something? It's station policy, look after the staff, look after our informants.'

'I'm not an informant.'

'Can I send her something? How about some flowers?'

'How about some toffees?'

Her jaw dropped a little. It had come over a little more sarcastic than he had meant. If there was one thing they didn't understand on this side of the ocean it was sarcasm. In Belfast everything was sarcastic. Even when it wasn't. He looked at her and smiled. 'Comedy is easy,' he said, 'toffee is hard. Can we just drop it?'

She looked at him for a moment, then gave a little nod. 'Sorry,' she said.

He nodded, then opened the car door. 'Look on the bright side,' he said, climbing out, 'I haven't even mentioned the love bite.'

They made a dash through the rain, Madeline holding her bag up to protect her hair, Corrigan with his hands shoved into his pockets. It was early afternoon. They pushed through the door, laughing the way people do when they emerge from a downpour into a

61

bar, shaking themselves and making whooshing noises like they'd achieved something.

There were seven guys, all of them at least in their sixties, sitting on stools near the door. They were swapping football stories and laughing. There was a barman, big stomach, white shirt, balding, serving up the drinks and laughing along, but his laugh sounded forced. There were about a dozen tables, none of them occupied. At first Corrigan thought that was it, but then Madeline nudged him and nodded up to the far end of the bar. He saw only a large TV, up in the corner, showing cartoons, but then he realized there was someone sitting both beneath and behind it, almost hidden in the shadows, a position that suggested an enjoyment of the privacy the distraction of the cartoon violence above allowed. They walked a little further up the bar until they were sure it was him. He was nursing a bottle of Budweiser and staring into the distance, at the whisky bottles stacked out of his reach on the other side of the bar.

Corrigan ordered three beers, then they took seats on either side of him. Corrigan put one of the bottles down before the old Indian. Tarriha's head nodded slowly and he looked wearily at Corrigan, then around at Madeline.

'What I'm thinking,' Corrigan said quietly, 'based on what little I know about you, is that you're a greedy, grasping old Indian, only interested in where the next dollar is coming from. So what I need to know is why you would disappear when there was six hundred dollars coming your way.'

His lips barely moved. 'Have I disappeared? I don't think so.'

Madeline put a hand on his arm. 'Madeline Hume, Channel 4 in Buffalo. Can you tell me what happened to, uh, this Lelewala? Do you know where she is? Why she went over?'

Tarriha looked to Corrigan. 'Tell your friend to get her hand off my fucking arm.'

'Get your hand off his fucking arm.'

Madeline moved her hand. 'I'm sorry, I . . .'

'Just tell me what she said,' Corrigan said. 'Then I'll give you the cash.'

'I don't want the cash. I want nothing to do with it. I want to be left alone.'

This time Corrigan put a hand on his arm. 'We had a deal. If you don't want to be paid for it, fair enough. But we still had a deal. Tell me about Lelewala. Tell me her real name . . .'

'It *is* her real name.'

'OK. Tell me where she lives. What she does. Why she . . .'

Tarriha pulled his hand away. When he spoke his voice was cold, old, and something about the way his eyes narrowed and his brow furrowed sent a shiver up Corrigan's back. 'She doesn't *live* anywhere, she doesn't *do* anything. Don't you understand? She *is* Lelewala. She's come back.'

16

It really wasn't any darker in Whiskey Nick's, but suddenly it seemed to be. The air drew in around them, the sports chatter failed, the mad colours reflected off the Bugs Bunny cartoon faded to grey; there was only Madeline and Corrigan and Tarriha. His voice was no longer that of the money-grabbing old cynic Corrigan had first been annoyed by, it was deeper, wiser, age-soaked but not dulled by the march of time. His eyes were focused not on the bar, nor on his small audience, but on the past. His fingers traced invisible outlines on the stained wood of the bar, as if he was dipping his fingers into a pond of memories.

'She has come back,' he said slowly, 'because there is a great evil abroad.'

'Evil as in . . .' Madeline began.

'I don't know. She doesn't know. She is scared. Scared of you, scared of me . . . scared of everything.'

Madeline leaned forward, catching Corrigan's eye, then looked at Tarriha. 'You don't mean she's *literally* come back. She hasn't just stepped out of the dark ages.'

'The *dark ages?*' Tarriha growled. 'What do you know about dark ages? *These* are the dark ages.'

Madeline shook her head. 'I'm sorry, but it doesn't seem that dark in Buffalo.'

'You do not know the legend of Lelewala?' he said.

Madeline shrugged: 'Native American Princess goes over Falls. I don't know *why*.'

'I will tell you the story.' Madeline started to speak, but Tarriha raised a finger to shush her. 'Sometimes,' he said, 'it is good to listen.'

Sometimes, Madeline's look said, *it is good to meet deadlines.* But she shut up. Corrigan took a drink. Tarriha lifted his own bottle and drank. He didn't swallow. Just poured it straight into his stomach. Then he set the bottle down and closed his eyes.

'Many years before you stole our land,' he began, 'Lelewala lived with her family on the banks of the Great Niagara. Her father was Chief Eagle Eye and her mother Najaka. You . . .' and he turned suddenly and prodded Corrigan, 'have seen her and you know that she is beautiful.' He removed his finger and closed his eyes again. 'She was young, full of fun and energy, and she wanted above all things to be married to her true love Sahonwadi . . .'

Sahonwadi. Sahon . . .

'A father never likes to lose his daughter, but Chief Eagle Eye knew that Sahonwadi was not only the bravest warrior of the tribe but also the brightest. And that he would look after Lelewala, and also be guided by her. So he gave his blessing to the marriage. Sahonwadi busied himself making their bridal canoe. Lelewala could not wait for the day that she would become his wife, and dreamed of bearing his children.

'But as the wedding drew near, a great sickness arrived in the village and soon many were dying. The young, the old, the warriors, so many were struck down by it. The tribal elders knew that they had to try and appease the great God Hinum so that he would take away the evil. A canoe was loaded with the finest foods the tribe could gather and it was sent over the Falls as a gift to Hinum. But it was not enough. Still the tribe continued to die. The witch doctors put on their masks and rolled their bones and after many hours they spoke in one voice: "The great God Hinum wants more! A great sacrifice must be made!"

'So it was that Chief Eagle Eye journeyed to Ta Wa Sentha, the holy place where Gitchi Manitou once spoke to his people. Chief Eagle Eye built a great fire and called on the Thunderbird to answer his prayers. After much time the Thunderbird came to him and told him what the sacrifice to Hinum must be.

'Heavy of heart, Chief Eagle Eye returned to the village and told the elders what the Thunderbird had said, and it was agreed that it would be done.

'The next day was Lelewala's wedding. She was getting ready in the longhouse when her father came to her and told her what the Thunderbird had said. He said he could not order her to sacrifice herself, but that it must be of her own free will. Lelewala was distraught, but she knew that she must do what the Thunderbird had said if the whole tribe was not to die. One life was nothing. She also knew that she must do it before Sahonwadi found out, because he would surely stop her. He was young still and in time would find another wife.

'Chief Eagle Eye led Lelewala to the water's edge, to the wedding canoe. There the village had gathered and there were many tears. She said goodbye to her father and mother and climbed into the wedding canoe. She rowed out into the river.

'Sahonwadi, preparing for his wedding on the edge of the village, saw Lelewala set out into the dangerous current and raced into the village. Only then did he learn of what had been decided. Lelewala heard him scream and looked back to see him climbing into another canoe; she cried to him to go back, but he would not listen. Soon they were both caught in the current and racing towards the edge of the Falls.

'He almost caught her. Near the end she reached out to him, and he to her, and their fingers almost touched, but then the mighty Niagara took her, and took him. And in their dying, the village was saved. The great sickness vanished.'

The old man opened his eyes, looked from Madeline to Corrigan, and then behind Corrigan. Corrigan turned as well and was surprised to find that the elderly sports fans at the bar had gathered about them, enthralled by the old Indian's story. Even the barman, leaning back against a stack of beer crates, looked as if he might be about to shed a tear.

'And she told you all this?' Madeline said, and her question seemed to break the spell. The old guys' faces suddenly became animated again.

'Great story, old fella,' one of them said as he turned back to the bar.

'Jeez,' said another, 'would you go over the Falls after your wife?'

'You've met her, wouldn't you?'

'You're damn right I would. Just to make sure she *was* fucking dead.'

They cackled; the barman pushed himself off the crates, wiped at an eye and said: 'Fucking bullshit,' and went down to serve the octogenarian jocks.

'She told me all this. Sure,' Tarriha said to Madeline, then angled

66

his bottle at the bar, looking for another. Corrigan waved down to the barman, holding up two fingers. Madeline hadn't touched hers.

'Well, if she died going over the Falls, how does she know that the village was saved?'

'*I* know that the village was saved.'

'Uhuh.' Madeline looked doubtful. 'So what date was this, about? I need historical verification, I need . . .'

Corrigan rolled his eyes. 'Madeline, please. There aren't *dates*, there aren't *records*. . . Tarriha, tell me if I'm wrong, but it's like a myth, isn't it? It's an old Indian story about the evil diseases white men brought to America, and this girl has gone over the Falls to protest at . . .'

'You mean it's an AIDS allegory?' Madeline asked.

Corrigan shrugged. 'Could be anything. AIDS. Indian rights. Pollution. Drugs. Nike Air Jordans. It doesn't matter; that's what you're looking for, isn't it? A good story.'

Tarriha shook his head slowly. 'You do not listen. *Allegory*. Huh. I have spoken to her. I spent the night in her room. She *is* Lelewala. Her body, her spirit, her broken heart.'

'Uhuh,' said Madeline.

'OK,' said Corrigan, 'supposing for the moment that she is. Why did she come back? What did she say?'

'Because there is a great evil . . .'

'But what is it? Specifically. Why would she suddenly . . .'

Tarriha suddenly slapped his hand on the bar. 'She doesn't know! All she knows is that she was sacrificed so that a great evil would leave her village. And all she knows is that she has come back because some great evil is walking this land again.'

'Can't she be a little more specific?' Madeline asked. 'Animal, vegetable or mineral? Is it President Keneally or Spike Lee or . . .'

Tarriha's eyes narrowed. 'You mock me,' he said.

Madeline's eyes narrowed back. 'On the contrary,' she said, her voice suddenly razor-sharp, 'I think you mock me.'

She pushed herself up off the barstool and lifted her bag. She looked from Tarriha to Corrigan and back. 'I never heard so much . . . *hokum*. I don't know why you've cooked this bullshit up between you or who you're hoping to fool, but it's not me, and it's not my station. There is a story, a damn good story, but this sure as hell isn't it. I think you know what it is and you're trying to hide it.'

Corrigan raised placatory palms. There was nothing flirtatious about her manner now. 'C'mon, Madeline, we're not trying to hide anything . . .'

She wasn't having it. She grabbed her bag off the bar. 'I'll find this Lelewala or whatever her name is, and I'll get the real story, OK? I don't need bullshit time wasters like you two, OK? I don't need it.'

She flounced off down the bar. Corrigan slipped a hand into his pocket, searching, then called down the bar after her.

She stopped. 'What?'

'Here's five dollars for the cab.'

'Fuck off!'

And she was gone, with the old guys whistling and whooping after her.

Corrigan almost followed. He got to the point of finishing his drink, wiping his mouth, nodding down at Tarriha. But then he stopped, sat and ordered another drink for each of them. Tarriha grunted in quasi-appreciation.

'What do you do with a woman like that?' Corrigan asked.

Tarriha nodded thoughtfully for a few moments, then said: 'Big stick.'

17

He had a few beers on him by then, so he went home.

Not home, but *home*.

Nicola opened the door to him. She smiled as best she could. Aimie ran out and up into his arms and he hugged her and she hugged him back and then complained about the stubble on his chin and the beer on his breath. She was out of his arms and away running into the back garden before he was even through the door.

'I worry about her attention span,' Corrigan said.

Nicola led him into the lounge. She seemed relaxed, but swollen. There was no sign of the Fat Man. Perhaps he was off getting his circus pants laundered. Usually Nicola wasn't much on housework, but the place was pristine. Then he remembered.

'The people came about the house?'

Nicola nodded.

'Any joy?'

She nodded. 'Therbeacertfychek . . .' She stopped. She lifted a notepad, flicked through half a dozen pages until she came to a clean one, then wrote: *There'll be a certified cheque with our solicitor in the morning.*

'Oh really.' He tapped his foot. He gave her a hard look. 'Don't you think you should have consulted me on this at all?'

She nodded. She wrote: *Sorry. Lovely people. They loved the house.*

'Big deal. How much did they sucker you for? If it's a cent less than three fifty I'll call them right back, get them to . . .'

She wrote it down. *$400,000.*

'No, seriously,' Corrigan said.

She smiled. 'Imseris.'

She wrote: *They love the view.*

'Nick, you have to stand on boxes in the loft to get a view. And

69

then only if the wind's blowing the trees in the right direction and the sun's out.'

A Niagara view is a Niagara view. Location, location, location. He thought to himself for several moments while she watched him. Then he looked up and smiled. 'I suppose you're pleased with yourself.' She nodded. 'So we split it two ways.'

'Three.'

'You said that clearly enough. If you think I'm giving that fat bastard . . .'

'Aimie!'

He stopped. 'Right enough.'

She wrote: *A trust fund.*

He nodded. He crossed to the back window. Aimie was on the swing, singing away to herself. Nicola came up beside him. She glanced behind her, then put her arm around his waist.

He wanted to tell her to take it away. Because, after all, she was selling his house and giving him a third of it and still fucking the fat guy even though he'd broken her jaw. But he liked it there. Around his waist. The warmth. 'Four hundred,' he said slowly, then gave a little whistle. 'And did they seem reasonably sane?'

Nicola nodded.

'Are we going to quibble about throwing the curtains in?'

She smiled, shook her head. They stood silently for several minutes, just watching Aimie swing. Then, for a little bit, he watched Nicola, watching Aimie. She was beautiful. *They* were beautiful. He bent down and kissed her on the cheek.

She grimaced and pulled sharply away. 'Jeezchrist,' she spat, her hand massaging her jaw.

'Sorry, I was only . . .'

'Jeez-zus,' she said again, patting her cheek. She bunched her fists up in frustration, glaring at him, then rushed across to her notebook. She flipped to a new page and wrote in big capital letters, *I'VE A FUCKING BROKEN JAW AND ALL YOU CAN THINK ABOUT IS SEX.*

Corrigan held his hands up. 'I wasn't thinking about sex! I just gave you a peck on the cheek!' And then he saw her eyes flit to Aimie in the garden, and knew suddenly what it was all about. The arm round his waist had been below eye level. But the kiss on the cheek had been in full view of his daughter. And his daughter had told Big Fat Fucker about the last kiss, and he'd broken her jaw. Nicola saw the realization dawn on him and looked away, embarrassed.

Corrigan tutted. 'You're scared of your own daughter.'

She shrugged.

'I don't understand you at all,' Corrigan said.

He was having a smoke by the Falls. Just enjoying the thunder. Not close enough to the edge to have the spray put out his cigarette, but close enough. He was thinking about Lelewala and how on earth she could have survived *that*. It was power. It was glory. It was Mother Nature and God, although of the two he only believed in Mother Nature. If there was a God and he had a big white beard, then he was Santa. And Santa was an anagram of Satan and that worried him.

He was prepared to believe in evil, but not in good.

Because nothing that was good ever happened to him.

Or if it did, it was taken away from him.

Lelewala had come back to fight evil. At least according to Tarriha. Maybe she would fight it on his behalf. Take on Big Trousers and sort him out properly. He had only been able to point his impotent Glock at him and inspire some bowel relaxation. It wasn't the same as breaking his neck.

He threw his cigarette into the water. Who was he kidding? He was the beaten man. Second best. Second best to a fat fundamentalist fucker. And Lelewala? Tarriha, for all his superb story telling, hadn't a clue where she was. If she wasn't chasing an evil spirit, she was probably drinking one. She had survived going over the Falls by a miracle, but had clearly been bonkers to go over in the first place.

His phone rang. It was Stirling. His voice was low, almost a whisper. 'I have good news, and I have bad news. Take your pick.'

Corrigan sighed. Then he got bumped from behind by a Jap tourist walking backwards trying to get himself and the Falls into a photograph while his wife barked directions. Corrigan growled. They looked uncomprehendingly at him for a moment, then bowed. Corrigan felt like a git. He smiled and waved an apologetic no harm done and started to walk.

'Sorry,' Corrigan said, 'start with the good. I need to hear some good. And speak up.'

'Can't. But the good news is I've decided against fronting this whole Pongo thing. The interviews. The limelight. It's not me.'

'Fair enough,' Corrigan said. 'What changed your mind?'

'The bad news.'

'Which is?'

'Pongo's just about to walk.'

'Excuse me?'

'You're excused.' There was a pause, and then: 'I'm sorry. I'm a bit freaked. I have to let him go.'

'You *have* to let him go.'

'Yes, sir, I do. With the Chief of Police at my elbow and the Barracuda showing his teeth.'

'Fuck,' said Corrigan, 'I'll be there in a minute.'

18

Thomas Vincenzi, a.k.a. the Barracuda, was as tall and gaunt as an undertaker. His suit was Italian and so was his demeanour. He wore *don't fuck with me* pointed black shoes and a watch heavier than a hard-boiled ostrich egg. He had the look of a man who had dealt with his fair share of nuts, and the bejewelled fingers of one who no longer had to. He said jump, people asked which cliff.

He was just coming through the door of the station. Pongo was beside him. Corrigan hurried up the steps and said: 'Where the fuck do you think you're taking him?'

'Inspector,' said the Barracuda, 'it's been a long time.'

'Not long enough,' said Corrigan. He pointed at Pongo. 'He's mine. We have him for murder. Maybe manslaughter. And we certainly have him for coke.' Pongo was looking at his velvet-slippered feet.

'No, Inspector, you have one Bernard Rawlins, a driver for the Pongo organization. He's just signed a confession admitting to the drugs and picking the girl up. Pongo was asleep through the whole thing.' He shook his head sadly. 'Happens all the time, Inspector, guys taking advantage of their employer. Ripping them off. Getting them a bad reputation. Particularly Negroes.'

He gave Corrigan a thin smile, then led Pongo down the steps. Pongo averted his eyes as he passed.

Corrigan went through the doors, fast. Chief of Police Adrian Dunbar was standing in the hall, talking to Stirling. He wore a beige suit and a monk's hairstyle, though only one of them from choice. As Corrigan approached the Chief turned towards him. Stirling took advantage of it to raise his fingers to his lips and mouth a pleading *shush*, but Corrigan ignored him.

'What the fuck is going on?' Corrigan spat.

The Chief looked at him dryly. 'Indeed, Inspector, what the fuck *is* going on?'

'We had a cast-iron . . .'

'You had nothing. You kept a superstar in solitary for eighteen hours, you denied him access to his lawyer, you prevented him from taking his medication, you failed to inform headquarters . . . indeed, Inspector, what the fuck *is* going on?'

Corrigan looked at Stirling, who raised an eyebrow. Just one.

'Pish,' said Corrigan. '*Medication?* Who the fuck is he . . .'

'Inspector . . .'

'Jesus Christ, the Barracuda, he's . . .'

'He's gonna hit us with half a dozen million-dollar lawsuits, and it isn't going to come out of your pocket, Inspector, it's going to come out of mine.'

'Chief, for fuck's sake, Pongo as good as admitted . . .'

'Inspector, I believe you haven't even informed the dead girl's parents.'

Corrigan cleared his throat. 'No, sir, I thought it . . .'

'Inspector, I want a full report on my desk by this evening. And then we'll see if we can get you a nice cleaning job somewhere, OK?'

He pushed past, out the door, and down the steps.

Stirling, at his elbow, said: 'You can clean my house, if you want.'

19

Stirling stared morosely out at the countryside. They were about twenty minutes out of town, heading for Fort Erie. The sun was making laborious jabs through the clouds like an over-the-hill boxer on the comeback trail. 'I just think you're taking things a little far.'

'I'm just checking it out. What harm can it do?'

'To my reputation or my chances of promotion?'

'Lighten up. It'll be interesting.'

Corrigan had come to a decision. He was the boss, at least for a while, he was allowed to come to decisions. The Barracuda's presence had swung it. Yes, he was probably one of the most powerful lawyers in the country. Yes, he could smack a million-dollar lawsuit on them without blinking. And yes, he was a Mafia lawyer. He was well known for it. He represented drug dealers and gangsters. He was a bad egg. A rotten egg. The black banana in the fridge. The skin on a custard. The mould on the bread. Corrigan knew it. Stirling knew it. The Chief knew it. So why was the Chief so anxious to pander to him?

'Because he's powerful,' Stirling said, 'and much as I hate to admit it, he does have a point. We've hardly done this by the book.'

'Because you wanted the glory.'

'Oh, blame me.'

'Only because it's *all* your fault.'

'You're my boss, you should have told me to wise up.'

'I only went along with it because you were hell-bent on getting your face on TV.'

'So? You didn't have to indulge me. And besides, I'm not the one going to get busted down to cleaner.'

'Don't bet on it.'

They'd thought about Pongo and his convention fantasy.

Corrigan had typed the names into the computer *again* and *again* his finger had hovered over the *send*. Stirling had looked at him and said: 'The Barracuda.' They'd both sat back and discussed how that changed things. And decided they had no idea how that changed things, except it made them even more hesitant about pressing the *send*.

Then Corrigan had a brainwave. And now they were looking at house numbers on the outskirts of Fort Erie.

'This is stupid,' Stirling was saying. 'It's just a horticultural convention.'

He rested his head against the passenger window. The last three months, Niagara had been dead in the water. Nothing. Zilch. They'd been reduced to busting drunk drivers and hookers, usually at the same time. Not a robbery in the whole region, hardly even a careless tourist whacked over the head and his money belt stolen. The only thing on their books was a stolen police car, and that was too embarrassing to make a big deal out of. Then suddenly there was the Indian fished out of the Niagara, then a little girl flattened by the Coke lorry and now a horticultural convention which might be a front for the biggest drugs convention in the history of organized crime. Or a platform for selling daffodils.

Stirling decided to wait in the car while Corrigan went and got embarrassed.

The house was big, but not as big as Corrigan had imagined. Maybe there wasn't that much money in books. The pool already had an autumnal look about it; indeed, the closer they got, it was the previous autumn's look. Leaves lay dank and black on the surface, hemmed in by a thick scum line. A few more years of similar neglect and they could start prospecting for oil. Corrigan ordered Stirling out of the car. He climbed out slowly, complaining, then trailed behind as Corrigan walked up a short flight of mossy steps to the door and pressed the bell.

'Your last chance, Frank,' Stirling said.

Corrigan ignored him. Stirling stepped up beside him and hammered on the door.

'Now you're part of it,' Corrigan said.

Stirling gave him a weak grin. Then there was a shadow behind the grimy glass and the door opened.

James Morton was looking pretty autumnal himself.

Like everyone else in the world, Corrigan had been glued to his television during the Empire State Building siege five years before. Like every dedicated policeman he was half jealous at not being involved, and half relieved. The President had survived, the kidnapper Nathan Jones had become a national hero and most everyone, save for all of the dead people, seemed to have prospered from it.

James Morton, the FBI Chief in New York at the time, had written the best-selling *Shield of Honor*, then retired from the Bureau and moved across the border into Canada to escape the continuing media frenzy. Soon after arriving he agreed to lecture students at Westlane Secondary School. He told them he was writing a novel. Corrigan had attended the lecture in an official capacity, his contribution the local angle on crime. What he had to say had seemed small and petty and deathly dull compared to Morton's exploits, but the former FBI man had made a point of congratulating him.

Now, standing in the doorway, Corrigan hardly recognized him. His hair had been tawny and thick, now it was grey and thin, his eyes seemed to live in dark hollows. Where there'd been a square FBI jaw, there hung loose flesh jagged by an unkempt beard. Corrigan didn't want to look too closely at it in case he found leaves there too. Suddenly his idea didn't seem so hot.

'I told you not to come,' Morton said, his voice nicotine-husky.

'I know . . .' Corrigan began.

'And I certainly didn't invite Hitler.'

But he stood back and nodded them in. He led them down a dark corridor to a conservatory at the back of the house. The whole place smelt of neglect. So, for that matter, did Morton. The conservatory windows were speckled with birdshit, which lent an odd, yellowed light to the proceedings. Morton dropped heavily into an armchair, then waved them on to a wicker lounger.

'You didn't give me much of a chance to explain,' Corrigan said.

Morton looked to the glass, then beyond to the overgrown garden. 'No,' he said quietly, 'perhaps I didn't. The singer. The crash. The conspiracy. What of it?'

'I thought you could clear something up for us. I mean, I have this list of names of people Pongo says are attending the convention. I thought maybe you could tell us whether you'd heard of any of them.'

'Haven't you got computers for that sort of thing?'

'Well, yes,' said Corrigan.

'He, uh,' said Stirling, 'said we'd get disappeared if we tried to check up.'

A little grin made its way slowly on to Morton's face, like a hedgehog searching for winter accommodation. 'Got you spooked, huh?'

Corrigan smiled weakly and handed the list over. Morton held it away from his eyes and squinted. His cracked lips began to move silently as he studied the names. After a little he looked back up at Corrigan, then his eyes flitted to Stirling and back. 'Have you told anyone about this?'

Corrigan's heart stopped. 'No, sir.'

'Good.' Morton curled the list up into a ball and tossed it across the room. It bounced off the top of a crowded wastebin and rolled under a table. 'Save yourself the embarrassment.'

'Fair enough,' Corrigan said.

'Do you know what the weak link in your story is, Mr Corrigan?'

'It's all weak,' opined Stirling.

Morton nodded, where Stirling had expected a smile. 'The weakest link, then?' Corrigan shook his head. 'I'm prepared to accept that drug dealers might feel the need to hold conventions. I accept that if they did they would have to disguise them as something else. And I don't see any reason why they shouldn't hold them somewhere nice and scenic and quiet where no one is going to suspect a thing. Holding it in Thailand would rather give the game away, don't you think?' Corrigan nodded. 'No, sir, the weak link is Pongo himself. Today's drug dealers are highly sophisticated, their deals involve billions, not millions of dollars. They are not drug *users*. They don't employ fuck-ups like your Mr Pongo, and they don't allow little girls to get killed. They don't exactly court publicity. No sir, I'm afraid you've been led astray by your guest. My advice to you is to throw the book at him, and make sure it's a big book for wasting your time.'

'And this Old Cripple,' Stirling ventured, 'you haven't heard of him?'

'I think I might have remembered a name like that.' He stood up. 'Gentlemen?'

There was an awkward silence while they gathered up their coats. Then Corrigan extended his hand. 'I'm sorry for disturbing you. I just thought ... well, you're a hero all over the world for what you achieved at the Empire ...'

As he shook hands Morton smiled sadly. 'I achieved nothing,' he said. 'The bad guy got away.'

'Well ... I just thought ... if there was anything to it ... you know, you'd probably want to get involved.'

'It's not that we're scared,' Stirling added needlessly, 'it's just not our area of expertise.'

Corrigan rolled his eyes.

'What exactly is your area of expertise?' Morton asked.

Stirling looked to Corrigan, who tried to raise a single eyebrow, but failed. He raised two. Stirling shrugged. 'Smaller stuff,' he said weakly.

Morton walked them to the door. On the steps he took a deep breath, as if he hadn't ventured outside in months.

'So you reckon we should just forget about it?' Corrigan ventured.

Stirling, already opening up the car, said: 'I've already forgotten about it.'

Morton nodded. 'Coke means paranoia, paranoia leads to delusional conspiracy theories. We spent a lot of years tracking them down at the Bureau, and usually they weren't worth shit. Sorry. I know things can get pretty boring round here.'

Corrigan nodded and walked down to the car.

'Drive carefully,' Morton called after him.

When they had gone Morton poured himself another drink then returned to his chair in the conservatory. He sat for a little while, thinking. Then he put his glass down and crawled under the table to retrieve the rolled-up list of Pongo's international drug dealers.

Corrigan stared moodily ahead as they drove. Stirling looked out of the side window. After a couple of miles Corrigan said: 'It's not that we're scared.' He rolled his eyes again.

'Sorry,' Stirling said. 'I was just trying to contribute something.'

Corrigan shook his head, then slapped the wheel. 'Well,' he said, 'that was a fucking big waste of time.'

'Told you,' Stirling replied.

'How old you reckon he is?'

'Who? Morton? Dunno. Sixty.'

'Try knocking twenty off that.'

'Seriously? Jeez.'

'Yeah, I know. He'll be in the morgue before the year's out.'

'What happened to him. Bad reviews?'

'Good reviews. Bad driving. Someone totalled his wife and kid. Out near St Catharine's, couple of years ago.'

'And he blames himself.'

'God no, blames the other son of a bitch. He was never caught. *She* was never caught. Whatever. Been hitting the bottle ever since.'

'Sad.'

'Yeah, it's sad.'

They drove on in silence for a while until Stirling said: 'What are we going to do now?'

'We're going to visit a dead girl's parents. We're going to write a report. Then we might as well go out and get pissed.'

Stirling nodded. He took out a cigarette and lit it. 'You're disappointed, aren't you?'

Corrigan shrugged. 'It would have been kind of interesting.'

'It would have been fucking dangerous.'

'Yeah. Well. We aren't going to know.'

20

The message from Nicola was distinct in its indistinctness. It began: *Corrganimsuhlnotfelunthbest, hekinduhskaruhsme...* and continued in a similar vein for two minutes.

Corrigan listened to the tape, then wiped it. He couldn't be bothered translating it. *You've dug your own grave, now you can lie in it.*

It was a little after 11 p.m., it was dark. It had been a difficult afternoon. The girl's parents had asked questions he did not have answers for. He had escorted them to the morgue. They'd done a good job with her, but death was death. There were few smiling corpses, but seemingly she always smiled. He had to tell them that a Negro driver had admitted the crime. And they'd said goddamn niggers. On the way back to their house he'd switched the radio on, maybe to take their minds off it, and for the first time in his life Corrigan heard one of Pongo's songs. It didn't mean a thing to them – he hadn't been allowed to tell them about Pongo's involvement – but it near forced tears into his eyes, and not just because it was crap.

He had left Stirling to do the report, but when he got back to the station he threw out most of what he'd written and had a go himself. If Stirling had put as much effort into it as into writing his now aborted press statement then it wouldn't have been so bad. He told him that. Stirling sulked. They bickered on and off throughout the afternoon. Their plan to get pissed wasn't mentioned.

Corrigan spent an hour driving around looking for Lelewala, but nobody seemed to know anything, least of all Tarriha, who was carried out of Whiskey Nick's legless and thrown in the gutter. He was sleeping it off in a cell downstairs in the station.

At home in his damp apartment, Corrigan lay in the bath, then lay on the sofa, then lay on the floor. There was nothing on the TV worth watching, his collection of CDs bored him. The owner of the apartment, Mrs Capalski, the Polish harridan, called by to collect the rent. To *demand* the rent. He always paid, and he always paid on time, but she always demanded it as if he was a student or a murderer or somebody equally disreputable. When she'd gone he took a bottle of whisky down from a cupboard then poured it into a silver flask and took a walk along the river, sipping. Thinking. Thinking about Northern Ireland, his real home, and why he couldn't go back.

It had been a typical Crossmaheart summer. Rain smacking like bullets into the metal sheeting that had served as the barracks roof since the bomb attack a month before. The arrhythmic rat-tat-tat was annoying, but at least it kept him alert. It was easy just to drift away in those long, silent nights. Watching, watching, watching *nothing*, then *something*, something that turned out to be *nothing*. Nothing between the last drunk rolling home from the Ulster Arms and the first hum of a milk float four hours later. He wasn't allowed a newspaper or a book or a radio, nothing that would distract; and ironically it was the lack of *distraction* that usually edged him towards sleep. Although not, of course, *to sleep*. That could be a fatal mistake. What it did encourage was a kind of horse inertia, standing up, eyes open, but unfocused, the mind and the memory in a slightly different, somehow better place. A place where he had something better to rest his arse on than a wooden bench, where he could tap his toe to the country and western that *he knew* oozed out of Radio 2 in the middle of the night. A place where he could unlock the door and lay out a saucer of milk for the tabby, *something* that was *nothing*, who always came sniffing just before dawn. But this night there was the rain, and it saved him. The recent spate of kneecappings in the town had made it difficult to get any of the local tradesmen to carry out repair work. The army sappers were trying to cope with the rebuilding of their own bombed-out base in Belfast and could only vaguely promise a date several weeks in the future.

He yawned. He was thinking of the girl in the hardware store who'd refused to serve him because he was a cop, but who'd still flirted shamelessly with him. The double-edged sword. They could arrange to meet, have sweaty dangerous sex, or she could lure him into a trap and her mates would blow his head off.

The rain stopped just as suddenly as it began. It wasn't over for the night. It was just God reloading. But it stayed off long enough for the summer heat to steam back up through the tarmac outside the station.

He was watching the steam, eerie in the dead-of-night silence, when the bulldozer came into view.

It was a good half-mile away along the Main Street. It stood out yellow like a fallen moon against the darkness, its bucket held high. There was no sound but the quiet hiss of the steam, and for several moments he thought he might be imagining it, that he had slipped into that other place. But no, it was there. And it was coming.

He hesitated. There was a slight incline on the Main Street and the bulldozer appeared to be freewheeling. It could just be a farmer or a builder getting an early start. But it was *too* early. Corrigan picked a pair of binoculars up off the otherwise bare table before him, and focused in. His mouth went dry. The driver was wearing a balaclava. It was summer and it was warm, and in this part of the world knitted winter garments meant only one thing. And behind the vehicle, *glimpses*. Shadows. The shape of a head. *Heads.* Feet. Shuffling. Jogging.

Ordinarily there was a garrison of twenty-five. Tonight there were just three. There was a police dinner in Belfast. A police dinner masquerading as a rugby-club dinner. Only someone, somewhere, knew their rugby, and now there was death coming along Main Street in the shape of a bulldozer with a bomb in its bucket and an IRA unit using it for cover. It had been tried before, at a neighbouring station. The bulldozer to smash through the wire fence surrounding the barracks. Then setting off the bomb and blowing the station to bits and the active service unit waiting impatiently to massacre any survivors.

Corrigan pressed the alarm button.

It was not so loud that they would hear it down the street. Thirty seconds long, and Constables McDermott and Hamilton were stumbling into the room before it had run its course. *The rain.*

They didn't speak, at first. They struggled into their green trousers and shirts. Their boots were off. They were strapping on their pistols. They looked out of the letter-box-shaped opening, and their faces blanched, and they knew.

'Shit,' McDermott said.

'Shit,' said Hamilton.

'Shit,' McDermott said again, 'what'll we do now?'

'Well, we could run away,' Corrigan said, 'but it mightn't look very good on our records.' He smiled. His lips, in *seconds*, had dried and cracked. The smile *hurt*. His heart raced. They had trained for this a hundred times, but they had trained with a full squad, not with a skeleton crew. The training had presumed at *least* equal terms. The presumption had been presumptuous.

Death was rolling down the Main Street.

Any second the bulldozer would lose the benefit of the incline. As soon as it hit the flat end of the street it would roar into life. And then death would be rushing *and* rolling towards them.

They ran out of the sentry post and into the armoury. They chose sub-machine guns. They attempted to load up with quiet proficiency. But it was impossible. They mad cackled as they forced the magazines in with shaking hands.

'This is fucking crazy,' McDermott said.

Hamilton giggled.

'One thing we gotta get,' Corrigan said.

'What's that?' McDermott asked.

'Outta this business.'

It was a two-storey building. A house. It had belonged to a butcher once. Apt, in hindsight. A big house with security cameras and a lengthy extension on the back, and Portakabins beyond that. All surrounded by sandbags and a huge wire fence. But nothing that would withstand the kind of force that was trundling along Main Street.

They left the armoury and ran through the canteen to the back of the station. They opened the door and hurried between the Portakabins to what they knew as the tradesman's entrance. It wasn't quite that. It was a small gate in the wire fence that they used occasionally for civilians who didn't want to be seen entering the station in full view of the public, and occasionally for smuggling out prisoners to waiting ambulances, prisoners who'd accidentally fallen down steps.

They weren't perfect.

And they were scared.

The back gate led on to the black remains of a burnt-out shopping centre. It had fallen vacant during the last economic downshift and been destroyed for fun by a passing arsonist. The police had discouraged any rebuilding, preferring to have a derelict rear buffer rather than renewed development that could be hijacked by the IRA.

Corrigan snapped open the lock, peered out, then ran first out on to the weed-strewn lane-way that ran between the station and the shopping shell, then on beyond and into the ruined structure. He not only had the benefit of age and experience, but the benefit of shoes. The other two hopped and winced and giggled as they raced across the ruined floor, jagging their feet on rusted cans and the smashed green glass of cider bottles. Above their heartbeats they could hear the rumble of the bulldozer. It was close, and closing.

Corrigan came to the crumbled far wall. Hamilton and McDermott ducked down beside him and peered out. They were almost level with the bulldozer. The driver was fiddling with the controls. The others – he counted six – were checking their weapons, still in its shadow. They too wore balaclavas. And carried big fucking guns.

They walked right past.

Corrigan suddenly felt better. They were behind them now, and undetected. They had the advantage of surprise.

According to the book they should shout their warnings now, read them their rights, arrest them before any damage was done.

But nobody had brought the book. And even if they had, the classification on the spine would say *fantasy*. It was not how they lived. It was not how they survived. This was war.

McDermott raised his gun. Corrigan put a hand on the barrel and forced it quietly down. He shook his head.

The driver jumped down from the cabin. He landed badly and went over, but he didn't yell. One of the others helped him up and then handed him a rifle. He leaned on it. The bulldozer continued on its way. It was about forty yards from the station.

The IRA squad spread itself out along the road in a loose

semi-circle, then crouched down on the damp tarmac. They had a new confidence now, based on the certainty that the station was under-strength and the revelation that the sentry post was either unmanned or the sentry was asleep.

They waited for the station to explode.

Corrigan could have stopped it.

But then there would have been no excuse.

The bulldozer rammed into the wire, dragging it inwards. It tore, it screeched metal on metal and nails on blackboards and then the bucket thumped into the front of the station and it blew.

Pooooowchhhhhhhhhhh . . . !

Corrigan and his men ducked down behind the wall. Grabbed on to it. Feared that it would collapse on top of them. The roar was tremendous. For a hundred yards on either side of the road windows imploded, roofs rose and rubble rained. Corrigan looked to the station, but there was nothing to see except a cloud of dust and a sudden spit of flame.

And then, after perhaps thirty seconds, just an awful silence.

The IRA waited for the first glimpse of the survivors.

The police waited on Corrigan's lead.

The residents lay silently in their beds, clutching each other, wondering if this was *the end* but too scared to inquire.

And then at a nod the gunmen stood and began to spray the ruined, burning building with bullets. They were happy that it was destroyed, unhappy that there were no obvious signs of life. They were pleased that they had struck another blow against the British presence in Ireland, disappointed that they were reduced to shooting bricks and mortar.

Another lull. Time to fade back into the welcoming countryside, bandit country, into the safe-houses, to hide their weapons in their underground bunkers, to clean and scrub and remove every trace of gunpowder. To return to work. To the fields. To the factory. To the pub. To the very Civil Service.

But then there was a voice from behind.

'Top of the morning to youse, lads.'

They turned, and in the act of turning, they died.

Corrigan, Hamilton and McDermott, shooting from the hip and evening up the score.

*   *   *

Corrigan spat into the river. There had been no medals. There had been a trial. For murder. The Crossmaheart Massacre. Proof of the police's shoot-to-kill policy. They had, of course, been acquitted. It was a British court with a British judge and no jury. Not guilty of murder, and the judge had refused to consider a lesser charge of manslaughter. They'd walked free, but they would never walk free in that country again. Too many people out for revenge. A danger to his colleagues. A whip-round and a quietly arranged transfer to a police force on the other side of the world.

What had he left behind?

Nothing.

What could he go back to?

Nothing.

What did he have here?

Nothing.

He looked at the river. He had reached the top of the Falls. Lelewala had rowed over. The Lelewala of legend. She had reached out to her lover, and he to her. But whom did he have to reach out to? And who would reach out for him?

He took another drink.

He had come to a decision.

He would have to join a dating agency.

21

Corrigan was always a light sleeper, even with the drink.

There was an instant when his eyes fluttered, ears pricked like a dog. *Something*.

Shapes in the darkness. A whisper.

He threw himself suddenly to one side, grabbing for his gun, forgetting that he no longer kept it by his bed, as he had in Ireland. As he fell he scrambled for another weapon, alarm clock, a paperback, but there was nothing. He hit the floor and rolled; he struck legs, there was a shot and a barked scared admonishment, and then half a dozen lights went on and there were eight men and eight guns pointed at him. He froze.

The police.

But not *his* police.

Corrigan blinked from murderous eye to murderous eye; beads of sweat on straining brows, fingers shaking on triggers; he had only luck and unprofessional hesitation to thank that he was not already dead.

All he could say was: 'What?'

His head throbbed; he tried to peer through the fog; what was . . .

They closed in, hauled him up on to the bed, threw him face down. Searched him. It didn't take long. All he wore was his underpants. They flipped him on to his back. He looked at them; he was shaking, and he could hear the shake in his faked laugh. 'OK. . . OK lads. April Fool. Though I should point out that it's September.'

They were rifling through his belongings.

They were wearing rubber gloves.

A forensics team.

Scenes-of-crime team.

Cops, in Niagara, and he didn't know any of them.

'Do you mind telling me what the fuck is going on?'

One of the cops raised the butt of his rifle and might have shattered Corrigan's kneecap if the guy in charge hadn't stopped him. He then tapped Corrigan's passport against his leg and said: 'OK, let's go.'

As they dragged him through the door Corrigan struggled for the first time; it had more to do with modesty than wrongful arrest; then something hit him on the back of the head, a fist or a gun, and he stumbled forward, but they had too good a grip on him to let him fall.

There were six vehicles parked in the middle of the road. He was hurried along to the third and placed in the rear seat. The leather was as cold as the handcuffs that pinched his skin.

'What's this about?' Corrigan asked again.

'Murder,' said the cop beside him.

It was like a thump to the head with a big stick, with a nail in the end of it. Penetrating his brain, lacerating his eyes, paralysing everything but his voice, and his memory.

'What the fuck're you talking about?'

The convoy travelled at speed, sirens blaring.

'Shut the fuck up.'

'You can't just say *murder* and leave it like that.'

'Shut the fuck up.'

'You can't just break into my house and search my arse and say murder and not tell me what the fuck this is all about. I'm a police officer for fuck's sake. This is my town.'

'Not any more.'

'I have rights. You can't just . . .'

They shut him the fuck up.

22

They uncuffed him, then shoved him into a cell, his arms and legs aching from the beating. A blanket landed on the floor beside him. It was grey and jagged and he picked it up and pressed his face into it, willing the nightmare to end. But when he pulled it away he was still in the cell, *his* cell, and there were fragments of grey fluff stuck to his stubbled face. There was a bed, mattress, no pillow, a table, two chairs, a bare lightbulb, linoleum floor stained with blood and cigarette burns. It smelt of . . . *Dettol*. The door opened and he looked up, hoping for a familiar face, but it was another stranger. Corrigan said: 'What the fuck is going on?'

But he was ignored. His arm was grabbed and his watch wrestled off.

Murder.

As the constable left the cell Corrigan heard a long stream of something loud and guttural. The constable was framed in the doorway, but behind him he caught the merest glimpse of Lelewala being dragged fighting and screaming into the next cell.

Corrigan leapt towards the door. He grabbed the constable back by the shoulder and yelled: 'What's going on?' in his startled face. 'What's she done?' he demanded.

The constable thumped him.

Corrigan tasted the blood on his lip even before his head cracked off the linoleum. And he could feel the bump on his head beginning to rise even before the boot thumped into his ribs.

He groaned and retched. The constable began to circle, looking for the next exposed area to strike. He found it: the lower back. Bending, he shot his fist into the soft flesh and Corrigan was face down. Then the toe of his boot in his arse.

He couldn't move. Then the constable was kneeling beside him. When he spoke his voice was a rough hiss. 'She was pregnant.'

Corrigan blinked uncomprehendingly. 'Lelewala?'

'Your wife.'

His body was suddenly racked by great involuntary shudders; it was as if his soul was choking. He spread his hands out on the floor of the cell, trying to hold on. But he could not. He was falling. He forced his eyes shut.

But there was no place to hide.

Nicola.

Nicola dead.

Nicola pregnant and dead.

He could not stop the tears. The shudders. Racked by pain and guilt and memories.

Please God. Please God no.

Hours later. Countless, miserable, lonely, cold, shaking hours later, a cop, a cop he knew, a cop who worked for *him*, came into the cell. Bringing in water. Looking uncomfortable. 'Jimmy . . . Jimmy,' Corrigan whispered urgently, 'what the fuck is going on? What happened to my wife?'

Jimmy put down the mug and looked at him awkwardly. 'Sir. Sorry. They told me not to . . .'

'Jimmy, for fuck's sake – my wife!'

'I know. I'm very sorry. But you shouldn't've . . .'

'I didn't do . . .' He was about to launch into an anguished defence. But he stopped himself. He took a deep breath. Steady. *Steady*. 'Jimmy, please, just tell me what's happened. Who the fuck are all these cops?'

Jimmy looked warily at the door. 'From headquarters. As soon as they found . . . Mr Stirling called them in as soon as he realized who . . .'

'Stirling called them in?'

'Yes, sir.'

'Fuck,' said Corrigan.

'Fuck indeed,' said a voice from the door, and he didn't have to look up. Chief of Police Dunbar. In beige suit and hairstyle, and still only one of them from choice. There was another beige suit with him. Younger, square-jawed, blue eyes. He nodded at Jimmy and Jimmy scooted out.

They entered the cell. 'Frank,' Dunbar said, 'this is Carl Turner. He's going to ask you some questions.'

Turner nodded at Corrigan, then pulled out a chair from the table and sat. He looked at Corrigan again and said: 'Sit.'

'Who the fuck do you think you're talking to?' Corrigan spat.

'A murderer,' Turner said.

Corrigan looked at Dunbar. 'There's no need for this,' he said. 'For godsake, I'm a friggin' cop . . .'

Dunbar smiled. 'Indeed you are. Which is why we have to be seen to be treating you the same as everyone else. If not worse.' He walked out of the cell, pulling the door closed behind him.

Corrigan slapped his hands against the cell door. He rested his forehead on it. His wife was dead. Nicola was dead. Aimie's mother. Dead. Dead. *Dead*. He took in a deep breath, held it, then slowly let it out. He turned and looked at Turner.

'Have a seat, please,' Turner said.

Corrigan walked across to the table and sat down. Turner was looking at the bruise already forming up on Corrigan's cheek. 'Fall?' he inquired, with a slight raise of his eyebrows.

'Aye,' said Corrigan. 'Shouldn't there be two of you?'

'This is just a preliminary interview.'

'Shouldn't someone read me my rights?'

'Someone did. Although very quietly.'

'Tell me about my wife.'

'Why don't you tell me?'

Corrigan shook his head. He stared at the table. 'She's dead,' he said quietly. 'Murdered.' Turner nodded. 'And you think I did it.' Corrigan looked up abruptly, anger suddenly flashing across his face. 'Although if you don't mind me making a wild suggestion, picking up the fucking fat bastard who broke her jaw might be worth considering.'

Turner ignored him. 'You have quite a background. Five murder charges.'

'Acquitted,' Corrigan said. 'Acquitted. Acquitted. Acquitted. Acquitted.'

'Still,' said Turner, 'makes you wonder. What brought you to Niagara?'

'I came for the waters.'

Turner smiled. 'OK. Where were you last night?'

'At home.'

'Talk to anyone?'

'No.'

'What time did you go out at?'

Corrigan shrugged. 'I went for a walk.'

'Meet anyone?'

'No.'

'When did you last see your wife?'

'Yesterday.'

'Last night?'

'No.'

'Tell me about Gretchin Solyakhov.'

'What?'

'Tell me about Gretchin Solyakhov.'

'You just told me everything I know about her.'

'How much did you pay her?'

'I didn't pay her anything.'

'So she did it for nothing? A crime of passion, then?'

Corrigan shook his head. Turner took out a packet of cigarettes and offered him one. Corrigan accepted and managed to stop his hands from shaking as he bent for a light.

'Frank,' Turner said quietly, 'you know how it works here. Make it easy on yourself. Tell us what happened; we'll do the best we can for you.'

Corrigan stroked his bruised cheek. 'Somebody already tried.'

Turner looked a little miffed, said, 'It wasn't *an order*. The guys get upset when a pregnant woman gets murdered.'

Corrigan closed his eyes. 'I didn't know she was pregnant.'

'Would that have stopped you killing her?'

'I didn't fucking kill her.' He sighed. He put the cigarette out. 'Do I get to see a lawyer?' he asked.

'Eventually,' said the cop. 'How did you meet Gretchin Solyakhov?'

'I have never met Gretchin Solyakhov.'

'How did you meet Bobby Doyle?'

'I came home one day, he was fucking my wife.'

'When did you last see him?'

'Yesterday. I went to see him because he broke my wife's jaw.' He paused, managed a weak smile. 'Look at that, a clue.'

'You threatened him.'

'Did not.'

'He broke your wife's jaw and you didn't threaten him?'

'I'm not a violent man.'

'He made a complaint about you yesterday afternoon. Down at headquarters. Something about a gun.'

Corrigan shrugged. 'I didn't threaten him. I gave him some advice.'

'Tell me about Gretchin Solyakhov . . .' Turner asked.

Corrigan rolled his eyes. 'What would you like to know?'

'Whatever you would like to tell me.'

Corrigan took a deep breath. 'She's a Russian immigrant.' A flicker of excitement crossed the detective's eyes. 'Her father was a scientist. Her mother mined lithium near St Petersburg. She studied classical violin at the Sorbonne.' Corrigan paused, as if he was having second thoughts about spilling the beans. Turner blinked hopefully at him. 'I would like to tell you that, but I don't know what the fuck I'm talking about. Who is Gretchin Solyakhov?'

'She's the woman who was pulled out of the Niagara.'

'Lelew . . .'

'She was found at the murder scene. In fact, beside the bodies.'

'Bodies?'

The officer nodded slowly, noting the surprise suddenly etched on Frank Corrigan's face.

23

Corrigan did not sleep. He lay on the bed and tried to stop the world from revolving and his heart from exploding. He picked at his fingernails. They had come earlier and taken samples from beneath them and now they felt uncomfortable. A lock of his hair. A syringe full of his blood. A gob of his saliva. It wasn't beyond the bounds of possibility that they would ask for semen too. They had given so little away. He had no idea how Nicola had died. Or the Fat Man. His wife was dead and they would ask him to wank in a bucket. He closed his eyes, rubbed the top of his nose. His face was grim and his mouth was tight, and it wasn't just the thought of masturbating to order.

Nicola.

On a slab.

It was a small-town police station and not usually that busy, but throughout the night the sounds of murder throbbed through the linoleum. Double murder was big. Double murder with a cop involved was bigger still, and double murder with a cop and a love triangle was biggest of all. Not that there was a love triangle: there was something to do with love, but it was formless and did not adhere to any of the established rules of geometry.

The big fat bastard was dead.

And of course Corrigan was implicated.

But Lelewala?

Lelewala?

At *his* house?

How? Why? He closed his eyes. He rubbed at them. What possible reason could she have for killing them? For even knowing of their existence? She had come back to fight a great evil. If the worst she could find was Nicola and Big Trousers then she was not only bonkers, but had a poor understanding of the state of the world.

He listened. He knew the station intimately. The nights he had spent here, working, drinking, seeking refuge from Nicola's infidelity. If you were quiet enough, if you stilled everything, then there were no bounds to what you could hear. Every whisper. Every creak. Every ring of a phone, the tramp of anxious feet. Words. Whispered. Shouted. Gossiped. Even *sung*. They left the cell light on. Every half-hour an eye appeared at the spyhole to check that he had not begun tunnelling out. Somewhere, somewhere, there was a TV playing. *It's A Wonderful Life*. Snatches of it.

At some point in time there came a soft tapping on the wall dividing him from Lelewala. He listened for a while, trying to detect if it was semaphore, but it was formless and arrhythmic. It could well just be the plumbing. He tapped some simple words in response anyway. Just *Hello* and *Nice here, isn't it?* He could picture her only as he had seen her at the women's refuge, naked and beautiful, and he found it difficult to equate such beauty, and such nudity, with death and horror. How could she? And why?

When he had finished tapping, he waited for a response. But nothing came. And then he wondered if the bizarre acoustics of the station were sufficient to relay his ghostly wall-taps to others, to detectives, and if any of them were intelligent enough to read them. He tapped: *I am ready to confess*. Then waited thirty minutes for a rush of feet outside.

When he was just on the verge of sleep, when his eyes finally, finally gave up the fight and reluctantly began to lower the shutters, they came back in and questioned him. Again and again. Turner, always, he was the constant, but other detectives too. None that he knew. It seemed like Chief Dunbar had moved half of Toronto's detectives in to grill him. But they got nothing more, because there was nothing more to tell. He got a little out of them: not that they volunteered it, but he could detect it from the pattern and content of their questions. That Nicola had been shot three times. Fat Trousers likewise. That Lelewala had been found at the scene, but no weapon. His gun had been checked by forensics, but was clean.

The door opened again. He was lying on his bed, eyes closed. He didn't even bother opening them, just rolled up into a sitting position and tried to stop himself yawning, because yawning somehow suggested that he was relaxed, and he was anything but. He was taut.

The voice said, 'Inspector, how are you?' and his eyes snapped open.

The Barracuda. Vincenzi. All tan and leer.

'What the fuck do you want?'

'You asked for a lawyer.'

'I asked for a lawyer. Not a fish.'

'Come, come, Inspector. Please. You need a lawyer. I'm the best in the business. Let me help.' He crossed the cell and put his immaculate leather briefcase down on the table. He flashed pearly-white teeth at Corrigan. 'The first thing we do is get you out of here.'

'The first thing we do,' Corrigan responded, 'is you tell me why you're really here. Court-appointed lawyers don't wear suits like that.'

'No, of course they don't.' He removed a yellow legal pad from his briefcase and a fountain pen from inside his jacket pocket. 'Let's just say I like to do charity cases from time to time. It keeps my feet on the ground.'

'You haven't got a charitable bone in your body. Try again.'

'OK, Inspector, you got me. Let's just say that a friend has asked me to represent you in this matter.' His pen hovered above the first page. 'Your full name . . . ?'

'A friend of yours or a friend of mine?'

'A friend.'

'Must be yours, because I think I'm seriously short of friends right now.'

'Your full name?'

'Just tell me,' Corrigan said, 'who the fuck it is?'

'Your friend, and mine, prefers to remain anonymous. Now . . .'

Corrigan sighed. 'OK. Have it your way. It's still no go. Look, Vincenzi, we know each other. We know the kind of people you represent, and there's a world of difference between them and me. For a start, I'm innocent.'

'I don't doubt that. But it's not me you have to convince.'

'Do you think for one moment that being tied up with you is going to help my case?'

'It can't make it any worse, Inspector. You hear that sound?'

Corrigan listened. 'What sound?'

'Vultures, circling. They're out to get you, Corrigan; you should take help where it's offered.'

'I haven't done anything.'

'That's what Joan of Arc said. Corrigan, your wife and her boyfriend are dead. You threatened him with a gun yesterday. You are a close acquaintance of the woman arrested at the murder scene.'

Corrigan nodded at the wall. 'Lelewala. She's an Indian Princess,' he said, somewhat hopefully.

'Her name is Solyakhov. Gretchin. She's from Georgia – that's Russia, not the States. Naturalized Canadian. Been here five years. Three convictions for prostitution, one for possession of cocaine. When she's not too stressed out she speaks perfect English. She didn't pull the trigger, either, Corrigan. Forensics cleared her. They have nothing on you, and nothing much on her. There is *no* evidence. So it's not going to take very much for me to get you out of here – if you just give me a little co-operation. Fire me by all means once you've got your freedom, but just let me get you out of here first, OK?'

Corrigan looked at him, confused still by his apparent enthusiasm. Then suddenly it came to him and he lay back on the bed and laughed.

'What's so funny?' the Barracuda asked.

'Tell me, Mr Vincenzi,' Corrigan asked, 'do you often beat your wife up?'

24

They released him shortly after breakfast. Theirs, not his.

It was a long, silent walk up the stairs and through the station, his cops, *his* cops, averting their eyes all the way. He picked up his watch. Somebody had brought him a suit from his apartment and a pair of shoes. He signed papers wordlessly, he listened while a detective he didn't know told him to stay in town. He was to report to the station daily. They were holding on to his passport. And his badge. And his gun. He was suspended on full pay.

At the doorway he stopped and looked back, looked at them all. Still, their eyes went to desks, to windows, to anywhere but him.

'Thanks,' he said quietly.

There were reporters outside. Camera crews. He hesitated. He could go back and ask about the rear exit. But no, he wasn't going to give them the satisfaction. He stepped forward and was instantly enveloped. He said nothing. He pushed through. A taxi had stopped to watch the commotion. He pushed through the throng to it and pulled open the door. He climbed into the back seat. The cameramen bustled around. The reporters shouted questions he ignored. The taxi did not move, even after he said, 'The morgue.'

'What're you doing?' Corrigan asked.

'Milking the publicity,' said the driver, and sat for a further minute. Then he nodded. 'That ought to do it. Morgue you say?'

Morgue. *Morgue.*

Cold.

Slab.

The attendant pulled her out. Autopsy stitches and pale, pallid, deathly skin.

But beautiful, still.

'Can you leave me with her?'

'No.'

Corrigan nodded. He put his fingers on her brow and ran them down her face. He touched her lips.

'She was shot three times,' Corrigan said.

The attendant nodded. He'd worked with him before. But he'd been a policeman then, not a murder suspect, and the difference in attitude wasn't subtle.

He kissed her on the forehead. Then he turned to the attendant and said: 'Thanks.'

The attendant nodded, then pushed her back in.

He walked to Turner House. With his collar up and the rain on his face so that you couldn't tell it from the tears. He had seen bodies before. He had killed people before. But never his own. She had no longer been his, but she would always be his. Sense and non-sensibility.

He was a cop; his first thought should have been: who?

But instead he stopped at Whiskey Nick's. It was on the way. He ordered a whisky. The octogenarian jocks were there, still, or returned. They looked at him, then they looked at the TV screen and they saw him there again. He sipped his whisky. He was coming out of the courthouse looking pale and disorientated. And then there was a reporter speaking to camera and it was Madeline. Madeline Hume. From Channel ... whatever. The sound was turned down. He could not read her lips. But he could watch them: red, full of life, not blue, full of *nothing*. His hand shook, he dropped his glass. It shattered on the floor. The barman looked at him. Corrigan said sorry again and hurried out of the door.

He rang the bell at Turner House and a spindly woman in a turquoise jumpsuit answered the door with a reassuring smile that fell away the instant she twigged him. He asked to see Annie and she shut the door. He stood for several minutes, giving her the benefit of the doubt. Then the door opened and Annie was there looking out at him.

'Hi,' Corrigan said.

'Hi,' said Annie.

There was no invitation. He shivered. 'I'd like to see my daughter.'

After a little bit Annie nodded. 'Sure,' she said, 'come on through.'

He walked through the door. The woman from before with the

shotgun was standing in exactly the same spot. 'Try anything funny,' she said, 'I'll blow your head clean off.'

'I don't do funny,' Corrigan said, and followed Annie through the house and into the kitchen. The house felt curiously empty. Quiet.

The kitchen was big in every way. Big workbenches and a cooker you could launch rockets from. Lots of catering-sized pots and pans and boxes and tins. 'You could feed the five thousand,' Corrigan said as they passed.

'Sometimes we have to,' Annie said, without a trace of anything.

'But not today,' Corrigan said. 'It's very quiet.'

'Quiet as a morgue,' said Annie.

She took him into the backyard. It had been turned into a playground. Swings. Roundabout. Slide. It was partially covered against the elements by a wooden extension. Aimie was swinging. Singing happily. She wore a red-and-blue anorak and a smile as wide as the Niagara as she saw her daddy approaching.

'She doesn't know,' Annie said.

There was a picnic table. Corrigan sat on the table with his feet on the seat while Annie went and got some coffee and juice for Aimie. He watched her swing and joked with her. Annie came back with the coffee and set it down.

'It is quiet,' Annie said, 'and I'm sorry. For saying that.'

'It's OK,' said Corrigan.

'We go through quiet periods. Sometimes it's the weather. Sometimes it's a sad film on TV. Or a happy one. Sometimes it's the news. Day Princess Diana died, they all shipped back to their hubbies.' She shrugged.

Corrigan, looking at his daughter, said: 'What do I say? How do I tell her?'

'I usually find the truth is best.'

He shook his head. 'She's five and I'm the chief suspect. I think not.'

Steady gaze. 'Did you do it?' To the point.

'No. Of course not.'

Annie nodded slowly. 'I liked Nicola,' she said. 'But she had a lot of problems.'

'A big fat one in particular.' He swallowed. He looked away. 'I think she still loved me. I think she wanted to get back with me.'

He looked back. Annie was looking at him strangely. He gave a short little laugh. 'Eternal optimist.'

'I don't think she did.'

'She *told* me she still loved me.'

'She felt guilty about what she'd done to you. But she didn't love you.'

'Excuse me?'

'We talked a lot over the past few months, Corrigan. It's what I *do*.'

Corrigan took a deep breath, then let it out slowly. He faked a reassuring smile for Aimie, then turned back to Annie. 'What are you trying to say?'

'I'm trying to say . . . I try to sort these women out. Whatever their problem is. Put their lives back together, or sort out a new one.'

'And?'

'She didn't love the fat guy either, if that's any consolation. She was going to take Aimie and move south. New York. Only she wasn't that strong, she needed an excuse to get out. Getting him jealous was one way, getting smoochie with you again so that he'd hit her and she'd be forced to move out. It happens a lot, Corrigan.'

'She *told* you this?' Annie nodded. 'She *used* me?'

Annie shrugged. 'We all use each other.'

'The conniving little . . .'

She dropped her voice so Aimie wouldn't hear. 'They're burying her, Corrigan.'

'Deep enough, I hope.'

'You don't mean that.'

'I fucking do.'

'No you don't.'

Aimie jumped off the swing and came running. 'Will you stop fucking cursing, Daddy?' she said.

Corrigan's jaw dropped. Annie Spitz guffawed.

A flustered Corrigan said: 'Where'd you learn that word, Aimie?'

'What word, Daddy?' She smiled as innocently and as knowingly as . . . *her mother*, and for a moment his heart stopped.

Corrigan shook his head. 'Doesn't matter, love,' he said, and stroked her hair. She ran to the roundabout and shouted: 'Push it, Daddy, push it!'

'Can you believe that?' he said to Annie.

'Heard worse from a lot younger.'

He smiled too then and crossed to give the roundabout a push. 'I wanted to thank you,' Corrigan said to Annie, 'for arranging the Barracuda.'

Annie nodded without thinking. Then she said, 'What barracuda?'

'Sorry,' said Corrigan, giving another push, Aimie shrieking as it speeded up, 'Vincenzi. The lawyer.'

'What lawyer?'

'The one that got me out. I presume he owes . . .'

'Sorry, Corrigan, but you've lost me.'

'You didn't organize a lawyer for me?'

Annie cleared her throat. 'No offence, but you may have murdered one of my girls. I'm not about to go arranging a lawyer for you.'

'Oh,' said Corrigan. 'Right.'

25

Annie was OK. She agreed to look after Aimie. At least until after the funeral. He had no idea when that would be. He had to pick out a coffin. Contact relatives. Explain. And all the while them thinking: *You did it.*

No, I didn't.

Well who did? Your girlfriend? The Indian?

She's not an Indian. And she's not my girlfriend.

Oh yeah?

She's a Russian hooker with a conviction for coke.

Coke.

Pongo.

The convention.

Tenuous.

He tramped home towards his apartment. It started to pelt with rain. He sought shelter under a tree and watched as lightning split the sky. It probably wasn't the best place to stand. But he didn't care. If he'd had an aerial he would have lifted it up above his head and challenged Mother Nature to strike him dead. But he didn't. He rarely carried an aerial with him.

Across the road a car stopped and a window zipped down. A woman shouted something.

He peered through the curtain of rain like a nosey relative. He splashed through the puddles and peered into the car.

'I said, can I give you a lift.' Madeline.

'Oh. Sorry. I thought you were looking for directions.'

'A cop to the end.'

'This is the end.'

'I know. Get in. I'll give you a lift. Where are you going?'

He hesitated. He wanted to say, no, fuck away off, leave me alone, but he also wanted to say yes, get me out of here, take me away. Keep driving. Keep driving till the sun gets his hat out and puts it on. 'I'm torn between killing myself, picking out a coffin for my wife or solving this dastardly crime.'

She smiled. 'I don't think I've ever heard anyone say dastardly before. Not out loud.'

'I think Sherlock Holmes did. Or if he didn't Watson certainly did.'

'Is that what you're going to do, solve the crime?'

Corrigan shrugged. 'The alternatives are too depressing. And try as I can, I just can't get very excited about killing myself.'

'Get in.'

He got in. She looked sympathetically at him. 'Thanks for the piece on the TV,' he said. Her smile faded. 'It looked really good, but I couldn't hear a word of it.'

'I'm sorry,' she said, 'it's my job.'

'I know.'

A car gave her a blast from behind. Madeline started to drive. 'Were you seeing your daughter?'

Corrigan nodded.

'How's she taking it?'

'She's not. Yet. I can tell her when I can look her in the eye and say I caught the fella that did it.'

'You think it was a guy?'

'You mean, do I not think it was Lelewala?'

Madeline nodded.

'No, I don't think it was Lelewala.'

'I don't know whether your loyalty to her is quaint or sad or suspicious.'

Corrigan shrugged. 'That's up to you.'

Madeline smiled. 'I think you're half in love with a myth. Except she's not a myth, she's a little miss. Close, but not the same. Gretchin . . .'

'Solyakhov, I know.'

'Convictions for prostitution and . . .'

'Coke. I know. What's your . . .'

'And didn't even survive going over the Falls. Nothing very mythical . . .'

'Didn't even survive what?'

'The Falls. She didn't . . . you *didn't* hear my report?'

'I told you. I was too busy looking at my dead wife.'

'Right. OK. I'm sorry.'

'The Falls?'

'The Falls. She didn't go over. That was part of my report. I turned up a couple of witnesses saw her being thrown into the river below the Falls.'

Corrigan drummed his fingers on the dash.

'You're disappointed, aren't you?'

'Why would I be disappointed?'

'I've seen her. She's a stunner.'

'She's not that great. When did *you* see her?'

'About half an hour ago. When she got released. I'm on my way to interview her.'

26

It wasn't an appointment. Madeline had tried to talk to her outside the station, coming out on the arm of her lawyer, one Thomas Vincenzi, a.k.a. the Barracuda, but had been brushed off. A cop with a Hitler moustache had begrudgingly released her home address to the lady from the press, but refused to answer questions.

Corrigan was surprised to find that Lelewala, Gretchin, *whatever*, lived only a few blocks from his own apartment. They probably used the same stores. Had rented the same videos.

It was the top apartment in a rickety three-storey house. The front lawn was strewn with rubbish.

'Pretty rich neighbourhood,' Madeline said.

'Sarcasm,' Corrigan replied, 'is the lowest form of wit.'

'I'm not being sarcastic. You see that stuff?'

She was looking at the rubbish in the garden. Corrigan looked closer. There was a CD player sitting on the lawn. And beside it there was a video. A microwave. Shirts. Shoes. Handbags. He looked back at the video. It was fractured. There was a dent in the grass where it had landed. As they got out of the car there was a sudden movement on the top floor. Then a crash as a television hit the ground and a boom as the tube exploded with a sullen thump.

Corrigan saw a familiar face looking out at them. He tutted. 'Mrs Capalski,' he shouted up, 'what on earth are you doing?'

She glared down at him. 'Oh my God,' she said, 'I knew you two killers connected. What the fuck you think I do? Ain't no killers stay in my apartment. I go to your place next, Frankie Corrigan. I throw your stuff outta window too.'

'Mrs Capalski, there's no need . . .'

A lamp exploded to the left of them. Madeline gave a little shout.

Corrigan walked forward, his shoes crinkling over broken glass.

He bent his neck back to talk up to her. 'I paid my rent, Mrs Capalski, I'm all up to date.'

'I don't give a fuck, Frankie Corrigan. Some bills you can't settle.'

'Mrs Capalski . . .'

'Don't *Mrs Capalski* me . . . that poor girl murdered.'

'It wasn't me, Mrs Capalski! Look at me, aren't I standing here? I'm innocent.'

'Mr Big Police Man, you not so high and mighty now. You kill your wife, you get the fuck outta my apartment.' She stepped back from the window.

Corrigan rolled his eyes. 'C'mon,' he said to Madeline, 'let's take a look.'

He started towards the door. 'Why don't we just wait here?' Madeline said. 'It's all coming down anyway.' Then she smiled and followed.

When they arrived at the top floor the door to Lelewala's apartment was open and Mrs Capalski was back at the window emptying out a drawer full of underclothes. She glanced round at them and said: 'You not the first.'

'I not the first what?' Corrigan asked.

'Come looking for her. I have no time for men with guns! You have a gun with you, Frankie Corrigan?'

He opened his jacket, showed her he was clean.

'What you do, leave it at the crime scene? Anyway,' and she took a break to fire a shoe out of the open window, 'I don't know where she is, if that's what you want. I tell you that for nothing. Or in fact I tell you that for five hundred dollars, 'cause if you think you gettin' your deposit back after this, you can go whistle up a fucking stick for it.'

'Mrs Capalski, *keep* the five hundred dollars. Tell me who was asking for her.'

'How the fuck do I know? Men. Men with guns. You know more about that sorta thing than me. They come round, threaten to shoot if I don't tell them where she is. I tell them with great pleasure, but I don't know where the fuck . . .'

She let fire with another shoe. Corrigan tried to get more out of her while Madeline nosed about the apartment. But she couldn't tell him anything beyond the fact that they looked like standard-issue hoods. She hadn't seen Lelewala for weeks. He switched tack. He tried to save his own apartment. It wasn't much, but it was all he had. And then even while he was arguing with her he started thinking about Nicola again and the house they had bought together. Would it revert to him now? Had the sale gone through? Would the purchasers change their minds now? Would the realtors amend the sales pitch from Niagara Falls views to Niagara Falls views plus free chalk outlines of murdered previous owners?

'I'm sure a simple notice to quit would have sufficed,' Corrigan said.

She looked at him. 'I'm an old woman, I don't need this shit. You betta get right round to your place, Frankie Corrigan, and clear it out, 'cause all your gear's going the same way as this hooker's.' She threw another shoe out of the window. 'I was like a mother to you . . .'

'I didn't see you from one end of the month till the next!'

'Didn't I rent you an apartment, good rate too? Didn't I feel sorry for you, thrown out by your wife, and make sure the refrigerator was working OK, and get a man to fix the window that broke when the last no-good bastard broke it with his basketball? Didn't I do that? I never asked for nothing in return, but rent. What do you do? You murder your wife and then the whole world knows I rent rooms to the son of the bitch who kills his wife and a fat person.'

'I didn't kill anyone!'

'I saw it on the news. You sure as hell killed someone!' She heaved another armful of clothes out of the window, then nodded across at Madeline. 'Hey,' she said, as if she was seeing her for the first time, 'who the fuck are you?'

Corrigan sighed. 'Just a friend.'

'Your wife not cold yet, already you have another woman.'

'She's just a . . . oh fuck it. It doesn't matter.' He walked across to Madeline and snagged her arm. 'You ready to go?'

'Sure.' She'd been looking in a duffle bag, which she hoisted up over her shoulder. 'Let's go.'

They hurried down the stairs, both of them smiling, though there was little to smile about. 'So,' Madeline said, 'we're not the only ones looking for Lelewala.'

'We?' said Corrigan.

Madeline smiled. 'We're a team now, aren't we?'

Corrigan cleared his throat.

'C'mon, Corrigan. What have you got to lose?'

'I don't know where to begin.'

She climbed into the car. Corrigan got into the passenger seat. 'I better get home,' he said, 'pick up my stuff. The lady's not for changing.'

Madeline nodded. 'I wanted to show you something first,' she said, pulling the duffle bag round into her lap, 'might change your mind.'

'That's theft,' Corrigan said.

'So call a cop.' She opened the top and pulled out a photo. It was Lelewala, maybe ten years younger, just a kid, with her parents, he presumed. Her father wore an army uniform and there were a couple of medals on his chest, but nothing to suggest he had attained any significant rank. Her mother wore the kind of smart pink dress that had been fashionable in the fifties, or last month in Eastern Europe. Neither of them looked as if they could summon up a rain dance for the Tuscorora Iroquois.

'You should have seen the bedroom,' Madeline was saying. 'Or should I say *the office*? Smelt of incense, and dope. There was a nice black satin sheet on the bed and a mirror on the ceiling. A packet of condoms on a locker beside the bed. Do you want me to go on?'

He shook his head.

'She's no Julia Roberts, Corrigan.'

'I thank heaven for little mercies.'

'Do you know what I think you are?' He looked at her, then shrugged. 'A romantic. You believe in love at first sight, and all that shit, don't you?'

'What were you going to show me?'

She smiled and returned her attention to the duffle bag. Her hand delved back inside it and felt around for a few seconds. Then she produced a book. A children's book. 'I found it in her room.' Thick, hard pages. On the front there was the picture of an Indian woman rowing her canoe over the edge of a raging waterfall. The book was called *The Legend of the Maid of the Mist*, and its author was one Tarriha Long Fellow.

27

She was waiting for him to say, 'Do you want to come in?' But he just got out of the car and walked towards his apartment. She wasn't sure if it was a curt dismissal, bad manners or simply that his mind was elsewhere. So she got out and followed and when she drew level with him he turned slightly and looked at her as if he was seeing her for the first time. A sad little smile appeared on his face. She said: 'Are you OK?'

He nodded. He led her up the back stairs and unlocked the door. 'Come on in,' he said. 'You'll have to excuse the mess.' He paused. 'And the guns.'

She saw two men standing just inside the door, pointing guns at them. Corrigan looked at them for several moments, then shook his head and walked between them. 'Just make yourselves at home,' he said. He crossed to a cupboard and pulled down a bottle of vodka. It was half-empty. Or half-full, depending on your outlook.

The men stood looking at her suspiciously for several moments, then turned to Corrigan. He'd taken down four glasses from the same cupboard and was starting to pour.

The tallest of the men had a Hitler moustache. He pocketed his gun and said: 'Sorry, Frank, it had to be done.'

Corrigan handed him a glass. He lifted the second and held it out for the other man. 'What changed your mind?' he asked.

The second man let his gun drop to his side. 'You sowed the seed. It just took a while to sink in.'

Corrigan brought the third glass to Madeline, then pushed the door shut behind her. 'Madeline. Let me introduce you. This is Mark Stirling. My erstwhile partner down at the cop shop, although latterly the man who had me arrested.'

'We've met,' Madeline said dryly.

'Have we?' said Stirling.

'And this is James Morton, formerly of the FBI and lately

dismissive of the biggest criminal conspiracy this country has ever known. Guys, this is Madeline Hume; she's a reporter from Channel 4. She's made me a household name, like Charles Manson.' He held up his glass and drained it in one. Then he wiped his mouth and said: 'Do youse want to form a fucking fan club for me, or what?'

Morton had shaved. He had washed. His hair was still long but it sat OK. You couldn't wash away fatigue and depression; Corrigan could still see that in his eyes, and there was a limited amount he could have done in a matter of hours about the saggy folds of flesh hanging from his jaw. But he looked one hell of a lot better.

Stirling was trying to justify himself. 'I had to do it. You know that. You would have done the same.' Corrigan looked at him. Stirling looked pained. 'Well you *might* have done the same.'

'I *might* have given you the benefit of the doubt.'

'C'mon, Frank. It had to be done. I thought they'd just send in a couple of detectives. I didn't expect the heavy artillery. The fucking place is swamped.'

'You're telling *me* this?'

'I know. I'm sorry. What can I say?'

'Sorry. Again.'

'Sorry. Again.'

Corrigan turned to Morton. 'And what brought you out of the woodwork?'

'He did,' said Morton, pointing at Stirling. 'He asked for help.'

'What happened to the paranoid delusions of a coke addict?'

'I didn't want to believe it. Then I did a little checking. I'm still plugged in to the system, even if I'm no longer a part of it. I was able to check names, movements, patterns of movements, movements of patterns. And when you see everyone moving in one direction then you tend to give a little more credence to what remain, essentially, the paranoid delusions of a coke addict. If you're right about the convention, and I believe you are . . . well, you're going to need all the help you can get.'

Corrigan nodded. From behind, Madeline said: 'What convention?'

They all looked at her. Then at each other. Morton said: 'Can you vouch for her?'

Corrigan shook his head.

'Thanks,' Madeline said.

'I want your word that nothing you hear goes outside this room,' Morton said. 'Unless we approve.'

Madeline pursed her lips.

'You're asking a reporter for her *word*?' Stirling asked.

'You mean it's off the record,' Madeline said.

'No,' Morton said, '*that* means you can write about it but not name your source. *This* isn't to be written about, talked about, *breathed*.'

'If I don't know what *this* is, I can't make that kind of promise. I mean, it might be in the national interest.'

'This *is* in the national interest. And that's precisely why you can't talk about it.'

'You'll need to tell me more.'

Morton rolled his eyes.

'Throw her the fuck out,' said Stirling.

'Madeline,' Corrigan said, 'do you want to hear this, or do you not?'

She sighed. She nodded. 'OK. I won't tell a soul. Promise.'

'*Promise*,' said Stirling.

'OK,' said Morton.

Corrigan poured himself another glass and pulled a chair out from the kitchen table. The others followed suit. They sat about the table, eyeing each other up like strangers at a high-stakes poker game. 'OK, Mr Morton, James, Jimmy . . . do you want to start? Do you want to tell us what you know about the convention?'

Morton nodded solemnly. He fingered his glass. Corrigan proffered the bottle; Morton hesitated, then shook his head. 'I want to tell you,' he said slowly, 'about TCOs.'

28

'TCOs,' Morton said. 'Transnational criminal organizations.'

Corrigan nodded. 'You mean the Mafia.'

'I wish it was that simple.' Morton leaned back in his chair, folded one leg over the other and looped his hands over the extended knee. 'Sure,' he said, 'if you think of organized crime you think of the Mafia. You think of Italy, the United States of course, maybe Japan. You know the Yakuza?'

Stirling nodded. 'Movie with Robert Mitchum.'

'I wish it was that simple,' Morton said, patiently. 'During the past few years we – that's the FBI – have recognized that organized crime is no longer something that is limited to a few countries. For all sorts of reasons.' He let go of his knee and began counting them off on his fingers. 'The rise of the global market for illicit drugs, the end of the Cold War, the breakdown of the barriers between East and West, the collapse of the criminal justice system in Russia and other states of the former Soviet Union, the development of free-trade areas in Europe and North America, the emergence of global financial and trading systems: the whole cartload. Put them all together and you realize that criminal organizations have had to develop into TCOs to survive.'

'It's difficult to talk about all this and then think of Pongo,' Stirling said.

'*Pongo?*' said Madeline.

'This is the problem,' Morton said. 'While you've been thinking about Pongo, I've been thinking about the struggle of the Colombian cartels to change their government's extradition policy. The attack of the Sicilian Mafia on the Italian state. The emergence of Russian criminal organizations, not only at home but in Western Europe and the United States. I'm thinking about money laundering and trafficking in nuclear material. I'm thinking about the Chinese triads, the Nigerians, the Turks . . .' He stopped, looked round the table. 'I can't emphasize enough the extent to which these TCOs violate national sovereignty, undermine democratic institutions, how they add a new dimension to problems such as nuclear proliferation and terrorism. I can't emphasize enough the *danger*.'

'And they're all in our backyard,' Corrigan said quietly.

Morton nodded. 'These organizations, they're like . . .' he clicked his fingers, looking for the right word '. . . a plate of spaghetti. Once in a while we arrest someone we're sure is important. And probably he is right up until that moment, but once we have him, he's suddenly no more than a tiny cog.' He smiled. 'Although I believe that's a mixed metaphor. I just need you to understand the magnitude of this. If you're right about this, it's the convention from hell.'

'What I don't understand,' Corrigan said, 'is why a convention at all.'

'And where Pongo comes into it,' added Madeline.

Ignoring her, Morton said: 'Why not a convention? Doesn't matter whether you're a dentist or a computer programmer or a toy salesman. People like to network, they like to find out about new developments in their field. Only these guys don't subscribe to *Drug Dealer and Money Laundering Quarterly*.'

'And they hold them, what, every year?' Stirling asked. 'Like the World Series?'

'Sure, every year. Started about seven, eight years back. You know Arruba? Sixty-nine square miles of everything the Caribbean should be, and every inch of it owned by the Sicilian Mafia. Literally. The Cuntrera Brothers, late of Siculiana, Sicily and Caracas, Venezuela, bought it out of the billion dollars they made from the North American heroin trade in the eighties. Hotels, banks, casinos, construction, building land, customs, the police and the prime minister. Bought up every one of them. So they felt safe inviting a few of their international allies for a vacation.'

'I'm betting there wasn't much vacatin',' Stirling volunteered.

Morton nodded. 'The Sicilians and Colombia's Medellin cartel agreed to join forces. Wham and you have a $300-million-a-year drugs colossus. Come the next year, word's out; everyone wants in on the deal. The American Mafias, the Russians, the Chinese Triads, the Japanese Yakuza, the usual suspects. There's a new spirit of co-operation, they sign non-aggression pacts, divide up the world, swap gossip. But as the convention gets bigger, Arruba gets smaller. They need a new venue, so it goes to Bangkok. Then New Orleans and Mexico City.'

'It's not really my field,' Madeline said, 'but I take it this isn't common knowledge, is it? How on earth do they keep it quiet?'

'No, it's not common knowledge. They buy people off. There's such a huge amount of money involved that there's few can resist it.' He looked at Corrigan. 'I'm surprised you haven't been approached.'

Corrigan smiled. 'Maybe they know better.'

'Or maybe they come at you a different way.'

'You mean my wife?'

Morton shrugged. 'Maybe. Anyway. Crime syndicates now vie for the honour of hosting it, the same way cities spend millions campaigning for the honour of hosting the Olympics or say the soccer World Cup. And once they have it, they guarantee complete secrecy, complete security. Which is why these murders interest me, and what they have to do with the Old Cripple.'

'Ah,' said Stirling, 'back to the Old Cripple.'

Morton laughed suddenly. 'The Old Cripple. It does have a certain ring to it, doesn't it? So definitely un-PC. The Old Cripple. He's hosting this year's convention in Niagara Falls.'

'Who on earth is the Old Cripple?' Madeline asked.

'He's Pongo's father.'

Corrigan told her about Pongo and the dead girl and the confession. Her reaction was, 'Pongo? Of the cute ... the great singles? I lost my virg ... Pongo?'

'One and the same,' said Stirling. 'Only he's not so cute any more. Next time he wipes his nose on his sleeve his fucking nose is going to come off, if you get my meaning.' She didn't. 'Cocaine,' he added. Madeline nodded.

'Which brings us neatly back to the Old Cripple,' Morton said, 'and what he does.'

'Which is what?' Corrigan asked.

'Jack of all trades. Master of most of them. He's an importer, exporter, facilitator, negotiator, arbitrator and killer. He's known as the Old Cripple, because, well, that's what he is. Blown up.

Years ago. Eighty per cent burns. Confined to a wheelchair. If anyone best represents the ideal that the disabled really can look after themselves, well he's the man.'

'If he's such a fucking big deal,' Stirling asked, 'how come he's living in *our* neck of the woods and we've never heard of him?'

'Because he's international. You won't find so much as a parking ticket on him here. He's global. We've been trying to get him for years. To understand him, you have to understand what he does and why he's held in such great respect. These organizations, they're going global, but you can't just throw businessmen together and hope they come to some agreement; there are too many natural obstacles. Language, culture, not to mention monstrous egos and a propensity for violence. The Old Cripple is like Henry Kissinger, Armand Hammer and the Pope rolled into one. Take the Mexicans . . .'

'I prefer not to . . .' Stirling said.

Morton laughed. 'OK, take the Nigerians. The Old Cripple has set up an alliance between the Nigerians and the Colombian cartels based on product exchange. The Nigerians are classic free-market entrepreneurs; they started out as couriers for others, but now they're major players in their own right. Cocaine and heroin. Nigerians supply heroin to Colombians in return for cocaine. This has helped the Colombians to develop their own heroin market while also allowing the Nigerians to sell cocaine in Western Europe.'

'And from it all, this Old Cripple takes a cut,' Corrigan said.

'Exactly.'

'OK,' said Stirling, 'you've got me curious about the Mexicans.'

'Much the same. He's brokered a risk-reduction alliance between them and the Colombians. The Mexicans have a well-developed smuggling infrastructure for the transport of goods and services across the frontier with the United States. The Colombians get their drugs into their primary market, and the Mexicans get a foothold in the cocaine business. More profit in cocaine than in marijuana, which is what they traditionally smuggled in. Or take people. I mean, we all know how many Mexicans come across the border illegally. The Old Cripple set up a deal between the Mexicans and the Chinese to smuggle Chinese along the same routes. We reckon there's some 2,000 a month coming across via Mexico.'

Corrigan refilled his glass. He offered another shot to Morton, but he turned it down. Stirling accepted. There was none left for Madeline. Corrigan stood and began to rifle through the cupboard. He produced an unopened bottle of Martini Bianco. 'Best I can do,' he said.

'Beggars can't be choosers,' said Madeline.

Corrigan broke the seal and poured her a glass. He offered some to Morton again. Morton raised his eyes and Corrigan apologized. As he was screwing the top back on Corrigan said: 'You seem to keep your finger pretty firmly on the pulse, for someone's been out of the saddle for so long.'

'Ignoring for the moment the mixed metaphors,' Morton replied, 'keeping my finger on the pulse has been one of the few things that has kept me going. I'm sure you heard that my . . .'

'I heard,' Corrigan said.

'You should form a club,' Stirling said, and then wished he hadn't. 'I mean, for mutual support, kind of thing.'

'What happened . . . ?' Madeline asked.

'I moved up here because I was sick to death of the media's obsession with the Empire State thing, not because I was tired of fighting crime. And then my family died in a car crash.'

'So, indirectly,' Stirling said, nodding at Madeline, 'it was your fault.'

'What is your fucking problem?' Madeline snapped.

'Journalists,' Stirling said, 'and the bullshit they . . .'

'Girls, please,' said Corrigan. 'We have to make a decision.'

'A decision?' said Madeline.

'Yes, a decision. What we're going to do. About the convention.'

Stirling rubbed his hands together. 'I should have thought that would be obvious,' he said. 'We're going to nail the fuckers.'

29

For a despairing alcoholic, James Morton was acting pretty chipper. He talked enthusiastically and animatedly about strategy, secrecy, observation and action. He was, of course, the voice of experience. He'd danced with the devil and written a book about it.

Corrigan was just a do-hickey cop by comparison.

Stirling's knee was jolting up and down with excitement.

Madeline produced a video camera from her handbag and started recording.

'Excuse me,' Stirling said, 'but what the fuck do you think you're doing?'

She removed her eye from the viewfinder. 'Fly-on-the-wall documentary.'

'I think not,' Corrigan said, reaching a hand out to block the lens.

She jerked it away from him. 'It's important,' she said, 'that there should be a record of this. To show that you got into this for all the best possible reasons.'

'Nothing to do with the fact that you work for a *television* station, of course,' Stirling said.

'Believe me,' Madeline replied, 'if this thing is as big as you all seem to think it is, you're going to want to have it on tape.'

'She may have a point,' Morton said. 'There should be a record. As long as you understand . . .'

'That I don't breathe a word until it's all over. I understand. I thought we agreed that already.'

'As long as you understand,' Morton repeated, 'that we agree on a four-way split on the profits. All the profits. I got fucked over on the Empire State deal. I mean, I did OK, but I could have done very OK if I hadn't signed away most of the rights. And *they* talked about making a historical record and accuracy and all the time they were selling the broadcast rights to Algeria. We need to agree this now or there'll be trouble further down the line. Frank?'

Morton looked to Corrigan, who was shaking his head. 'I'm interested in finding out who killed my wife and stopping this convention. It doesn't matter a fuck to me about Algerian television rights.'

'But *it will*, once it's over.'

'Believe me,' Corrigan said, 'it won't.'

'Frank,' Stirling said, 'don't be too hasty. Algeria's a big country.'

Corrigan rolled his eyes. 'OK. Right. International television rights. We split them four ways. OK? Is that OK?' Madeline nodded reluctantly. 'OK, now let's concentrate on some of the minor details like . . .'

'Who's going to play us in the movie,' said Stirling.

'. . . finding out a little more about this convention,' said Corrigan.

'Pongo may be our best route into it,' said Morton. 'If we can get to him.'

'We can get to him,' Corrigan said confidentially.

'Are we presuming,' Madeline said, 'that your girl Lelewala . . .'

'My girl?'

'That Lelewala and the murders are tied into this convention?' Corrigan looked to Morton.

'I would tend to think they must be tied in,' Morton said. 'Niagara's too small for all this shit to be happening at the same time and they're not connected in.'

'So we need to go after her as well.'

'Sure,' said Morton. 'And we need to start working on the Old Cripple.'

'We need,' Corrigan said, 'more men. And women.'

'What do you think?' Morton asked. 'Will your guys at the station work with you on this?'

Corrigan shrugged. 'It'll be hard for them if Dunbar's cracked down. I don't know. Mark, how was I doing in the popularity stakes? Do you think some of them would put their careers on the line to help me nail this . . .'

'Mmmmm?' said Stirling, suddenly aware that he was the focus of attention.

Corrigan knocked his fist on the table. 'Hello? Anybody in?'

'Sorry,' said Stirling. 'I was thinking about Brad Pitt.'

'What?' said Madeline.

'For the movie.'

'Jesus,' said Corrigan.

'To play who?' asked Madeline.

'Well,' said Stirling, and gave a shy little shrug.

Madeline started to laugh. 'You've got to be joking.'

'It's a thought,' said Stirling.

'It's a stupid thought,' said Madeline.

'Please yourself,' said Stirling. 'I won't tell you who I picked out for you.'

'Please,' said Corrigan, 'could youse just pay a little attention? Jesus! My wife has died! And you're talking about fucking film stars! Now come on!'

'OK,' Stirling said. 'Sorry.'

'Sorry,' said Madeline. 'Sorry.'

'OK,' said Corrigan. 'Now, the first thing we need to . . .'

'Kathy Bates,' said Stirling.

30

Stirling was just coming up from the cells when he saw Gretchin Solyakhov leaving the station, her dark hair tied back, her short black leather boots clicking on the tiled floor. He hurried across to the reception desk, all the time looking at her through the glass as she hurried down the steps.

The cop behind nodded and said: 'Yeah, I know.'

'What was she . . . ?'

'Notifying us of her change of address. Condition of her bail. Beats me how a broad as good-looking as that could get tied up in all that shit.'

Stirling took a look at the address and followed her out of the door. She had climbed into a battered Oldsmobile. As she drove off Stirling lifted his mobile and called Corrigan at his apartment. His former apartment. Mrs Capalski had called by. She hadn't mellowed any. Now he was packing his bags, with Madeline's reluctant assistance.

'How's it going?' Stirling asked.

Corrigan glanced at Madeline, standing with CDs in her hand, and shook his head. 'We're arguing over what I should keep and what I should throw out. And I don't know her from Adam.'

'I told you she was trouble. And speaking of trouble, Gretchin Solyakhov just walked past me.'

'Lelewala?'

'No, Gretchin Solyakhov. I have her new address if you want it.'

Corrigan clicked his fingers at Madeline for a pen. She looked daggers at him, then lifted her handbag off the floor and produced one. 'Thanks,' Corrigan said, then 'Shoot,' into the receiver.

'I wish you wouldn't say that,' Stirling said. 'Rainbow Motor Lodge, apartment sixteen. Do you want me to take a run out there . . .'

'No. I need somewhere to kip anyway. I may as well take a look out there.'

'Uhuh,' said Stirling.

'Uhuh yourself. How's the recruitment going?'

'Slowly. The *Come and Hear the Pregnant Wife Killer Justify Himself* spiel isn't exactly going down a treat.' Stirling thought about what he'd said for a moment. Then gulped. 'Sorry. But we'll get there, don't worry.'

Corrigan drove. Madeline sat on the passenger seat, weighed down with plastic bags. The back seat and the boot were filled with plastic bags as well.

'You've never heard of suitcases,' she was saying.

'My wife got custody,' Corrigan replied.

'*And* the child?'

'And the child.'

'You didn't fight her for it?'

'*It?*'

'Her. Aimie.'

'You obviously don't have children. Or if you do you hate them.'

'No. I don't have children.'

'You should. Aimie's the best thing ever happened to me.'

'So you must have been pretty angry when you lost her.'

'Angry enough to kill my wife. *Sure.*' Corrigan shrugged. 'Nicola was just better equipped to look after Aimie than me.'

'Equipped? We're not talking stereotypes here?'

He started to deny it, then stopped and smiled. 'OK. We *are* talking stereotypes. But then stereotypes aren't stereotypes for no reason.'

Madeline tutted. 'No, clichés aren't clichés for no reason. Stereotypes are just stereotypes. And wrong.'

Corrigan glanced at her. 'How *did* you get that love bite? You obviously don't have a boyfriend.'

They sat in the car park for a little while, watching apartment sixteen, but there was nothing to indicate anyone was at home. Then they walked into reception and asked for apartment fifteen. The manager, an elderly woman with pink hair, smiled at them and said: 'Happy memories for you?'

'No,' Corrigan started, 'I just liked the look . . .'

Madeline cut in, smiling warmly. 'The best. We came here a few years ago. Didn't go out for four days. Didn't even see the Falls.'

'Aw,' said the manager, 'that's sweet. I presume your wife didn't know, Inspector?'

'I . . .'

'Terrible business, terrible business that. You don't remember me, Inspector, do you?'

'I . . .'

'Had a burglar, couple of years back. You were very helpful. Caught the son of a bitch too. Yes, very helpful. If it's any consolation, I don't think you killed her.'

'Well, thank you, ma'am.'

She handed him the key.

They moved his stuff into the apartment, all the time keeping an eye on next door. On the third run, Madeline struggling under a bag of his CDs, the door opened and Lelewala looked out, her eyes flitting off Madeline to scan the car park. Madeline gave her half a smile and continued on through to where Corrigan was putting crumpled t-shirts into a drawer. Lelewala had been well shielded by the Barracuda on her departure from the police station and walked with her head down; plainly she had no recollection of being confronted by Madeline.

'It's her,' Madeline whispered and thumbed behind her.

Corrigan, seeing nothing out of the open door, whispered: 'Did you . . .'

Madeline shook her head. 'She looks like she's waiting for someone.'

Corrigan crossed the room, peered out, then quietly closed the door.

In one of the plastic bags she found another bottle of vodka. She showed it to him. 'Do you drink a lot?' she asked.

'No.'

'You seem fond of vodka.'

'The bottle is full and the seal is intact.'

She broke the seal. She took a mouthful. 'I was never one for stakeouts, if that's what this is.'

'You get used to them. Although I don't normally bring my worldly possessions with me.'

She went into the bathroom and got two glasses. She poured two drinks and gave him one. They sipped. 'Straight vodka,' she said over the rim of the glass, 'with a murder suspect in a cheap motel. Mother would turn in her grave.'

'Cheering drinks as we set out to save the world from a sinister criminal conspiracy. Your mother would make me wee buns.'

They turned at the sound of a car door closing. They hurried to the window. The blinds were two-thirds closed, just enough for them to watch without being seen, and to see without being completely sure what they were seeing. It was a trade-off, but in the end it didn't matter, because there was no doubt about whom they were seeing.

Madeline, with Corrigan pressed up behind her, let out a low whistle.

'The jigsaw thickens,' Corrigan said.

The Artist Formerly Known as Pongo was climbing out of a battered-looking jeep. He wore a plain black tracksuit and wrap-around shades. He hurried across the gravelled car park, shoulders bunched up, head down, hands thrust into the pockets of his tracksuit bottoms. He knocked on the door next to theirs. It opened, and they heard an excited little squeal.

Corrigan raised his eyebrows. 'Somebody loves him.'

About five minutes later the sounds of sex began to filter through the wall.

Madeline sat awkwardly on the bed. Corrigan remained by the window. The love making grew louder.

'Disappointed?' Madeline asked.

'About what?'

'About Pongo making love to your girl.'

'She's not my girl. And I'm not disappointed. Although the thought of anyone wanting to make love to that coke-warped pixie does make my stomach turn.'

'So what do we do now?' Madeline asked.

'Listen,' Corrigan suggested. 'See if we pick up any important information.'

'It doesn't seem right.'

But they'd no choice but to listen. It was that loud. And growing in intensity. After several further minutes of it, Madeline said: 'Should it last that long?'

'Done properly.' Corrigan smiled. He turned back to the window. Another car had just pulled in, crackling across the gravel. It stopped parallel to Pongo's.

'Fuck,' said Corrigan, 'it's getting like fucking Piccadilly Circus round here.'

Madeline hurried across. She peered across at the new car. Its boot was open. Four heavily-built men in long coats were gathered about it. When they turned and began to walk towards Pongo's apartment she saw that each of them was carrying a gun.

31

Corrigan's throat was suddenly sand-dry. From the next room came the sounds of urgent fucking ... they were yelling at each other, thinking they were whispering sweet nothings but actually shouting frenzied fuck words, lost in it ... the way he had never been able to let himself go ... he had made love quietly, like a student in a library, not scared of talking, but overawed by the ... *what the fuck am I doing*... the gunmen were splashing through the neon reflection of the motel sign towards Lelewala's room.

'Oh Jesus,' Madeline said, her voice low, scared, 'do you think they're ...'

Corrigan dashed across the room to his underwear drawer. He pulled it open, slipped his hand in and withdrew his .38. He had somehow neglected to trade it in when the new Glocks arrived. He raced back to the window. For a moment he thought he was too late, that they were already past, but then he heard the careless thump of their shoes on the wooden walkway outside and their dark forms began to cross the rain-streaked glass. They were not delivering pizza.

Corrigan glanced at Madeline, raised his gun to the window.

'I hope you're going to ask them to put their hands up.'

'That's what a cop would do,' Corrigan said. 'I'd take cover if I were you.'

Then he crashed his gun through the glass and pulled the trigger in one fluid movement. He wasn't trying to hit them, just to scare them off. The crack of a bullet and ...

'Oh God! Gretchin! Go! Go! Go!'

... footsteps clattering on wood, the splashy thud of heavy hitters hitting saturated gravel, and from next door, ignorantly lost in lust ...

'I can't! I can't! I can't!'

'You must! You must! Gretchin! Please!'

And then Corrigan dived for cover, taking Madeline with him, as the rest of their window came crashing in around them. There had been no gunshots. *Silencers.* Corrigan jumped back up and fired twice into the darkness and then ducked again as a high-pitcher zinged past his ear and embedded itself in the wall behind him.

'No more!' from lust central.

'More!'

'Please!'

'Oh!'

'Oh!'

'Oh!'

'Oh!'

'Oh!'

'*Pongo!*'

'Don't call me ... oh!'

Corrigan peered over the windowsill. They were running back across the gravel to their car, which was already reversing towards them. Corrigan fired twice more. Then he pulled open the door, and fired again. He pulled the trigger again, but the six-clip was done and the other was back in his underwear drawer.

Then suddenly he was spun round, shot.

He stumbled out of the doorway, across the wooden walkway, and sprawled drunkenly on to the soaked gravel.

The frantic escape was suddenly cancelled. The reversing vehicle screeched to a halt. Corrigan heard muffled curses as the car doors opened. He tried to raise himself, but a bolt of pain shot down his arm. His gun lay just a few feet away, but the pain ... if he could just get it, aim, maybe they would ...

His good arm was kicked from under him. His face hit the dirt. There came a low laugh and a distant ...

'Finish him.'

He looked up at them, but couldn't see the faces of his killers. He closed his eyes and tried to think of something nice to die with, but nothing would come apart from the rain and pain and the gravel.

There was a click and he said goodbye ... then a crunching sound and the beginnings of a yell and something hot sprayed against his face.

There was no pain, no pain at . . .

He opened his eyes as the scalped head of his executioner toppled towards him. He rolled to one side and the corpse crashed to the ground where he had lain. Hands gripped him and he winced as they hauled him to his feet.

Indians. *Native Americans*. Twenty or thirty of them. Out of nowhere. In costume. With bows and arrows and spears and tomahawks and painted masks hiding their faces . . .

They were holding two very scared-looking men in big suits.

One of the Indians looked him up and down. He was the only one not wearing a mask, and his face was scarier than all of the others combined. Tarriha.

One of the other Indians called across, 'Hey, what'll we do with . . .'

The old Indian looked at the hoods, then pulled his hand across his throat.

The Indians pulled knives across the hoods' throats. They went down without a word, and their blood began to bubble in the puddles.

Corrigan, dizzy, felt himself falling. But they held on to him. The old Indian turned back to him. 'Don't worry,' he said, 'you done good, mister. You come with us now. It is time to talk to Lelewala.'

32

They pushed the Artist Formerly Known as Pongo, the Georgian Formerly Known as Lelewala and the Irishman Formerly Known as Inspector down on to the floor of the first mini-van as it approached the Rainbow Bridge. On the other side was the United States and its own tattier, less commercial version of the town of Niagara Falls. Corrigan groaned as he hit the floor. One of the Indians shushed him. The pain in his arm was getting unbearable. Everything looked and sounded fuzzy. Lelewala shivered against him. Pongo was tutting. Over and over and over again. Corrigan could only hope that Madeline had escaped. Hidden under a bed or in the shower. That or she was lying on the floor of the apartment with her throat cut.

The van slowed and a window was wound down. Corrigan heard the roar of the Falls. A border guard peered in, surprised to see the Indians returning so soon, and still wearing their masks, all save for the little old driver.

'What's up, pops?' the guard asked.

'Powwow double-booked,' Tarriha said. 'Agent gonna get fired.' The guard smiled and waved them on. The second and third vans too.

They came off the bridge and raced on through the town and out past the university before turning on to the Tuscorora Reservation. As they entered the gates a palpable air of relaxation descended on the little convoy. Lelewala was helped up on to a seat, Corrigan and Pongo were left where they were. The masks came off and the Indians began to talk excitedly among themselves. Corrigan couldn't make any sense of it.

Tarriha pulled the lead vehicle into a parking space in front of an elongated wooden shack and jumped out, already barking commands as the other vehicles drew up. Corrigan was pulled out, followed by Pongo then Lelewala. As he stepped down Corrigan recognized one of the Indians as Barry Lightfoot, his acquaintance from the Egg Scramblers; Lightfoot saw him too, but averted his eyes quickly and turned away. There was a little gasp from Lelewala. Corrigan turned as the first of the dead hoods was dumped on the ground. Two more followed, like sacks of potatoes. It was too dark to see their faces. One of the Indians took hold of Corrigan's good arm and led him towards the wooden shack. Lelewala followed.

Siren wailing, Stirling roared into the forecourt of the Rainbow Apartments. Madeline had called in a blind panic from a callbox several blocks away, screaming and crying. They picked her up, calmed her down and left her in Whiskey Nick's with a whisky.

There were three other cop cars already in the car park. A gaggle of locals stood on the opposite sidewalk. James Morton sat beside him, looking pensive. As he pulled up Stirling saw Chief of Police Dunbar emerge from one of the apartments, talking animatedly to another officer. Glass glinted on the walkway.

'What'll I say?' Morton asked.

'Stay in the car. Don't say anything.'

'They're bound to ask.'

'Say you're my cousin. From New York.'

'That sounds dumb.'

'I know. Feel free to come up with something better.'

Stirling crossed the gravel towards Dunbar. Morton got out and sat on the bonnet. As Stirling stepped on to the walkway he saw that the wooden slats outside the door were stained black. He stopped, ran his foot over the deck like a bull ready to charge.

'What's up?' he asked.

Turner, another of Dunbar's blow-ins from Toronto, looked suspiciously across the car park at Morton.

'About an hour ago the manager heard gunshots,' Dunbar said. 'Locked herself in the back room, didn't come out until she'd counted to forty thousand.' He thumbed back. 'There are bullet holes in the back wall. Forensics are digging them out.'

Stirling shook his head. 'Any idea who . . . ?'

'Your friend Corrigan moved in this afternoon.'

'*Corrigan?*' He did his best to sound surprised. 'Jesus. Is he . . . ?'

'Come on through.' Dunbar turned and led him into the

apartment. There were scene-of-crime people at work. The bed was made but creased. There was a half-empty bottle of vodka on top of the television and black plastic bags stuffed with Corrigan's possessions lay on the floor.

'I heard he got kicked out of his apartment,' Stirling said.

Beside the TV there was a small table, two chairs and a *Niagara Falls Visitors' Guide*. On top of the guide sat a human scalp. Blood from it had seeped into the guide, dyeing the pages red.

'Shit,' said Stirling.

'Shit indeed,' said Dunbar.

Stirling bent to examine it. It looked as if somebody had taken a hammer to a huge black spider. 'It's not Corrigan's,' Stirling said.

'I know,' Dunbar said. 'But doesn't it suggest something to you?'

'Somebody's got a sore head.'

'Indians,' Turner said.

'Indians *take* scalps, surely? They don't leave them.'

'Maybe real ones do,' Dunbar said. 'Somebody masquerading as an Indian mightn't.'

'Gretchin Solyakhov,' said Turner.

'Corrigan checked in with a woman this afternoon,' Dunbar said. 'Now they've both skipped and there's a scalp sitting here. That's another murder they're tied in to. I want them picked up, and I want them picked up *now*.' Dunbar shook his head. 'I was willing to give him the benefit of the doubt before, but this time I'm going to bury him.'

They walked back outside. Morton was off the bonnet now and kneeling in the middle of the car park examining the gravel. His finger hovered an inch off the ground, tracing the outline of something. Stirling tried to ignore him, but Turner nodded across. 'Who's your friend?'

'Cousin,' said Stirling.

'Is he a cop?' Turner asked.

'Yup,' said Stirling. 'Up from New York.'

Turner glanced at Dunbar.

'Traffic cop,' said Stirling.

Morton looked round for the first time. 'Sorry,' he said, 'lost a contact lens.' He stood up and kicked at the gravel. 'Shit,' he said, 'like looking for a contact lens in a shit load of gravel.'

He walked across to them, still shaking his head.

'So,' Turner said as Morton joined them, 'how's the traffic in New York?'

'Busy,' said Morton.

Driving back to Whiskey Nick's to pick up Madeline, Stirling said: 'What'd you find in the gravel?'

Morton looked at him. 'Nothing.'

'You were looking at something when we came out.'

'I was looking for my contact lens.'

'Seriously?'

'Seriously.'

'Oh. Right.'

33

The Long House was dark and smoky. At the far end of the hall the Indians were already ordering drinks from a bar. Barry Lightfoot was putting quarters into a slot machine. Corrigan, Pongo and Lelewala were ushered into chairs set about a pine table. The bleeding in Corrigan's arm had not stopped. A medicine man Tarriha introduced as Doc arrived after five minutes, puffed with running. He was a thin man in his late fifties; he wore bifocals and a floral waistcoat and he smelt of whisky. He began to dab at the bullet hole with what looked like an old dishcloth. 'Exactly where did you do your training?' Corrigan asked warily.

Doc smiled, revealing a mouthful of imperfect teeth. 'Right here. My father taught me everything I know, and his father taught him, and before that his father taught him. It goes on like that, right back to long ago.' Then he crinkled his brow and said: 'I'll be back in five minutes. Need some special medicine for that.' He hurried away.

Lelewala was looking about the walls of the Long House. They were adorned with masks and drums and dresses and tomahawks and murals. She was entranced. And so was Corrigan. She was every bit as beautiful as he remembered. Her hair. Her face. Her eyes.

Pongo removed a small compact from inside his jacket and examined himself, before starting to fix his hair. *Pongo and Lelewala. In bed. Screwing.*

Tarriha raised a hand. 'Do you recognize this place, Lelewala?' he asked.

Lelewala nodded vaguely, her eyes never leaving the walls. 'It is very old . . . I think.'

Tarriha nodded sagely. 'Nineteen fifties. We're gonna knock it down and build something doesn't leak. Just as soon as the government comes through with a grant.'

'I thought . . .'

'Yeah, you been here before.'

She was confused. Her eyes flitted from the wall to the bar. 'I remember . . . dancing . . .' Her eyes settled on Corrigan. A shiver went up his back 'Sahonwadi . . .' she said softly.

Corrigan shook his head helplessly.

'Our wedding dance . . . ?' she asked.

Tarriha lifted a bony finger and pointed up the hall to the bar. 'No,' he said, '*his* wedding dance.'

Standing holding a beer glass and grinning sheepishly at them over its rim was a porky, balding Indian with a thin and fresh scar running down one side of his face.

'I don't understand . . .' Lelewala began. Then stopped. She raised a hand to her face and began to trace the outline of his scar on her own pale skin. 'I don't . . .'

'You cut him, OK,' Tarriha said.

'Me? I didn't . . .'

Tarriha looked back to the bar. Then he smiled kindly at Lelewala. 'You were here last week,' the old Indian said. 'Walter Running Bear's stag party. We hired you as an exotic dancer. Stripper. Popov brought you.'

'Popov?'

Tarriha nodded. 'Gavril. Gavril Popov? You remember none of this?'

She shook her head vaguely.

'Walter, as normal a guy as you would hope to meet. Works as an accountant at the Niagara casino. Lovely wife, though she nearly wasn't, after you got your claws into him. You strip good, big crowd, love it, only Walter has a lot of whisky, all of them do, very drunk, thinks he's Crazy Horse. He wanted to fuck you after the show, but you weren't interested. They tried to talk him out of it, but he came at you, ripped your clothes, tried to . . . well, you cut him pretty bad. You got crazy yourself; we felt pretty bad. Gave you one of our old ceremonial dresses to wear. Worth a goddamn fortune. Popov pretty damn angry you don't fuck, I tell you. Throws you in the goddamn Niagara.'

'I don't remember any of this.' She slumped down against Pongo.

Pongo made a face and pushed her away. 'I don't know what

135

fucking drugs you're all on,' he whined, 'but I'll have to be going home soon. My father will be expecting me.'

'The Old Cripple,' said Corrigan.

Pongo gave a little shrug.

Tarriha ignored him. He was looking at Corrigan. 'Tell me,' he said softly, 'what you know about the Ga-go-sa, or in your tongue, the False Faces?'

'Nothing,' said Corrigan. He was tired and he was confused. Lelewala shook her head, although it barely moved. The Long Room had grown quieter. Some of the drinkers had drifted off, others had settled into a poker game. But they were seated close to the only door and Corrigan noted that there was always one of them with his eyes on Lelewala.

Tarriha took a long gulp of his beer, then settled into his chair. Corrigan could feel another story coming on.

Tarriha fixed his eyes firmly on Lelewala. 'We, the People of the Five Nations, of the Tuscorora Iroquois,' he began, 'have always believed in the existence of the Ga-go-sa, the False Faces. They are demons without bodies, simply faces, hideous faces, so demoniacal as to paralyse all who behold them. They have the power to send plagues and pestilence among men, and to devour bodies. To this day we believe implicitly in the existence of these demons.' He paused, his eyes pinholes, probing for a response, but there was nothing, only a blank gaze. He licked his lips, took another drink. 'Upon this belief was founded a secret organization called the Falseface band, to appease these demons and to arrest pestilence and disease. The members of the band wore masks of equally hideous appearance. They were all males, save for one, who was a female and called Ga-go-sa Ho-nun-nas-tase-ta, or the keeper of the Falsefaces ...'

Corrigan raised a tired eyebrow. 'You're not suggesting that ...'

'Listen to me. Like so many things, the Falseface band has fallen on easy times. My people are not rich like other Americans, but they do not starve. They do not have to hunt to survive. They have grown fat and soft like the white man, present company excepted. And instead of keeping the old traditions alive, the Falsefaces have become ...' and his lip curled up and sharp yellowed teeth glared out '... *a social organization*. They dance.

They play poker. They put on their Falsefaces and they talk about hockey and mortgages and airbags.'

'Like masons,' said Corrigan, 'without the hockey and airbags.'

Tarriha nodded gravely. 'Their low point, and their turning point, was the attack on this woman, a dancer, an *erotic* dancer. For many years there has been no mistress of the Falsefaces. But when this dancer's dress was ripped, she was given instead to wear a dress not worn for more than fifty years, not worn since the last Ho-nun-nas-tase-ta died. I saw that it was given and tried to prevent it, but I am old and sad and I have given up fighting. I thought, let it go; it does no good here.

'But when you brought the dress to the casino, told me that there was a crazy woman who had nearly drowned in the Niagara, I had to find out more. And when I talked to her she talked to me in a language that has not been spoken in such a way for many, many years, and told me things that had not been spoken of for many, many years.'

Lelewala was looking at the ground.

'What're you saying?' Corrigan said.

'That something happened when she was thrown into the river. The river recognized the mistress of the Falseface band and summoned the spirit of Lelewala, and the spirit of Lelewala swam into her and has now returned among us to fight the great evil that is coming.'

Tarriha sat back, his eyes darting from Corrigan to Lelewala and back. 'And with her return to us comes inspiration and leadership and power. Now the Falsefaces are a true band of warriors again, sworn to protect Lelewala, sworn to strike fear into all those who would seek to harm her. Every one of them will lay down his life for her.'

Corrigan took a sip from his bottle. 'Even Walter Running Bear?'

'Even Walter Running Bear,' said Tarriha. Then added, 'Especially Walter Running Bear.'

Doc reappeared suddenly at Corrigan's side. 'Sorry,' he said, 'took me a while to find . . .'

He delved into a cloth bag that hung at his waist and removed a fistful of what looked to Corrigan like dead leaves that had lain in a drain for six months. Doc smiled reassuringly. 'Old Indian cure,' he said. 'My father taught me this, and his father before him, and before that his father, and beyond that it gets pretty damn hazy. Tomorrow morning you'll wake up . . . well tomorrow morning you'll wake up, which you might not if you lose any more blood and I don't do anything about it.'

'I really would prefer a second op . . .' Corrigan began, but before he could finish Doc had slapped the dank muck against his arm. Corrigan let out a shout and tried to pull away but Doc had clamped the arm tight between his left arm and his chest.

'There now,' Doc said, pushing the mush deep into the wound, 'just let that seep in a bit and you'll be good as new.'

Corrigan just managed to get to his feet, but he couldn't free himself. He swayed. Suddenly his legs would no longer hold him. He tried to say something, but the words would not come. He saw Lelewala looking concerned, Tarriha smiling confidently. Pongo was ignoring him completely; instead, he stared at Lelewala with a new light in his eyes.

It was starting to get dark. Corrigan's head lolled back and he felt himself falling. His last thought was: *I'm fainting like a girl.*

34

Maybe it was to save him the embarrassment. Maybe it was the way they always worked. Or probably it was just where they happened to track him down. They'd probably been to the station, questioned, seized; maybe the bank as well. They rang the bell, spoke to his wife, then she called up the stairs that there were two Internal Affairs guys here to see him.

Stirling's mouth was dry. He hadn't slept. He hadn't eaten. He'd drunk quite a bit. It was the wrong thing to do with the convention underway, with Morton trying to blend in down at the hotel, with Corrigan missing and possibly dead, and Madeline the reporter waiting to meet them all underneath Skylon Tower, but he couldn't help it. He had come to the sudden realization that people were dying all around him and he wasn't coping with it. He shouted that he'd be down in a minute, then began to pull on his uniform.

Internal Affairs.

He was a police officer and a gentleman, and he would deal with it as such.

Or perhaps not.

He had a good idea what they had on him, and he knew he was finished.

Or perhaps not.

Sometimes you have to make choices.

Stirling's head throbbed. Maybe they weren't Internal Affairs. Maybe they were the Old Cripple's men, come to murder him. He was scared and he was regretting everything and anything. Since when was the biggest criminal conspiracy in history any of his business? He was about parking tickets and mugged tourists, not the Sicilian Mafia. He had his gun in his hand. Other cops, in this situation, other cops he knew, would have blown their own fucking heads off rather than face Internal Affairs. And now they were downstairs making small talk with his wife and taking everything in, everything that looked new and shiny, like his wife. And she didn't have a clue. They were being warm and friendly and charming and preparing to stick the knife between his ribs, metaphorically perhaps, actually maybe. What could he do?

He checked his weapon. He laughed. He was a policeman. He wasn't going to shoot them. Not unless they pulled guns first, in which case he'd be entitled, and even then he doubted if he'd pull the trigger.

Of course they weren't going to kill him.

They were here because someone had tipped them off that his wife had a rapidly diminishing two hundred thousand dollars in her bank account. And she had no idea where it had come from.

They'd take him back to St Catharines, or Toronto, and throw the book at him, several books, the complete set. He'd tell them about the convention. They would steal his thunder and lock him up. He stood up. He was wearing his holster, but he left it empty; he tucked the gun into the back of his trousers. They would see it empty and relax. If they were going to kill him, they'd be thinking fish and barrels. Good. Let them. He was confused. Before, everything had been black and white, and mostly just white. Internal Affairs were drinking coffee in his front room and thinking *why, that's an expensive brand of coffee.*

It was time to go. His wife had called him three times already. He took a deep breath, then left the room and walked slowly down the stairs.

'Mark,' his wife beamed up, 'these nice men have come all the way from Toronto to see you.'

Morton spotted Stirling crossing the car park outside the Skylon Tower. He was in uniform, but he was twirling his keys nervously round. And of course he was. So was Morton, and not just from running out of small talk with Madeline, sitting opposite him in the café.

He came through the door, ignoring the looks of the tourists, wondering what a cop wanted. He pulled out a chair and sat down. He nodded at Morton. Ignored Madeline.

'What's up, Brad?' Madeline asked.

'Everything,' said Stirling, ignoring the barb. 'Internal Affairs. They called by the house.'

'What did they want?' Morton asked.

'Coffee. What do you think?' He put his head in his hands. 'I don't know why the hell I got into this.'

Morton, sipping his coffee, put down the cup. 'You got into it because Frank Corrigan's your friend.'

Stirling peered out from between his fingers. 'Who told you that?'

'C'mon,' said Morton, 'what did they say? It couldn't be that bad if you were able to walk in here. Internal Affairs haul ass first, ask questions later.'

'They're outside. In the car.'

'You brought them with you?'

'I brought them with me.'

'What for?'

'Coffee. What the fuck do you think? I just needed time to think.'

Madeline laughed. 'You said, pull over here guys, I need to go think over a cup of coffee.'

'No. Not quite.'

'It's the not quite bit I don't like,' said Morton.

'They started coming on all heavy.'

'Don't tell me this, Mark.'

'Threatening and pushing and sticking fingers in my face.'

'Mark, please.'

'What else could I do?'

'What else did you do?'

'They're in the car.'

Morton's mouth dropped. 'You didn't . . .'

Stirling followed the drop, then suddenly smiled. 'C'mon . . . whaddya think I am . . . ?'

Morton sighed. 'Christ, Mark, I thought for a minute you . . .'

'You think I'm crazy? No, they're in the car. Or in the trunk, to be more precise.'

'Fuck,' said Morton.

'Hands are cuffed.'

'Fuck.'

'Mouths taped.'

'Fuck.'

'I know. I kinda thought that while I was doing it. But I'd no choice.'

'You'd plenty of choice.'

'I know, but none I could live with, but this one.'

'What are you going to do with them?' Madeline asked.

'What are *we* going to do with them?' Morton said. 'I guess we're in this together.'

Stirling nodded appreciatively. Madeline rolled her eyes. 'I suppose,' Stirling said, 'that we have several options. I take the car and sink it in the river. I tell them it's all been a huge misunderstanding and let's be friends. Or we can leave them where they are until we bust the biggest criminal conspiracy in the history of the world and then they'll climb out and thank us. What do you think?'

Morton examined his fingernails for several moments, and then looked sheepishly up. 'How deep's the river?' he asked.

35

They walked down to the basement to wait. Usually there was a bustling amusement arcade down there, but it had been closed for refurbishment for the past three weeks and the manager had kindly lent Stirling the store room down at the back. Kindly, for fear of being locked up over his unpaid parking tickets.

They endured thirty minutes of scuffing their shoes in the dust and thinking no one was going to turn up. And then they did, almost as one, as if they'd arrived in an air-conditioned bus like the rest of the tourists. Maybe thirty of them, shuffling down the stairs, then nervously crossing the floor of the arcade, casting suspicious glances at the lifeless computer games and the pellet guns on string and the bumper cars lying idle. Stirling waved them through the open doors of the store room. They were all volunteers, but they came through them like they'd been tipped off about the showers at Belsen.

Stirling knew most of them. Three brother cops – *but for how long?* – a barman, the guy that took the tickets at the House of Frankenstein, the guy from the drugstore who'd sold him the condoms that had split (he now had twins), Corrigan's pal Maynard Dunn from the *Maid of the Mist*. They took their seats where they could, perched on cardboard boxes and wooden crates and upturned bumper cars. They chatted quietly among themselves, then fell silent as Morton closed the doors and looked expectantly at Stirling. Stirling looked expectantly at his audience. The audience looked expectantly at him. There were a lot of expectations in that room – high, low, mid-range – and then there was Madeline with no expectations at all but the lens of a video camera poking out of her handbag, capturing it all just in case.

The information they'd been given had been so vague as barely to qualify for the word vague, or indeed the word information. They thought it had something to do with community service.

Volunteering to lay a treasure trail or mend a fence or provide transport for a fancy-dress parade. Stirling looked at their soft faces and fat, pink bodies and shook his head. He wasn't looking for any of that. He was looking for heroes.

Or suckers. It didn't matter much as long as they'd do the job or die in the attempt.

Stirling raised his hands for quiet, though there was no need. 'I expect you're all wondering why I called you here under such, ahm, unusual circumstances.' There was a nodding of heads. 'Well, thing is, this is kind of unofficial. As you all know, there's been a lot of trouble in the town over the past few days. Murders. My friend and colleague Frank Corrigan lost his wife.' He looked at their pink faces for a hint of sympathy, but none was immediately apparent. No matter about the rights and wrongs of it, once you were arrested, you were as good as guilty. That's the way it worked. Always had, always would. There was curiosity there, maybe a little embarrassment, but no sympathy. He looked down the room to Morton, standing with his back against the door and his arms folded. He got the thumbs-up. Stirling nodded. 'You may have heard a lot of things. I know how news gets around. Maybe you saw it on TV.' He glanced at Madeline, who glowered back. 'I just want to put you straight, and then tell you why I've asked you all here this evening. First off, Frank didn't kill his wife. Truth is, we don't know yet who did, or why. But what we think, what we really think, is that her death is somehow tied in to the convention that's taking place in town right now.'

'The horticultural convention?' Maynard asked from the front row.

'Yes, Maynard, the horticultural convention.' There were murmurings, nudges. Stirling drank it all in. He wanted to *shout* his plan out loud. Raise his fist and call them to arms, lead them into battle. But he didn't. He sucked on his bottom lip and kept it calm, because his only chance was to win them over with *calm*. 'Except it's not a horticultural convention. They're drug dealers. The biggest dealers in the world. They're TOCs.'

'That's TCOs,' Morton said from the back, and began to walk down between the upturned fruit machines to the front. 'Transnational criminal organizations.'

'TCOs,' said Stirling. 'The Mafia, the Yakuza and a dozen others you never even thought of. This is James Morton from the FBI. You may recognize him from the Empire State Building siege in New York. He's here to help us.'

'Us?' said the man who sold tickets at the House of Frankenstein.

'Yup,' Stirling said ebulliently, 'we're going to form a special citizens' task force.'

Murmurs.

'Uh, Mark,' said the ticket taker from the House of Frankenstein, his head bent to one side as if he'd a sore bolt in his neck, 'isn't that the kind of thing the police should be doing? We, uhm, don't know much about, you know, murder and drugs 'n all.'

Stirling was considering his answer when Morton, nodding vigorously, stepped in to fill the vacuum. 'Yes, sir, that would be the ideal solution. Unfortunately it is not an option. The people who are running this convention are, how shall I put it, *extremely* influential. The police have been bought off.'

One of the cops at the back jumped to his feet. 'Ain't nobody bought me off!'

Stirling waved placatory hands. 'We're not saying that, Bill, we're saying higher up. In Toronto. That's why we've been flooded with out-of-town cops this last few days. You gotta admit that's a bit strange.'

'If I remember right, Mr Stirling, you called them in.'

'It was the right thing to do at the time,' Morton said.

'I called in officers from outside this district because my superior officer was suspected of a crime. He was subsequently cleared of any involvement in that crime. You all know Frank Corrigan. He's a good guy.'

'I heard he killed a whole bunch of people back in Ireland,' the pharmacist called.

'And his wife was pregnant,' said one of the other cops.

'How many of these drug dealers are we talking about?' Maynard asked. 'You want us just to walk in there with a couple of shotguns and arrest them?'

'About a hundred and fifty,' Morton said.

'Jesus!'

'I know . . .' Stirling said, waving his hands, 'I know . . .'

The guy who sold tickets at the House of Frankenstein jumped up. 'Those guys from the convention – and they ain't all guys – they're in my place every day. They don't look like drug dealers to me. In my place they were talking about flowers.'

'Believe me,' Morton said, 'they *are* drug dealers.'

He looked at Stirling. Stirling shrugged. Morton rubbed at his brow, then he launched into an explanation of what transnational criminal organizations were. He tried to keep it short and to the point, but the less he said the more ominous they sounded, and in trying to clarify and soothe he made them sound even worse. He was losing it. In his heyday it had been no problem inspiring the troops, because generally they *were* troops and up for it. Now he was trying to inspire hick cops and people who sold tickets at tourist attractions and it clearly was not working. As he talked, their jaws slowly dropped and a grey pallor seemed to descend over their pink faces. When he'd finished there was an ominous silence.

'Fuck it, Mark,' Maynard said, ignoring Morton, 'you don't need us. You need like ... like SWAT teams ... or Mounties ... I mean, if what you're saying is true, you've got to be able to take it higher up. Somebody will listen.'

'Maynard, I told you, they've been bought off. *I've* been bought off, for Christsake.' He let out a sigh, looked to the ground. He told them about the money that had appeared in his wife's bank account and the bullshit about a legacy from a distant relative she'd never heard of and the visit of the Internal Affairs guys. 'Same thing happened to Frank Corrigan. He's had his house up for sale these last few months, nobody interested, then suddenly he gets an offer he can't refuse. Turns out the buyer is a police inspector from Toronto. Narcotics division. Quite innocent on the face of it, but look a little closer ...' He shook his head. 'We have $200,000 in our account and nobody's asked me to do a thing for it. But they will. And that's why I can't call in a fucking SWAT team.'

'You could hire one, with that kind of money,' Bill the cop said.

Maynard rubbed at his chin. 'So we'd be taking on the Mafia, the Triads ... *and* the police?'

'Yup.'

'And you're suggesting we ... y'know, use *guns* and all?'

'Yes, Maynard, I certainly am.'

'Against the Mafia *and* the police?'

Stirling rubbed at his brow and looked at Morton for support. Morton gave a little shrug. Madeline was staring at the floor.

'I never said it was going to be easy,' Stirling said. He opened his hands to them. 'I won't hold it against any of you if you don't want to help out. I'll leave that to your conscience. But I want you to consider two things. One, what would you do if your wife or sister or son or daughter got murdered, and you couldn't do anything about it because they had enough money to buy off the cops? And two, we're all just ordinary guys living up here, and life is pretty easy. Sure we could just sit here and let all these gangsters waltz about town like they owned it, but wouldn't you just love to stand up to them and say, "Not in my town, mister." To take them on, beat them at their own game? Didn't you see *High Noon*? Didn't you feel sorry for Will Kane, getting no support from the townsfolk?'

'Mark,' the guy from the House of Frankenstein said, 'I kinda identified with the townsfolk.'

'I'm keen to help out . . .' the pharmacist said, 'but, the Mafia? Don't they take, y'know, contracts out on people . . . ?'

'You gonna put the whole town in a witness-protection programme?' a guy at the back shouted. 'Give us all new identities? We like it *here*.'

'We're not exactly the fuckin' A Team.'

'I ain't fired a gun since I was sixteen. And I shot myself in the foot then.'

'I missed my fuckin' foot, that's how bad a shot I was, tried to escape the draft.'

'There was no fuckin' draft in Canada, Bob.'

'That's how fuckin' stupid I was.'

There was laughter all round. And then it died out and they looked at Stirling and Morton and shifted, embarrassed, in their seats.

Stirling tried one last time. 'I know you all have families. I know that this will be traumatic. But when you're seventy . . .'

'I *am* seventy . . .'

'Yes, Paddy, I know . . .'

'Still spell my own name . . .'

'Yes, Paddy, but say when you're eighty, and you *can't* spell your own name, when your grandkids ask you what you did when the people of Niagara rose up against the bad guys, what're you going to tell them?'

'Probably won't recognize them. Haw, haw, haw.'

Stirling massaged his forehead again. 'I've told you everything I know, and I'm asking for your help. It's up to you now. All I can ask is that if you feel you can't do it, well no hard feelings, but promise me you won't tell anyone what you've heard here today. Not even your wives. *Especially* your wives.'

They giggled at that.

'If you're gonna help, raise your hand.'

Bill, one of the cops, raised his hand. Then the seventy-year-old. Then Maynard.

That was it.

'OK,' Stirling said, 'thanks for coming. And remember, not a peep.'

Disappointment was etched on his face. Morton felt bad for him. He'd presumed. He'd expected. He'd been let down. The crowd stood awkwardly, then began to move out of the store room. Stirling's jaw remained firm and his smile fixed, and he shook a lot of hands as they filed out, avoiding his eyes, mumbling excuses as they passed.

As their footsteps faded, Morton nodded at each of the remaining volunteers. All three of them. Add in Corrigan, Stirling, Madeline and himself. He took a deep breath, then clapped his hands together and forced a smile. 'OK,' he said, 'looks like it's all down to the Magnificent Seven.'

36

Corrigan woke with a start in the middle of the night. There was a hand on his brow and a soothing voice, with a hint of the East. 'There now, it's OK. It's *OK*.'

It took him several moments to calm down. It had been a dream, a nightmare, the creature, like a dragon, rising out of the water to devour him.

He blinked about him. There were two beds. There was a bedside light throwing a weak light about the room. The curtains were open and a brighter light came in off the moon. He was soaked in sweat. He did not feel *right*, and it wasn't just the arm. *She* was there, patting him down with a towel. He was wearing nothing but his underpants. He stopped her hand, pressed it against the towel against his chest and said: 'I'm OK.'

She smiled, unsure of him.

'Have I been . . . ?'

'A few hours. You're very hot. You should go to a hospital.'

'I'm OK. Where's Pongo?'

She shrugged. 'I think he left. They're not interested in him. They're interested in me.'

He still had hold of her hand. He looked into her eyes and said: 'And who are you?'

She looked away. 'I am whoever they want me to be.'

'*They*?'

'Whoever pays the money.'

'I don't understand.'

'I am prostitute. I suck cocks.' She took her hand away, but did not leave his side. She had the sad face of a beautiful woman forced to make her living giving blow-jobs to fat single guys and thin married men in seedy motels up and down Niagara's main strip.

'As a matter of interest,' Corrigan said, 'how much do you charge?'

'What? For blow-job? Seventy bucks.'

'Isn't that . . . expensive?'

'You pay for quality.'

'Seventy bucks, huh?'

She looked at him, and he was suddenly all flustered and avoiding her eyes. She smiled but he didn't see it. 'You know,' she said, 'I think you are a nice man.'

He smiled sadly at her. 'Do you remember me?' he asked. 'From before?'

She nodded slowly, and for a moment he thought she might be thinking about her Indian village, but she said, 'The women's refuge.'

'What do you remember?'

'How I got there?' She shrugged. 'I suppose Popov hit me and . . .'

'What is he . . . your pimp?'

'No . . . yes. He is my husband. And my pimp.'

'Oh.' Corrigan pulled the quilt up around him. He shivered.

'But I think maybe I will get a divorce. Throwing your wife into the Niagara and making her suck cocks for a living is not what I had planned when I came to live here.'

'What did you want to be?'

'I wanted to be an actress. I still do.'

'I'm sure you will be, one day.'

'Thank you. I hope to act with the great David Hasselhoff. *Knight Rider* and *Bay Watch Nights*. In California,' she said, 'such dreams come true.'

He nodded thoughtfully for some moments. An actress. Of course.

'What about Pongo?' he asked.

'What about him?'

'You're having an affair with him.'

'No, I'm having sex with him.'

'Isn't it the same thing?'

'No. He pays me money, I have sex with him.'

'That's all there is to it?'

'What more could there be? You've seen him.'

'I thought . . .' Corrigan sighed. His head was starting to throb now, just to keep his arm company. He closed his eyes. 'What did you think,' he said quietly, 'of what Tarriha said, about the False Faces?'

Lelewala shrugged. He *still* thought of her as Lelewala. Gretchin didn't sound right. It didn't even sound Georgian. It sounded *Sound of Music*.

'When you were screaming and shouting in the women's refuge, it wasn't Iroquois you were screaming and shouting. It was Georgian or Russian or whatever your mother tongue is, wasn't it?'

She shrugged again.

'And yet, and yet you spoke about Sahonwadi. You looked at me and you spoke about Sahonwadi. How was that?'

'I don't know.'

'There was a book about Lelewala in your apartment.'

'You were in my apartment?'

'I'm a police officer. Of course I was in your apartment. As you were in mine. My wife's.'

She looked away. 'Yes. I know.'

'You didn't kill her, did you?'

'No.'

'So who did?'

She shrugged.

'You were there. You must have seen who . . .'

'I don't know!' She reared up suddenly and for a moment she was possessed of that same fiery spirit he had first encountered in the women's refuge. 'I remember the bodies! I was very afraid! I do not know . . . !'

And then just as suddenly she began to cry, and the tears extinguished the fire.

For some reason it is awkward standing and crying. It is a thing that should only be done sitting down. She slowly lowered herself back down on to the bed, her shoulders shaking and tears rolling down her pale cheeks. Corrigan pushed himself up off the pillow and put his hands on her shoulders. 'Now there's no need . . .' he began, but stopped as she moulded herself into him. She shivered. He shivered. He kissed the top of her head.

'I'm sorry,' he said. 'It was . . . my wife.'

'I know. I'm sorry.' She sniffled. 'But I did not kill her . . .'

'I know,' Corrigan said, though he didn't.

'I do not know . . . I do not know what is happening to me . . . I black ... I black out. I go away. I wake up in places I do not remember.' She rocked against him. Then again she tried to pull away. 'I do not take drugs! If that is what you are thinking!'

He kept hold of her, calmed her down with soft words, although he knew she had a conviction for drugs. It didn't mean anything. He smoked dope occasionally and it didn't make him a murderer.

Or did it?

When she had relaxed again he asked softly: 'How long has this been happening?'

'Since I went in the river. That is why he scares me, the old Indian with his talk of spirits and False Faces. There is *something*. Something that takes me over. I don't want it to happen, but it does. All I want to do is go to California and act with David Hasselhoff.'

He began to rock her. Although he felt miserable, he had slept. As far as he knew she had sat up with him. Before very long she began to doze against him. He rocked on. Thinking about Aimie on a swing and Nicola on a slab.

When he was sure she was asleep, he carefully set her back on the bed and pulled the quilt up over her. He switched the bedside light off and looked down at her for several moments in the soft moonlight. She was sleeping peacefully. She was beautiful. Bonkers, clearly, but beautiful.

He needed to find a phone. He was convinced that he had blood poisoning. Not from the bullet, but from the mush Doc had pressed into his arm. He tried the door. It was locked. He tutted, although he was quite pleased that there was a door at all. He'd expected a wigwam or something vaguely *tribal* but it was a small, pleasant apartment. The window, although unshuttered, was bolted closed and locked. He pressed his face to the glass and looked out. For a moment he couldn't really make anything out, then slowly shapes began to form up in the darkness. The room was on the ground floor of a block of apartments built around a paper-strewn courtyard. There was a point of red light some distance away and for several minutes it confused him, moving about like a firefly, and then it crossed a lit window across the courtyard and he saw the outline of a man with a rifle in his hands and a cigarette in his mouth.

A guard on patrol. Corrigan waited until his circuit of the

courtyard brought him past his window, then tapped the glass. After a moment's hesitation the cigarette tip moved towards him, and a face peered into the room.

It was Barry Lightfoot. When he saw that it was Corrigan he stepped back from the window and shrugged apologetically.

'Barry,' Corrigan said, cupping his hands against the glass, 'what the fuck is going on?'

'Plenty,' said Lightfoot.

'I didn't think you were into all this Indian shit.'

'I'm not. And it's not shit.'

'That doesn't make sense.'

'What does?' He looked suspiciously around him. 'I gotta go.'

'Wait. Barry. Listen. I need to get to a hospital.'

A hint of a smile appeared on the Indian's face. 'Yeah. I know. We're gonna have to get ourselves a real, qualified doctor. Doc kills more than he cures. I expect you have blood poisoning.'

'So you'll call me a . . .'

'Can't do that, Frank. Sorry. I'm sure Tarriha will call one for you in the morning if you're still with us.'

He turned away. 'Barry!'

He stopped, hesitated, then turned. 'What?'

'Tell me what's going on. My wife's dead.' He paused, then for emphasis added, 'Dead.'

'I know. I'm sorry.' And he was sorry. Big sad eyes. 'But it's nothing to do with us. We're just protecting Lelewala.'

'Protecting her from what?'

'Anything that comes along.' He walked off.

37

They went back to the Long House for breakfast. Ham and eggs.

There was something about the new day, bright and crisp, that imbued Corrigan with a new sense of hope, and it wasn't just because he hadn't died during the night. When he'd tried the door of the room that morning, it wasn't locked. There was no sign of Barry Lightfoot or any other guard; Indians who passed the open door as he peered out, women with children off to school, smiled and said hello.

Lelewala was still asleep. He went into the bathroom and closed the door. He carefully peeled the bandage away from his arm and examined the bullet wound. It had scabbed over during the night, but it was dry and looked clean. There was a razor sitting in a cup, so he used it. He took a shower. He wasn't thinking about anything but the heat of the water and how to tackle the world's greatest criminal conspiracy when the plastic shower curtain moved back and a naked Lelewala slipped in beside him.

He said, 'Oh,' and got an erection.

She put her arms round him and kissed him. Softly.

'Oh,' he said again. 'What was that for?'

'That was for nothing,' she said, then lowered herself to his groin. 'But this is for seventy dollars.'

He just said: 'Gosh.'

It was not a word that had previously figured in his vocabulary, but it was certainly the most appropriate. It took him several seconds to recover, seconds during which she *started*. When he stopped her, and he did, it took all the will in the world, plus some borrowed from cold and distant planets elsewhere in the galaxy.

He pulled her back up, cupping her face in his hands, the power shower battering both of them. 'You don't have to do that,' he said.

'You don't like it?' Sad and doe-eyed.

'*Of course* I like it . . . but . . . goodness' sake . . .'

'Then let me, please. Seventy dollars.'

'No. No. No. Please.'

He moved her to one side and stepped out of the shower. He picked up a towel and tied it round his bulging groin. He shook his head. 'Why on earth would you want to . . . I mean . . .'

'I was only joking,' Lelewala said, 'about the seventy dollars.'

'What?'

'Joke. I do it for free. In Georgia I was known for my sense of humour. Perhaps it does not travel well. You will reconsider now?'

'I don't understand.'

'My English is not good?'

'Your English is perfect. I just don't understand . . .'

'You are Sahonwadi.'

'Excuse me?'

'You are Sahonwadi.'

'I am Frank Corrigan. Sahonwadi is a myth. Lelewala is a myth. And even if they're not, they're both dead, long ago.'

'Why is it then, *Frank Corrigan*, that I remember you, that I remembered you even before I ever saw you. That when I woke up in the women's refuge, I recognized you.'

'I don't know. Lele . . . Gretchin . . . you used to live round the corner from my apartment. It's not inconceivable that we've crossed paths before.'

'I know that we've crossed paths, Frank Corrigan.'

'Not like that.'

'I feel it.' She gave a little shrug and stepped back into the shower. 'Do you still say no?'

'Do I still say no to what?'

She looked down at his towel. The erection had not noticeably diminished.

'What is this obsession with having sex?'

'It's what I do.'

'I thought you were an actress.'

'Not yet. For now I suck . . .'

'Cocks. Yes, I know. And no . . . I don't . . . well I do . . . but it's not right. My wife's dead, I've been shot in the arm and we only met last night.' He laughed. 'I'm not that kind of a guy.'

She shook her head, then pulled the plastic curtain across again. As he turned away she said: 'Yes you are, Frank Corrigan.'

38

Tarriha was right. The False Faces were a social organization. The Long House was practically empty. They all had jobs to go to, in town, across the border in the casino, in the generating stations. There was little work on the reservation. Tarriha came across with a cup of coffee. He looked as refreshed as a hundred-and-five-year-old man can. He smiled at Lelewala. 'Apartment OK?'

She nodded.

'Arm OK?'

'Fine,' Corrigan said, 'but we have to go.'

Tarriha frowned. 'Go where?'

Lelewala looked at Corrigan. 'West,' she said.

Corrigan smiled. 'Hollywood,' he said. Lelewala smiled at him. Maybe he would go with her. He could meet David Hasselhoff, and punch his lights out.

'You can't do that,' said Tarriha.

'Can,' said Corrigan.

Tarriha's leathered face assumed a wise old great-great-grandfatherly expression as he looked at Lelewala. 'We have to protect you. We can't protect you in Hollywood. Can hardly protect you in Niagara. Much better you stay here. We can protect you here. No problem.'

Lelewala sucked on a lip. 'I appreciate the help you've given me . . .'

'Last time, woman died.'

'What?' said Corrigan.

'Last time she went to Hollywood, she died. Came from Hollywood too, but she went back, we told her not to, she died.'

'Tarriha, what are you talking about?'

He eased himself into a seat opposite them. 'Yellow Hair,' he said, smiling at the memory. 'Marilyn.'

'Marilyn?' said Lelewala.

'Marilyn,' said Tarriha.

'Marilyn?' said Corrigan.

'Marilyn,' said Tarriha. 'Monroe.'

Corrigan put his head in his hands. 'Tell me this,' he said, peering out from between his fingers. 'Are magic mushrooms in season? Or are you just friggin' nuts?'

'No,' said Tarriha, 'she was nuts. Because she went back to Hollywood. And they killed her.'

'Who killed her?'

'The Kennedys.'

'Fuck,' said Corrigan. He stood up, pushing his chair back. It toppled over. 'Look,' he said, 'I appreciate that you saved my life, but we really have to get going.'

Tarriha's narrow eyes narrowed further. 'Inspector,' he said slowly, 'the police are looking for you. Others want to kill Lelewala. Stay here. Be safe.'

Lelewala looked at Tarriha. 'Even in Georgia we know the great Marilyn Monroe.'

'Do you know why they killed her?' Tarriha asked.

Lelewala shook her head. Corrigan sat down again. He sighed. 'Tell me. Tell me why the Kennedys killed Marilyn Monroe.'

'Because we weren't there to protect her. And the same will happen to Lelewala.'

'What?' Corrigan asked, exasperated. 'The Kennedys are going to kill her?'

Tarriha's eyes narrowed. 'You mock me,' he said.

'No,' said Corrigan, both of them aware that they were treading familiar territory, 'I think you mock me.' He nodded at Lelewala. 'Let's go,' he said.

She moved, but only slightly. She looked helplessly at the old Indian. 'I'm sorry,' she said, 'but I have to . . .'

He wasn't listening. He was fishing in his wallet. It was made of rough, barely treated leather, as if he'd ripped it off a cow's hide and merely folded it up and put it in his back pocket to dry where it wouldn't be disturbed. Corrigan drummed his fingers on the table. Lelewala reached across and stilled them and he smiled oddly at her. He had the strangest sensation that he wasn't ever going to go anywhere without her again. He shook his head to get rid of the foolish thought. But it stayed where it was, and glowed.

Tarriha produced something folded and began to unfold it. It was a photograph. Black-and-white and creased and old, but he flattened it out on the table with his fist then slid it across the surface to them. They both peered at it.

'Marilyn,' Tarriha pointed out, needlessly. 'False Faces,' he added, equally needlessly.

It was. They were.

Twenty False Faces. Wearing the gear.

Corrigan said: 'Marilyn Monroe was . . .'

'She was filming *Niagara* . . . June 1951, with Joseph Cotten. Jean Peters. She first did the walk. The Marilyn walk. Henry Hathaway directed.' A pin-thin finger touched one of the False Faces. 'That's me,' Tarriha said. 'Day off, they came here. See what she's wearing?'

Lelewala lifted the picture, stared at it. 'That's my dress,' she said.

'Our dress.' Tarriha took the photograph back and began to fold it carefully. 'The mistress of the False Faces dress. She wanted to try it on. Fitted her as it fitted you. Like a glove. Although, of course, not a glove. Last living woman to wear it before you. She became honorary mistress, Ga-go-sa Ho-nun-nas-tase-ta Monroe. She's dead now. So will you be. I tell you no lie.'

Corrigan was drumming his fingers again. 'What we have here, Tarriha, is a souvenir snap of a film star visiting the local Indians. Nothing more, nothing less. It proves nothing.'

'She's dead, isn't she?'

'Half the fucking world is dead since then.'

'She was Monroe, Ho-nun-nas-tase-ta.'

'Yes, I'm sure she was. But she was still only . . .'

'She phoned.'

'She what?'

'She phoned me.'

'What are you on now?'

'Night she died. Last call she ever made.'

'Tarriha, all the calls she made are documented. I know this. She didn't phone you.'

'Yes she did. Callbox. Down the block. Round the corner. She told me.'

'She told you what?'

'That it was down the block and round the corner.'

'But what the fuck did she tell you?'

'That they were trying to kill her.'

'That who was trying to kill her?'

'The Kennedys.'

'Fuck.'

'Or the Mafia. She was a little confused.'

'I'm a little confused,' said Lelewala.

'You and me both,' said Corrigan. He stuck a finger out at Tarriha. 'What's your point, chief?'

'That she wanted to come home.'

'Home?'

'Here. Where she felt safe.'

'Jesus,' said Corrigan.

'And when she spoke, she spoke in Tuscorora.'

Corrigan rolled his eyes. 'I don't believe this.'

'Please,' Tarriha said, reaching a wizened hand across the table and placing it gently over Lelewala's clasped fingers. 'You must stay. This is a place of safety. We can protect you here.'

'Protect her from what?'

'The evil that walks this land.'

'This time,' Corrigan said, 'I've had enough.'

Nobody tried to stop them leaving. There was nothing to pack. Corrigan and Lelewala stood in the car park looking at the road that stretched ahead of them through the reservation and a couple of miles distant into Niagara Falls.

'I don't suppose,' Corrigan said, 'that you have a quarter on you so I can call a cab?'

Lelewala shook her head.

She waited in the pleasant early-morning breeze while he went back to ask Tarriha as politely as he could manage if he could use a phone. Tarriha nodded magnanimously.

While Corrigan waited for the taxi company to answer, Tarriha came up and stood at his elbow.

'You are young and you are foolish,' he said, gravely. 'But you are in love, Sahonwadi. And you will return.'

Corrigan looked him in the eye. 'Give my head peace, would you?' he said.

39

Lelewala held his hand and looked out of the window. They had only just turned out on to the highway and already she felt tense. He reached across and caressed her cheek. 'It'll be fine,' he said.

She nodded weakly. 'What if he's right?' she said.

'He's not right. He's just a senile old man lost in some myths. Forget him. You'll be fine.' He began to sing 'California Here We Come'; she smiled, but she didn't look convinced or entertained and his singing soon trailed off.

The taxi driver was eyeing them up in the mirror. Corrigan said: 'Something wrong?' and he averted his eyes. But he knew.

He dropped them at the Rainbow Bridge. Corrigan gave him a dollar tip, but he suspected it wasn't enough to prevent him calling the police. They nosed around a tourist office at the foot of the bridge for ten minutes until a bus pulled up and disgorged a crowd of unruly Poles, then mingled with them as they queued to have their passports checked before crossing over into Canada.

Corrigan guessed right. The guards, almost overwhelmed by the sudden influx, waved them all through after checking just the first half-dozen.

A couple of minutes' walking across the bridge and they were back in Niagara Falls. Corrigan found a phone box and made a collect call to Stirling. There was no response. He called Madeline's mobile number. She said she'd be there in ten minutes. In five a silver-grey sedan pulled up and three hoods climbed out. Lelewala froze against him. They removed guns from the pockets of their blue tracksuits and tried to look menacing.

'Hello, Gretchin.' A rich, high voice came from within the vehicle, and then a moment later the body it belonged to appeared. Lelewala immediately looked to the ground.

He was tall and bald and his four front teeth had gold crowns. He had a smile like melting butter. His suit was black with thin lapels and he wore a red AIDS awareness ribbon, which was pretty noble for a pimp and gangster like Gavril Popov. He raised his finely manicured hand to her hair and began to caress it as if it was a cat, then slowly bunched his fist about it and pulled her close. He was about to hiss something at her, but was distracted as one of his three hoods raised his gun at Corrigan, who was coming forward with his own fists bunched.

'No,' Popov said simply. The hood didn't fire, but he didn't drop his aim for one second, even as Corrigan came right up to him, as close as he could without the barrel of the gun getting stuck between his ribs.

'Get your hands off her,' Corrigan began.

The hood traced his pistol up Corrigan's shirt, on to his chin, and then poked it into his eye. Corrigan reeled back. The guy went after him, punched him in the stomach, then chopped at his head as it came down. Corrigan hit the road with a thump. He felt hands on his body checking for a gun. When he opened his one good eye, blinking back sympathetic tears for the other, he saw that Lela wasn't even looking at him. And then a shiny head came into his moist and hazy line of sight.

'You tell the Old Cripple, Gavril Popov take his woman back, that's all. Ceasefire still holds, OK?'

Corrigan struggled to his knees. 'She's not yours to take . . .' he gasped.

Popov smiled and the sun, flashing off his teeth, blinded Corrigan further. He turned to Lelewala. 'Get in the car.'

She got in the car. She didn't look at Corrigan. In a second the sedan was off. Corrigan remained on his knees in the middle of the street watching after it, watching the back of Lelewala's head. He was still sitting there watching it a minute later – it was a long, straight street – when another vehicle braked suddenly behind him and blared its horn; he was suddenly back to reality and pushing himself up off the ground and nodding apologies at the driver when he saw it was Madeline. She had the window down and was shouting something he couldn't hear because his ears were full of noise. Just noise. Rushing blood. He staggered to the window and said: 'What?'

'Get in! We can follow them!'

And he bounced off the bodywork round to the passenger door, pulled it open and jumped in. She gunned the engine and they were off.

She looked across at him and smiled. Her cheeks were rosy with excitement. The same red hair cut short. The same little turned-up nose. *Why would they be any different?*

'You look like death warmed up,' she said.

'Thanks.' Popov's car was about three hundred yards up on them, turning left out of Garner Road on to Lundy's Lane.

'Half the world's looking for you,' she said.

'That'll be an exaggeration.'

'OK. Half the cops in Toronto.'

'I can live with that.' She offered him a cigarette. He accepted it gratefully and began to twiddle with the car lighter.

'That,' said Madeline, 'is the radio.' She flicked a lighter for him.

He accepted gratefully, again. He put the cigarette to his lips, still breathing hard, and sucked hard. The experts were wrong, of course. Smoking was good for you. He was living proof. He could feel the goodness soak through him. 'So,' he said, having reduced the cigarette to a butt with one elongated draw, 'what's been happening?'

'Not much. We've formed a private army to storm the Old Cripple's mansion. He's hosting a ball tomorrow night. Everyone will be there.'

Corrigan nodded, eyes on Popov's car as it ran a red light. Madeline slowed.

'I give you permission to go on red,' he said.

She waited until it changed. The sedan was still in sight. 'I don't want it to look like we're following.'

'We're not following,' Corrigan said, 'we're pursuing.'

'There's a difference?'

Corrigan nodded thoughtfully for several moments. 'Spelling, mostly.' He took another cigarette from the box sitting on the dash. 'So,' he said, lighting up, 'how many have you managed to recruit for this private army?'

'Seven,' she said. 'Including you.'

He nodded. 'You ever handled a weapon before?'

'A gun?'

'Yes. A gun.'

She shook her head. 'But I'm willing to learn.' There was another set of lights, and this time the sedan came to a halt. Madeline pulled up two cars behind. She looked across and he saw that the lightness had vanished. There was concern and a little bit of anger. 'Are you going to tell me what happened to you?' she said. 'I was worried sick.'

'About me?'

'Yes. OK?'

'I'm touched.'

'Well?'

'Well what?'

'Tell me! I saw those men killed! Their throats cut! I was hiding under the bed and an Indian came in and left a scalp on the bedside table! I thought you were dead! Now *tell* me!'

The lights changed. She moved the car forward.

'I can't,' Corrigan said.

'*What?*'

'You'll have to speak to my agent.'

She laughed, in spite of herself.

'I'm OK,' he said.

'The Indians . . .'

'Just wanted to protect her. Despite what *you* might think, they do seem serious about her being Lelewala. They think she's come back to fight evil. And there's certainly no shortage of evil.'

'The Old Cripple and the convention.'

'The Old Cripple and the convention. And yer man up ahead. Gavril Popov. Her husband and pimp.'

'Oh,' said Madeline. 'Disappointed?'

An hour later they had been parked for fifty minutes outside the bus station on Erie Avenue. Corrigan had his one good eye trained on an apartment above the pizza parlour that faced the station. Madeline watched it too, occasionally folding or unfolding a bus timetable which she had propped up against the steering wheel as if she couldn't make up her mind whether to leave town or not. They had watched Lelewala, Popov and the hoods enter the pizza parlour then disappear behind the counter. A few moments later they'd seen them briefly at one of the top windows, then the curtains had been abruptly pulled. There had been nothing since. Nobody had looked out of the window to check on them, or on anything. The apartment was rundown; paint peeled, one window boarded up, a hand-painted FOR SALE sign taped to the board.

After a while Madeline said: 'What say I go over there and ask to buy the place?'

Corrigan pondered it for a moment. 'I think not. We just need to be patient.'

'Patient for what? We've been here an *hour*.'

'What's an hour? What else would you be doing?'

'An hour's a lifetime in television.'

'This isn't television.'

'It will be.'

He told her about Lelewala and her blackouts. Madeline thought she sounded like a schizophrenic. Corrigan was in two minds about that. He stared morosely at the apartment. She was up there. Popov had thrown her in the Niagara. A husband who sent her out to hook. 'He could be doing anything to her up there,' Corrigan said.

'You're right. It's been an hour. It's too long. Give me the phone.'

She handed him her mobile. 'I hope you're not phoning the cops,' she said.

He shook his head. 'The Indians.'

'The Indians? They *kidnapped* her . . .'

'They've also sworn to protect her.' He phoned the Clifton Diner and asked for Barry Lightfoot. There was a lot of noise in the background. Voices raised and wood splintering.

'Barry,' said Corrigan when he finally lifted the phone, 'sounds like there's a fight going on.'

'There is. Flower arrangers arguing over who sits where. Who is this?'

'Frank Corrigan.'

'Oh.'

Corrigan explained the situation briefly.

Barry Lightfoot was deeply, deeply embarrassed.

Corrigan said: 'Let me get this completely clear, Barry. The False Faces have sworn to lay down their lives to protect Lelewala, but only at weekends?'

'Uhm, yes,' said Barry.

'Does that include Fridays?'

'Fridays after five.'

'Are you kidding me?'

'Uhm, no. We all have jobs. It's pretty much a social thing, Corrigan. We're coming into powwow season, lotta dances, lotta public appearances. It's difficult to get the time off.'

'Right. Thank you. Thank you very fucking much.' He cut the line.

'So what do you say?' Madeline asked, taking the phone back. 'I go in and ask for a twelve-incher, or is that what Lelewala is doing?'

'You aren't funny,' Corrigan said.

They looked at the building a little more. There was a young girl, maybe seventeen, working behind the counter, although there wasn't much work. There had been only two customers since they'd arrived. They'd disappeared from their line of sight for ten minutes – possibly there was a waiting room off to the left – before emerging with red-and-white-striped pizza boxes.

Madeline lifted the mobile and began pressing numbers.

'What're you doing?' Corrigan asked.

'Ordering a pizza.' She nodded towards the shop. The telephone number was painted beside the sign. The sign said: PIZZAS, which must have taken a while to think up. 'Hi. I'd like to order a . . .'

'Sorry, ma'am, but we're closed.'

'Oh . . . but it's lunchtime.'

'Closed for refurbishment and training, ma'am.'

'You couldn't just squeeze one out for me? I'm starving.'

'Sorry, ma'am.'

Madeline clicked off, raised her eyebrows. 'Restaurant,' she said, 'closed for lunch.'

As she put the phone down, a car pulled up just in front of them. Corrigan tensed, ready for anything, but ultimately helpless, as a puffy-faced guy in a too-tight t-shirt and red trackpants climbed out. He ignored Madeline's car and hurried across the road to the pizza shop, his hands deep in his pockets and his eyes on the ground. It was the guy who sold tickets at the House of Frankenstein on Clifton Hill. Corrigan knew him of old. He was about to say so when Madeline said: 'I know him, he was at our recruitment meeting. Wasn't interested.'

They watched as the guy stopped outside the shop, looked at the sign above it, rubbed at his neck, then entered. He placed his order, then disappeared off to the left. Ten minutes later he reappeared with a box under his arm. He hurried across the road to his car. As he slipped the key into the door Corrigan appeared at his elbow.

'Dr Frankenstein, I presume,' he said.

'What the fuck . . .' the guy shouted. Then he saw who it was and said: 'Oh shit.'

Panic and fear were written in big thick letters all over his face. There was plenty of room. It was a fat face, with thick cheeks and ping-pong-ball eyes. 'Please don't kill me,' he said weakly.

Corrigan took the pizza box off him. It was extremely light. 'What are you, on a diet?' He flipped the lid. There was nothing inside. 'I don't see no pizza.'

'No, well.' There were damp patches under the arms of his t-shirt. He looked despairingly at Corrigan. 'You gotta understand, since my wife had the baby, things ain't been the same.'

'Excuse me?'

'She's not interested. Was yours like that? Before she died, I mean.'

'What're you talking about?'

'Making love. She's just not interested. You can't blame a guy; once in a while you gotta . . . y'know . . . do the business.'

'You . . . ?'

The man who sold tickets at the House of Frankenstein glanced back towards the pizza shop. 'She's the most beautiful woman I ever seen. That kinda helps.'

'You . . .'

'Y'know, it's nothing to be ashamed of. Even with the handcuffs.'

'What fucking handcuffs?'

'She's handcuffed to the bed. You don't pay any extra for it, but it does give it a certain . . .'

Corrigan got hold of him by the lapels and slammed him against the car. 'She's being held prisoner, you stupid bastard,' he spat.

Fear dripped off the man who sold tickets at the House of Frankenstein. 'Please don't kill me,' he said again.

Corrigan tutted. He let him go. There was no point in taking it out on him. 'Get the fuck out of here,' he said. He pulled the car door open and bundled the quaking wreck into the driver's seat. 'Just get the fuck out of here,' he hissed, and slammed the door shut.

As the man who sold tickets at the House of Frankenstein fumbled to get his keys into the ignition Corrigan hurried back and knelt by Madeline's window. 'He has her handcuffed to the fucking bed. He's had her in there less than an hour and he's already had three punters in with her. What kind of a fucking animal is he?' She just looked at him. 'I'm going in,' he said.

She tried to open her door.

He held it shut. 'Alone,' he said.

'They've got guns, Frank.'

He ignored her. He was already halfway across the road.

She scrambled out of the car after him. He was already past the counter and the protesting pizza girl and thumping up the stairs by the time Madeline reached the door.

She went to follow him, but the pizza girl blocked her way. 'Get out of the way,' Madeline said, 'I'm a journalist.'

In the big chart of threats, it didn't rank very high. The pizza girl snarled and pushed Madeline in the chest. Madeline pushed back. In moments they were wrestling, and then they both hit the ground. As the girl scrabbled at her Madeline realized she was only a slight thing. It was not hurting. She moved to one side and punched the girl in the face. The girl stopped suddenly, surprised, and checked her nose for damage. Madeline bucked under her and she went flying over her head, crashed off the open door and lay still.

Pleased with herself, adrenaline pumping, Madeline jumped to her feet and had just set foot on the first stair when the gunshot rang out.

She stopped, peered up the darkened stairs, then turned and ran away.

40

Lelewala was doing her nails.

He was blinking through the pain and Lelewala was *doing her nails*. She was looking at him, but she might as well have been looking at a very slow-moving programme on television. He tried to speak, but it came out as a thick croak and she barely blinked before returning her full attention to getting those nails *just right*. He started to drift away again . . .

There was movement to his left. It was getting brighter now. Before, there had just been a light around Lelewala. Why was that? Why was she bathed in light, like an angel? Like an Indian princess come to rid the world of evil? Or because she was sitting by the window . . . his thoughts were jumbled and the movement to his left was a distraction that . . .

Slap.

And sting.

And the room was suddenly properly bright and Lelewala was asleep on a couch and there was a face leering into his and there was a blinding glare.

Teeth. Golden . . .

Slap.

And sting.

And he was back and his whole arm hurt, not to mention his face, but he was back and Gavril Popov was standing there. Corrigan tried moving, but he was tied, and it hurt. There was blood on the floor. His hand. He looked at his hand. It was crudely bandaged. The bandage was soaked red.

'Ah now,' Popov said. 'You come a-storming upstairs like that, what can you expect but to be shot? You lucky I choose only to shoot you in the hand. I shoot you in the head we would not be having this conversation.'

'I . . .'

'Yes indeed. Gretchin tells me you save her life. Very good. There should be a reward. Perhaps in heaven. Tell me, were you ever down a Russian coal mine?'

Corrigan shook his head.

'No matter,' Popov continued. 'This Old Cripple. He been giving *me* a hard life. All I ask is to be left alone to carry out my business. But no, that is not good enough. And what is more, his son, this Pongo, this *singer*, he doesn't pay. Now that's not good business. That's the comedy, isn't it? The Old Cripple, he's Mister Drugs, but his son has to come to me for his fix. Funny, yeah?'

Corrigan nodded and looked away. Looking at Popov made him uncomfortable. His eyes were out on stalks. There was spittle at the corners of his mouth and sweat on his brow. Corrigan had dabbled enough to recognize the gabble. Motormouth was on speed. It wasn't the worst thing in the world, unless you were a psycho to start with. He looked at Lelewala. She was still sleeping. He wondered how she could ever have fallen for someone as obviously disturbed as Gavril Popov. But then she was hardly the full shilling herself.

'You know how much Pongo owe me? One million dollars.'

'That's a lot of drugs.'

'One hundred thousand for the drugs. Nine hundred thousand for the interest. That's snow business, Mr Policeman, and now I'm afraid I must cut off your finger.'

Corrigan's head shot back. 'What?'

'Choose a finger, any finger. What's the difference? You lost one already; I shoot it clean off . . . not clean maybe, tell you, fuck, there was bits of it everywhere, but anyways . . . what hand you write with?'

'What are you . . . ?'

'Do you know there are fifty ways to say steal in Russian?'

'I've never . . .'

'So what's it to be? Little finger, index finger? Take a thumb if you want, though you never pick up a pen again. Who needs pens? All computers these days. You decided yet?'

Popov made a grab for Corrigan's left hand. Corrigan pulled it back as far as he could. Popov giggled.

'Why the fuck would you want to cut one of my fingers off?'

'I don't *want* to. I *have* to. Business necessity. You fuck my wife, you tell her she great actress, she wanna run off to Hollywood and marry David Hasslefree. That mean you owe me, buster, and all you got damn nothing in your pants and that's not enough. So I ask myself, who will pay to get you back, and there's only one answer, so I cut off your finger and send it to the Old Cripple and say, hey, send me a million and I'll give you the cop.'

'I don't understand the logic of this.'

'Logic? Logic? This isn't no Mr Spock situation, Frank Corrigan. Maybe the Old Cripple pay quick, you get to stitch it back on again. I hear they do great things these days. Do great things in Russia too, stitch it back on the wrong hand. That's Russia for you. Thank God I got out. Do you know how many gangs there are in the Russian Republic alone? I tell you. Five thousand. Too busy, too dangerous. Here, things are just nice. And dandy. But I gotta eat. I gotta wife to keep in the custom to which if it were possible to be it would. I say. So now, to the finger.'

He turned and surveyed the apartment. 'You know, I rent these apartments with furnish, good money, but I never check for knives. Still, not a thing you ask straight out: Mr Landlord, will you provide me with sharp knives for cutting off fingers? OK, let me see.'

He moved into the kitchen and began pulling at drawers. He produced a succession of implements: a ladle, a fork, a potato peeler, then waved a spoon at Corrigan: 'No!' And laughed his gold-tinged laugh. Corrigan strained at the ropes, but succeeded only in jagging his shot arm. He groaned.

He hissed at Lelewala: 'Lelewala!'

But she was still out of it.

'Damn no good!' Popov slammed a drawer shut and slapped his hand on the counter. 'Never a knife when you need one. Maybe I wait until my boys come back; they sort me out with a knife. You met my boys?'

Corrigan nodded.

'Good boys. Growing boys. They've gone to meet Ken.'

'Ken?' Corrigan said weakly.

'Ken Tucky Fried Chicken! Them boys can't do a thing without their food. So tell me about the convention then, sweetie.'

Corrigan took a deep breath. 'What convention?'

Popov stomped across from the kitchen and whacked Corrigan

across the face with the spoon. Corrigan saw stars. David Hasselhoff.

'You stupid fuck. I take your whole fucking hand. I cut it off and stick it up your ass and send the whole fucking lot to the Old Cripple and say Happy Christmas.'

He whacked him again. As Corrigan was shaking the pain out of his head Popov turned suddenly and studied his wife. 'It is a great pity . . .' he said, waving the spoon in the air, 'she is so beautiful . . . she is . . . how do you say . . . ?' He clicked the clicking fingers of one hand. 'Horses run free . . .' He looked to Corrigan for assistance. He clicked the fingers again. 'Unstable. It is a great pity. This is the land of the free, is it not? Yet will she ever be free? I think not. How will she ever earn enough money to be free if she act the crazy woman all the time? She owe me, Mr Policeman.'

'She's your wife, for godsake.'

'All the more reason. If you can't trust your wife to pay her debts, who can you trust?'

'How much does she . . . ?'

'One million dollars.'

'That's a lot of . . .'

'That's one hundred thousand for getting her into the great land of the free . . .'

'And nine hundred thousand dollars interest. I get the picture.'

'You want a picture? I can get you pictures of her. Videos too. She very popular. Why not, she very beautiful, but she never going to pay it off if she acts the crazy.'

'How much does she owe you now?'

Popov thought for a moment. 'She hardly scratched my surface. Work it out yourself. Fifty dollars a guy, six guys a day. It gonna take her . . . what you say? Ten years. Plus you gotta take into account the depreciation in her good looks over that period, so maybe you can't charge fifty; maybe forty, maybe thirty towards the end. Fifteen years, maybe. But she pretty good on schedule, then she fucks up a gig and talks lots of Indian shit so I have to throw her in the river. What way is that to pay off your debt? I should cut one-ah her fingers off too, teach her not to . . . but yeah, I know. You can't do that to your wife. Look at her; isn't she beautiful asleep like that, although I had to knock her out?

Women, yeah? Always on your back, when they should be on theirs, paying off their debt to my society. So who told you?'

'Who told me what?'

'That I upset about the convention.'

'I never mentioned . . .'

'Well you wrong. I tell you, I like a quiet life. You think I want to get mixed up with those guys? All that shit. No way. I had enough of that in Moscow, I came here to get away with it. They can carve up the world all they like; ain't none of my business. All I want is to be left alone and my million dollars. Pongo owes me that. He ain't got it; the Old Cripple owes me it. What does he do when I ask for it? He tries to kill me. So he's not my friend. And if he's not my friend, you're my enemy. And then suddenly he's my friend again, says if I shut up for a month until convention is over, he'll give me the million. Fair enough.'

'Fair enough,' Corrigan ventured, looking warily at the spoon and desperately towards the door for some sign of assistance.

'Fuck no way!' Popov yelled suddenly. He slammed the spoon against his own leg. 'No one tells Gavril Popov to shut the fuck up for a month! I got clients. I got girls. What's he want, they cross their legs for four weeks? No way. I got customers. I show him how Gavril Popov keeps quiet.'

And then he stopped, looked at Corrigan, and for a moment seemed to consider shutting up, that he'd said too much. But it wasn't possible. 'So, I kill your wife.'

There was nothing Corrigan could do. He was tied securely, he was shot in the arm and the hand, he'd been assaulted with a spoon and he was about to have a finger severed, or even a thumb. There was nothing he could do to this man who had killed Nicola. Nothing except: 'Why?'

'Accident. Of course I did not know then that she was policeman's wife. All I want is to show the Old Cripple that I'm not to be fucked with, only my girls. So, what I do, I pick out the worst guy, the one who hurts my girls the most. He pays top dollar, but he hurts my girls, then says sorry, sorry, like it's all right. So this guy, big, big, fat guy, he phones up, asks for Gretchin. Now she not long outta the Niagara and her brain is all messed up, she don't wanna go, he beat her last time, but I say, you gotta go.

She has a lotta money to pay off so she ain't got much choice. I wait in the car outside, I figure if I hear her scream, then I gotta right to teach him a lesson. So I hear her scream and I go in; he's beating on my wife and I shoot the fucker. Except right then his wife arrives home unexpected and sees it all and so I shoot her too. Except I didn't know it was your wife also, and anyway the police are coming and Gretchin she's been knocked about so much she has a fucking fit and she won't move her ass and so I have to leave her. But luckily all she does is talk the turkey anyway, and get off with it, so happy faces all round. Except your wife. Her fat man, not a good fat man at all. Lucky to be rid of him, if she was alive. Explain OK, Mr Policeman?'

Corrigan nodded.

'Good, now I cut off the finger, yeah?'

41

Madeline's heart was pounding, and it wasn't for Corrigan. It was for the convention. It was for making her name. Corrigan's death – and she was sure he was dead – merely confirmed the importance of it all. And if it was really that big, then Channel 4 in Buffalo just wasn't big enough for the story. It was national. International. It was *Hollywood*.

Split the rights? *Certainly.*

Show me the contract, buster.

A verbal contract ain't worth the paper it's written on.

A Hollywood quote.

She'd done everything she could. Called the cops, alerted them to the shooting above the pizza shop. Zipped round to Stirling's house. Told them the terrible news about Corrigan. They'd looked at each other helplessly and resolved to destroy the convention.

Stirling's wife, young, trim, under the thumb, was turning out sandwiches for the Magnificent Seven, though they were only six. Morton was teaching them how to use their guns, how to shoot and roll and stab and fight, as if you could do it in half an hour. And she was getting it all on video without their realizing. She'd seen *The Magnificent Seven* as a kid, so she knew the possibilities; Yul Brynner had turned a bunch of dozy Mexicans into an efficient fighting force, although admittedly there had been one hell of a lot of them, *and* they'd been defending, not attacking.

A window exploded to her left and she let out a scream. Then the seventy-year-old, Paddy Crossen, grinned sheepishly across and apologized by waving the gun cheerily in his hand. Another shot went off and the Magnificent Six were diving for cover.

They would die.

There would be a record of it. A tribute to their bravery. But not without more videotape.

She made her excuses and drove back into town to pick up some more tape. What she really needed to pick up was a cameraman, then she could send him in with the élite fighting force and maybe just pick the tape up off his body afterwards if he didn't make it. But if he did, it would mean he'd make a claim for a share of the profits, so she resolved to do it all herself. Awards, fame, Hollywood, *money*.

She wasn't really a mercenary, she was just ambitious.

She wasn't really heartless, she'd just been hurt in the past.

And if she was pushed she'd probably admit to a girlfriend that she really fancied Frank Corrigan, but he was probably dead, so what could she do about that except produce this film as a fitting tribute to him?

She tutted and slapped the steering wheel. All these thoughts. Adrenaline. Keep calm. You're taking a risk. You'll probably get fired. Or arrested. But go for it. Make your mark.

She looked at the houses. The cars. The taxis. The conventioneers were in town, staying in private villas or luxurious hotel suites, carving up territories, making shipping arrangements, drawing up hit-lists, sealing rifts, promoting designer drugs, designing designer drugs, doing drugs, stealing drugs, planning to do and steal drugs. She'd seen some of them herself, sitting in the car with Morton while he snapped away and she resolved to steal his film.

Like Waldo Aponte Romero walking across the tarmac at Niagara Regional Airport, his Lear jet parked behind him, his flowered shirt hiding bullet and knife scars and his broad smile hiding the viciousness that went hand in hand with his high rank in the Medellin drug cartel.

Or Giuseppe Lottusi, bald, beefy, weighed down with gold chains, standing at the head of a chartered Greyhound bus, instructing the members of four Mafia families to relax, enjoy the convention but not to take no fucking prisoners if it came to it.

Or former Politburo member Geidar Aliev, head of the petroleum mafia, the fishing mafia, the fruit-and-vegetable mafia, the caviar mafia, and for the purposes of this trip, the export mafia, all in Azerbaijan, standing fuming in the lobby of the Skylon Brock hotel because his rooms were double-booked.

Or Chiang Kai Smith, the former Hong Kong Triad assassin, now domiciled in New York, coming by taxi with his three brothers because they could afford to *and* give a tip, bringing with them big plans to shake up the Koreans. Morton, for so long out of circulation, seemed to know it all and took an obvious pleasure in telling her. Maybe he was trying to scare her. If he was, he failed. It excited her. It was all she could do to stop herself going up to Chiang Kai Smith with her camera and saying, 'Welcome to Niagara Falls. How's the drugs business?'

So many angles. So many stories. So much money.

Her route to the camera store took her past the pizza shop where Corrigan had been shot, and she peered across, wondering what was going on outside it. There were people standing in a circle, watching something. She slowed, tried to see; there were two people on the ground. Fighting. Or at least one of them was. They were . . . both women. The girl from the pizza shop. Fighting again. She tutted and parked the car and hurried across for a closer look, positioning the lens of the video camera out of the little gap in her handbag so she wouldn't miss a thing.

She was just in time to meet the Big Circle Boys.

They'd made the short drive down from Toronto, expecting to pick up a cheap motel room or four, but were having some trouble. They weren't A list, making their money mostly as sewer rats – transporting illegal aliens – or from smuggling heroin across the border into New York – so they didn't qualify for complimentary rooms at any of the better hotels. They didn't even have direct invitations to the convention, but were hoping to blag their way in to one or other of the many fringe meetings taking place around town.

They'd started out as Red Guards a generation before, bright young soldiers who'd been purged by the People's Liberation Army and treated like hardened criminals, and as a consequence they'd become hardened criminals. Smuggled into Hong Kong and then to Canada, they'd made their name through a series of violent armed robberies in the mid-seventies. Now they were trying to move a little further up market. Instead of buying from a local wholesaler, they wanted to buy direct from the Golden Triangle of Laos, Burma and Thailand. They were sure if they just got to meet the Old Cripple he could arrange this for them.

But every room in town was taken and they were a little upset. Cheng Chui-Ping especially. Even bloodthirsty Chinese women gangsters get period pains. She was fed up tramping from one dive to the next, and she was cramping. So she led her men down Clifton Hill in a blind fury and came across the pizza shop. She thought maybe food might help with the pain and tried to place an order, but the young girl behind the counter said they were closed. In fact, the place looked like it was permanently closed. Of course she didn't know that upstairs there was a bullet hole and Corrigan's bloodstains on the floor. Cheng Chui-Ping demanded to see the manager, her demand was refused. The girl was pulled out from behind the counter and chopped. She ran screaming out on to the sidewalk, and people stopped to watch as she got chopped again. She tried to scramble away but the Big Circle Boys wouldn't let her go. The blows kept raining down. Cheng Chui-Ping was enjoying herself now and her boys were laughing.

The pizza girl's face was a mask of blood.

Madeline stepped out of the crowd and said: 'I think she's had enough.'

Cheng Chui-Ping turned on her heel and chopped Madeline across the throat. She was unconscious before she hit the ground.

42

Corrigan was clawing back towards consciousness, trying to figure out what time it was, and then how to read a clock. It involved a big hand and a little . . . finger.

Fuck.

And only then did he feel the pain. He opened his eyes very slightly. He had already lost one finger thanks to Popov shooting him; now, clearly, he had lost another. There was a different bandage on his hand, made of a different material – patterned and thick like a curtain – but the blood had soaked through it as well. If he did not die from losing fingers at a steady rate, he would die from lack of blood. Where was Doc and his black mush when he needed him?

Popov's boys had returned and now sat rolling joints. The place stank of greasy chicken and burped beer. He felt sick. His head pounded. Popov was at a table, counting money. Lelewala remained motionless on the sofa. He watched her chest for several moments, mostly to check that she was still breathing. He closed his eyes again. Dizzy. The room was starting to revolve.

There was a voice from the window and: 'Someone's coming.'

The hoods crowded around it. Popov continued to count. Corrigan just turned in time to see Lelewala's eyes close again. Sweat dripped off his brow.

'Limo. Stretch. White.' Then an anxious pause. 'It's Pongo. He's alone.'

Corrigan pulled deftly at the rope that secured him to the chair. It was tight and it bit into his arm and he fought manfully to suppress a yelp.

There came the sound of rapid footsteps on the stairs, and then a light tapping on the door. The boys drew their guns. Popov finished counting then slipped the money inside a battered holdall and placed it under the table. He placed a discarded KFC box on top of it.

One of the boys opened the door carefully, made double extra sure that Pongo was alone, then ushered him in. Pongo was wearing a white suit with large lapels and flares. He was *way* ahead of fashion. As he was frisked he nodded at Popov, then gave Corrigan and his bandages a cursory glance before fixing his attention on Lelewala. He was holding a small suitcase in his hand. It was leather and shiny and didn't look as if it had ever been down an airport conveyor belt. He held it up.

'I brought two million.'

'Ah now,' said Popov, 'like milk to my ears. Your father, he a generous man.'

'One million to pay off my debts, one million for your wife.'

A look of surprise crossed Popov's face. 'For *my wife*? I think the wires are cross. I send Old Cripple a finger, warn him to pay up for sick cop or I'll spill the tin of beans on his convention, you arrive with too much money and want to buy my wife. You've been at the marching powder again.'

'I'm quite serious,' Pongo said. He set the suitcase on the table before Pongo and unlocked it. He lifted the lid up, then let it drop back. Popov and his boys clustered around. Corrigan couldn't see what was inside, but from the impressed whistles coming from the boys he guessed the money was all present and correct. 'The cop's got nothing to do with us. He isn't on the payroll. Chuck him in the river for all we care; you seem to specialize in that. I want to buy your wife. What difference does it make to you? I've been renting her this last six months.'

Popov pulled the lid closed, nearly trapping one of his boys' fingers. A glint of teeth appeared wide across his face, but if it was a smile it was an evil one. 'You pretty damn funny, Pongo. The Old Cripple must be plenty upset, yeah?'

'Yeah, plenty upset. I had to talk him out of sending half a fucking regiment down here to blow your heads off. He doesn't like being blackmailed.'

'Well maybe next time he send me an invite to his party, not keep me locked in the coal shed.' He turned and looked at Lelewala. Her eyes were open now, and looking distastefully at Pongo. 'You really serious? Why buy when you can rent? Change the model every few weeks, eh?'

'I have my reasons.'

'How about you tell me those reasons, eh, Pongo boy? What, you going to make beautiful music together, eh? It would be a first.' Popov cackled. Then he stopped abruptly and his eyes narrowed. 'What the Old Cripple want my wife for?'

'It's nothing to do with him. *I* want her.'

'She's a pain in the vertebra.' Pongo shrugged. 'You're not in love with her, Pongo boy?'

Pongo shrugged again.

'That is so sweet,' said Popov. His hoods nodded in agreement. 'How can I resist? OK. I give her to you for one million. You're a good customer. What they call a wanker.'

'Banker,' said one of the boys.

'So you take her with you. You tell Cripple Features, thanks for the cash. I tell you what, you take Mr Policeman with you too. Two for the price of one. Then you come back and see me when you need some dust, yeah?'

Pongo nodded.

Lelewala looked on, aghast.

43

Pongo drove with his face pressed against the windscreen, trying to keep them on the road as the limo battled against the torrential rain. A corker of a thunderstorm had blown up while he was in captivity. Every few seconds lightning snaked out of the sky, throwing bursts of electricity into the country and western music that eased out of the radio, as if the fiddlers had suddenly discovered feedback.

Corrigan's fever was eating him up. When they'd untied him he'd tried to say something smart, but instead of wit there was bullshit, and not even as witty as that. Gabble. Babble. Something, at least, that Popov could relate to.

His legs would hardly support him. The hoods had to carry him down and throw him in the back of the limo. Lelewala had helped him sit up, and now he lay slumped against her shoulders, his good arm thrown round her and his bad arm throbbing in his lap. She touched his face. 'We have to get him to a hospital,' she said.

'*Hospital*,' Pongo muttered.

'I used to have some of your records,' Corrigan said, head lolling. 'But then I grew up.'

'Shhhhh,' Lelewala said.

'Actually,' Corrigan continued, 'that's a lie. I haven't grown up.' He started to laugh, and then he started to retch.

Pongo tutted. Lelewala stroked Corrigan's brow. His eyes rolled back towards her, struggling to focus. 'You've bought her,' he said. 'If I'd that kind of money I'd buy one too . . .' Corrigan smiled. 'You're free of him now . . .'

Pongo signalled and turned right. Corrigan groaned at the movement. A hospital. It would just be nice to sleep. Sleep for a long time, maybe just wake up once in a while to see if any more fingers had been lopped off. He closed his eyes.

Nicola. He wondered if they'd buried her yet.

If somebody had told Aimie.

If Aimie thought she'd been deserted by everyone.

She was only small, but she wasn't stupid.

Aimie.

Aimie.

'I killed them,' Corrigan said.

'What?' said Lelewala.

'But there's been no violence since.'

'He's delirious,' said Lelewala.

'So am I,' said Pongo.

'So am I,' said Corrigan.

'Are we nearly there?' Lelewala asked.

'I'm nearly there,' said Corrigan. 'I shot them in the back.'

'You shot who in the back?'

'Them. The IRA. Shot them in the back. Getting our own back. But you can't say that in court.'

'Shhhhh,' said Lelewala.

'Nearly there,' said Pongo, peering ahead.

But they nearly weren't. Lelewala rubbed at a misted window. Pongo had turned off the highway and now they were starting to bump along an unlit and neglected stretch of road. Soon the car began to slip and slide and she knew that the road had descended into a dirt track. She could see nothing but black and raindrops, but Lelewala knew it, she sensed it. She shivered. It wasn't the massed evil of her fits and furies, but there was a hint of it.

Pongo stopped the car.

Corrigan said: *'Je ne regrette rien.'*

Pongo got out. He pulled Corrigan's door open and dragged him out by his shot arm. Corrigan yelled. Lelewala yelled too and scrambled after him. Corrigan landed in the mud, soaked already. Lelewala crouched by him. They were in a field. It was pitch-black save for the car's lights, pointing away into the darkness.

Lelewala screamed: 'What are you doing?'

'Throwing out the garbage,' Pongo said, calmly. He produced a gun. Corrigan was shaking his head, shaking his fevered brain about, trying to calm it. The cold. The damp. What was he doing in a . . .

He looked at the barrel of the gun and Pongo's tear-stained face. No, not tears, raindrops.   ●

Raindrops keep falling on my head. Butch Cassidy and the Sun . . .

'No!' Lelewala yelled. She stepped in front of Corrigan.

'Get out of the way!'

'No!'

'Get out of the fucking way!'

'No!'

He stepped closer, then moved to the side, trying to get a clear line of fire, but she moved with him.

'You can't do this, Pongo.'

'Get out of the fucking way!'

'No!'

Pongo shot wide. Lelewala jumped, but stayed in place.

'Move out of the fucking way, Gretchin!'

'No!'

They stormed at each other in the rain. Lightning lit the scene. Corrigan began to lose focus again. Pongo turned suddenly away. 'Fuck you then,' he said.

Lelewala let out a big whoosh of air and knelt beside a fading Corrigan. Pongo swivelled back, deceptively quick for a cokehead, and slapped her hard. She went tumbling into the sludge. Pongo raised his gun and aimed. She threw herself back at Pongo, knocking him sideways just as he pulled the trigger, and the bullet zipped just to the right of Corrigan's ear.

He threw her off again. Raised the gun. He was about to fire, then hesitated because she hadn't attacked again. He turned slightly. 'What?' he said.

'Let him live,' she said, 'and I will stay with you for ever.'

'You *are* staying with me for ever.'

'But I will sleep with you and love you and make you the happiest man ever. Not just fucking.'

'It's the just fucking I'm interested in.'

'And we will make beautiful music. Isn't that what you want?'

Pongo raised the gun again. Paused. He looked at her, beautiful and bedraggled and angry and full of love for someone else. That didn't matter. 'Can you sing?'

'Like a bird.'

'What sort of a bird? If it's a seagull, you're no fucking use to me.'

'My people say that I sing like ...'

'What people?'

'The village. My father ...'

Pongo laughed. 'You're really serious about all that Indian shit! I love it!' He waved the gun at her. He was dying for another blast of coke. The realization of where he was and what he was doing suddenly dawned on him. He was getting soaked and there was no one to hold an umbrella over him. There was *mud* on his shoes. 'Get in the car, Gretchin!'

'Not until you promise ...'

'OK, OK! I fucking promise. Now get in the car!' She hesitated. Pongo looked at Corrigan flailing helplessly in the mud. He shook his head. He pocketed the pistol. 'Get in the car,' he said.

Lelewala hesitated. 'You'll shoot him.'

'I won't touch him.'

She took a deep breath, looked despairingly at Corrigan, then turned away. Pongo knelt down beside Corrigan. 'I told you about the fucking convention,' he hissed, 'and you fucked it up.' He stood up, glanced back at Lelewala, climbing into the car with her back to him for the moment, then kicked Corrigan hard in the stomach. As he turned to leave he stamped Corrigan's hand down into the mud, then tutted as it oozed up over his sole. And soul.

In a few moments Corrigan heard the engine. He could barely move his head in time to see the tail-lights disappear into the rain-swept darkness. For some reason he was wondering how he could ever manage to scramble eggs with one arm.

44

He staggered and he fell, he staggered and he fell. He got dirt in his nose and eyes and shoes and it seeped through his bandages into his bullet hole and no-fingers. He ached and sweated and bled and puffed and ran and cried.

The country lane seemed never ending, but it could only have been a few miles – long miles of rain and lightning and exhaustion – and by the time he stumbled out on to the highway and began waving his one good arm about like a madman and his other painful arm like a fool, he was as near to dropping down dead as a reasonably sane man at the end of his tether can be without actually dropping down dead. It was at this point that a cattle truck came thundering out of the storm like Noah's Ark with a very strict door policy. It stopped. Just. There were some moos from the rear.

As he climbed up into the cab and shut the door, the driver took a long look at him and said: 'What the freakin' hell happened to you?'

Corrigan slumped gratefully down into the seat. Between deep breaths he squeezed out: 'I got kidnapped by a Russian gangster who shot one finger off then cut off another and posted it to the Old Cripple. Then the Artist Formerly Known as Pongo came and bought the Russian's wife, the Indian Princess Lelewala, for a million dollars and got me as a free gift. Then he dumped me in a field and shouted at me for not doing something about the horticultural convention.'

The driver nodded. 'Where can I drop you?'

Stirling lived on the edge of town. Corrigan fell out of the lorry a couple of blocks away and thanked the driver profusely. He'd given him a cup of coffee and a cigarette, and the combination of caffeine and good healthy smoke made him feel ten times better. Maybe not ten. Three. Possibly two. But better.

The rain was still pouring out of the heavens, and it was the saving of him. He was five houses down from Stirling's when he saw the car sitting across the road from the house, two guys inside, both of them smoking. He checked the number plate. It was one of *his* unmarked vehicles. Corrigan pulled the collar of his mud-caked jacket up and walked on, and with the battering of the raindrops and the misted breath inside the car they either didn't see him or dismissed him as a local hurrying home. When he'd continued up the block a hundred yards he chanced glancing back, but there was no movement from the car. He turned the corner then slipped up the first driveway he came to and began to double back along the back gardens.

When he got to Stirling's he was so tired he didn't have the energy to knock on the door. He sat on the back step for several moments, just to summon the energy, and Stirling's wife Cindy found him there an hour later when she went to let the cat out. She screamed as a mud pie with legs tumbled into her kitchen. Stirling came running, gun out, Morton close behind him.

They dragged him in. He mumbled something they couldn't make out. They heaved him into the bathroom and stripped off his clothes and showered him down, then put him in a bed upstairs. Cindy, composed again, cut the bandage off his hand and looked at the wound. They all did. They shook their heads.

'Fester is the word that comes to mind,' Morton said.

'He needs to go to a hospital,' Cindy said.

'He can't,' Morton said. 'They'll arrest him. Then they'll arrest us.'

'Then we'll call a doctor,' Cindy said. 'He needs medical attention. He's not dying in my bed. We'll have to move house.'

'If we get a doctor, *they'll* see him.' Stirling thumbed at the window. 'They'll guess there's something going on.'

'They already know there's something going on,' Cindy said. 'That's why they're outside.'

They stood looking silently at Corrigan for several moments. He was pale and his breathing was laboured. There was a bubble blowing in and out of his nose.

'Jimmy Hatcher,' Cindy said suddenly.

'Jimmy Hatcher?' said Stirling.

'Who's Jimmy Hatcher?' Morton asked.

'The Vietnam vet. He could do something.'

Stirling thought for a moment, then nodded. 'Good thinking, Batman,' he said.

Morton looked confused. 'What on earth could a Vietnam vet do for him?'

Stirling turned and hurried down the stairs. 'Tell him,' he called back.

Cindy smiled patiently. 'Jimmy was trained as a veterinarian by the army. Served in Vietnam, looking after army dogs. He's mostly retired now, but he lives just round the corner. He still does a few days a week. He'll have medicines. Antibiotics.'

Morton shook his head. 'Frank Corrigan isn't a dog.'

'Well,' said Cindy, 'that remains to be seen.'

Stirling gave Jimmy Hatcher a lot of bullshit about under-cover ops and the need for secrecy. Had really to persuade him to clamber over fences and through hedges to get to the house the back way. Jimmy was in his early sixties and wore his long grey hair in a ponytail. He huffed and puffed as they hurried through the down-pour. He was a sixty-a-day man. Joints, not cigarettes. He was the original *I-been-smoking-this-stuff-for-thirty-years-and-I'm-still-not-addicted* man. When he saw who it was he said: 'He's wanted for murder, isn't he?'

Stirling nodded. 'But he didn't do it.'

'You sure of that?'

'I'm sure.'

As he started to probe the wound Corrigan winced and began to come round. He blinked at them for a confused minute. Then he shouted 'Lelewala!' and tried to get up.

They pushed him back down. He dozed for another half-hour, then opened his eyes again just as Jimmy Hatcher was finishing up. Jimmy smiled benevolently down at him. There was a joint in his mouth. 'Good news,' he said, 'we can save the arm.'

Corrigan looked about him warily, trying to remember. *Pongo and Lelewala.* His hand was freshly bandaged. He blinked at the spaces where the fingers had been and croaked: 'What about my fingers?'

'You type with two fingers, or all ten?'

'All ten.'

'Remind me not to read any of your novels.'

'I'm not a novelist.'

'It's a figure of speech. You play the piano?'

'Some.'

'Let me put it this way. The melodies may be a little lacking.'

'Melodies were never my strong point.'

'Good. Well at least now you have an excuse. What happened to the fingers?'

Corrigan looked regretfully at his bandaged hand. 'One was shot to bits. The other was cut off. How long could it survive without me?'

Jimmy shrugged. 'Depends.'

'On what?'

'On whether it's packed in ice. On whether it's been kept in sterile conditions.'

'What if it's been stuck in an envelope and posted?'

'Then you can wave goodbye to your finger. But relax. It could be worse. I took a bullet out of your arm – remarkably clear of infection. I wish I could say the same for your hand. Like the annual germ convention. I've given you a strong antibiotic that should sort it out. Although, of course, it's not specifically designed for humans.'

He smiled, lifted his medical bag, then turned from the room. Cindy went after him. Corrigan blinked from Stirling to Morton.

'Don't ask,' Stirling said.

Corrigan drifted again. He was on a picnic with Aimie and Nicola. By the edge of the Niagara. Aimie was pointing and then suddenly he was running and there was Lelewala paddling over the edge of the Falls. He yelled at her to go back and she looked up, she wanted to, but it was too late, she was sucked over the edge and Corrigan screamed, and then he woke up and he *was* screaming. He looked desperately about him, drenched in sweat, and his eyes came to a halt on Stirling, standing at the foot of the bed. There was sunlight streaming through a gap in the curtains.

'Take it easy,' Stirling said.

Corrigan was breathing hard. He examined the room again. Then his hand. He gingerly felt the space where his fingers had been.

Stirling sat on the edge of the bed. 'How're you doing?' he asked softly.

'OK.' Corrigan ran a finger through his dank hair. 'I know who killed Nicola.'

'I know you do. Gavril Popov.'

'How the fuck do you know that?'

'Hey, I'm a policeman.'

'No, *how do you know it?*'

'You've been shouting his name all over the house. But you can fill me in on the details.'

He told him everything he could remember. Stirling nodded sadly throughout. 'A pity,' he said at the end, 'that you didn't have a wire on you. But don't worry. We'll get him. Once we sort the little matter of the convention out.'

Corrigan sighed. 'What about Madeline?' he asked suddenly. 'I left her sitting in the . . .'

'She's in hospital. But don't panic. She got chopped by one of the conventioneers. She's OK. Just in for observation. She's fine.'

'The stupid bitch didn't try to interview one of them, did she?'

'She tried to stop one of them beating someone up.'

'OK. Fair enough. She mentioned something about *The Magnificent Seven.*'

'Yeah. We go in tonight.'

'That's complete madness.'

'I know. It was your idea.'

'God. I wish none of this had ever happened. I was quite happy with my wee life. And look at you, looking after a murder suspect. You should just wash your hands of it, Mark, go back to the way you . . .'

'I got a visit from Internal Affairs.'

'Seriously?'

'Seriously. They accused me of accepting a $200,000 bribe.'

'Well, you're standing here, so you must have convinced them otherwise.'

'No, actually, they're locked up in the boot of my car.'

'Very funny. How did you . . . ?'

'I'm not joking, Frank. They *are* in the boot. The car's in the garage. Every six hours Jimmy Morton puts on a balaclava, yanks up the door and throws some sandwiches in, then he bangs it down again.'

'Jesus. What do they say? You must have asked them what's happening?'

'Are you nuts? I'm not talking to those guys. They can put you away for life.'

'Mark, they're in your boot. You're *already* away for life.'

'Well if I'm already away for life, I'm certainly not talking to them; they'll come for me in the afterlife. They don't know anything, Frank, they're only following orders.'

Corrigan shook his head. 'What does Cindy say?'

'I explained it all to her. She thinks we're mad, but she still makes the sandwiches. This would be really funny if it wasn't so fucking serious.'

'I know.'

'Frank, are we wrong about this?'

'No. I don't think so.'

'That's not very reassuring.'

'What else can I say?'

Stirling shrugged. 'Dunbar's guys are watching the house.'

'I know. Do you think he tipped off Internal Affairs?'

'Doesn't matter. I'm still up that particular creek where paddles are in short supply.'

'You and me both, kid. You and me both.'

45

There was a plan. And it stank. It was madness, and he'd thought of it. If he could walk, there would indeed be seven of them. Seven against one hundred and fifty. Take control of the Old Cripple's mansion while the closing-night party was in full swing. Then wait for the shit to hit the fan. Madeline would broadcast live from the scene, and at the very least it might prevent Dunbar from shooting them.

What had he been thinking of?

It was a fantasy. A small fighting unit of earnest do-gooders taking on the bad guys. But it was three cops, one of them with a bullet hole in his arm and two fingers missing. It was a retired FBI man battling alcoholism. It was a man who piloted a tourist boat. It was a reporter. And it was a seventy-year-old who could just about spell his own name. It would be the death of them.

It wasn't going to work. It wasn't pessimism. It was reality.

He ached and he was drowsy, but he had to get moving. Stirling had left to go to work, to sweat it out until zero hour. Bill, the other cop in the Magnificent Seven, had picked him up so that he wouldn't have to take the Internal Affairs guys in his boot with him. Morton slipped over the back fence and picked his car up two blocks down and went to check on the layout of the Old Cripple's mansion. Cindy made some sandwiches. She had volunteered to join the Magnificent Seven but had been turned down. The Magnificent Eight didn't sound right, they joked. Corrigan's job was to rest up, then lead them into battle.

Instead he got up. Cindy was vacuuming in the front room. He slipped past into the kitchen, then carefully opened the side door into the garage. He closed the door just as quietly behind him and stood silently in the dark for several moments, listening. It was a double garage and the car sat in the middle. The muffled sound of conversation came from within, but nothing he could make out.

He stepped softly up to the vehicle, then suddenly slammed his fists down on the boot. Twin yells came from within.

They recovered quickly.

'Is that you, Stirling? You fucking son of a bitch! When we get outta here we're going to nail your hide to the fucking traffic lights.'

'We're going to fuck you over so badly you'll be fucking fucked over . . . really badly. You fuck.'

'You let us the fuck out of here. You fuck.'

'It's Frank Corrigan.'

They fell silent. Then one of them said: 'Don't kill us.'

'I'm married,' the other said.

'So was I,' said Corrigan.

'Right enough,' said the first. 'We were very sorry to hear about that.'

'We've nothing against you, Frank. Murder isn't our concern. We're only interested in bribery and corruption within the force.'

'That's right, Frank. Nobody paid you $200,000.'

Corrigan drummed his fingers on the boot. 'Yes they did,' he said. 'Bought my house at way over market value, paid it into my wife's account.'

'We didn't hear that.'

'No concern of ours what someone pays for your house.'

'Free country.'

Corrigan slammed the boot again. They both yelped.

'How'd you find out about the money in Stirling's account?'

'We gotta tip,' said one.

'Who from?'

'Can't say.'

'Boys,' Corrigan said, 'it'll take me precisely thirty seconds to hook up a hose to the exhaust and feed it into you. In five minutes you'll be sleepy, in ten minutes you'll be dead.' He slammed the boot again. 'So just answer the fucking question.'

'We don't know! It was just a tip-off!'

'Was it internal or external?'

'I don't know!'

'Internal! I think! I'm not sure!'

'What do youse know about the convention?'

'What convention?'

'What about the Old Cripple?'

'The who?'

'About Dunbar being on the take?'

'Chief of Police Dunbar?'

'Are you serious?'

'No,' Corrigan said, 'I'm only having a fucking laugh.'

He turned away from the car. He pulled open the garage door, only this time not bothering to mask it.

'Where are you going?' a worried, muffled voice called after him.

'To get the hose.'

As he stepped into the kitchen and closed the door Cindy appeared in the doorway. 'I thought I heard . . .' She stopped and looked him up and down. 'What do you think you're doing? And why are you wearing my husband's clothes?'

'I have to go out, Cindy,' Corrigan said. He was wearing a blue tracksuit with a hood. He'd found it in a cupboard. It fitted just right.

'They told you to rest. The doctor . . .'

'The vet . . .'

'The vet told you to rest.'

'He gave me dog medicine. I'm going out to sniff around.'

Cindy smiled. She was a lot younger than Stirling. She was still at college. Stirling arrested her one night for pulling some girl's hair in an argument over a boy, and the boy was forgotten about by the time he dropped her off home with a caution and a date. 'I've made some sandwiches if you want some.'

Corrigan nodded and stepped aside as she walked across to the fridge and pulled out a plate piled high with thick American ham, not like the wafer-thin efforts at home. He picked two up. She switched the kettle on for coffee.

They sat on either side of a pine bench that sat in the corner of the kitchen. There was a bowl of fruit with blackening bananas and bruised grapes sitting in it. 'This would be very nice,' Cindy said, 'if there weren't two men trapped in the boot of my car. I can't even go shopping.'

'I know,' Corrigan said. 'But it'll all be over by tomorrow.'

'I don't want my Mark to die.'

'He won't.'

'He's a wonderful father. He's a wonderful lover.'

'He won't die.'

'I go along with everything he says because I love him. Even making sandwiches for Internal Affairs guys he locks in his car and leaving my children in the house with a murder suspect. No offence. Nickie was a friend.'

'I know. I heard she was planning to skip town.'

Cindy nodded.

'She didn't love me or the fat guy.'

Cindy shrugged.

'Was she going to take Aimie with her? Without a word?'

'I think she was going to leave Aimie. With you.'

Corrigan shook his head. 'Jesus,' he said, 'didn't she love anybody?'

'People are complicated. She changed. She felt tied down.'

'You're only eighteen and you only met her half a dozen times and you know more about her than I do. What are you studying? Psychology or philosophy?'

'Marine biology.'

'Figures,' said Corrigan. He put a sandwich in each pocket of his tracksuit bottoms. He stood up. 'I have to go.'

'Coffee's nearly ready.'

'Sorry,' he said.

She smiled weakly. He stopped and kissed her on the top of the head. 'Don't worry about him, he'll be fine.'

'You can't promise me that.'

'Yes I can.'

She looked into his eyes. 'What are you going to do?'

'I don't know. Something. Right at the start Mark said this was too big for us and I laughed it off, but he was right.'

He turned for the back door.

'Frank?'

He stopped. 'What?'

'Take another sandwich.' She had the plate in her hands. 'And don't do anything stupid.'

'I'll meet you halfway.'

He took a sandwich.

46

Over the back fence. It was daylight, so he had to move more carefully. Everybody seemed to be at work. There were some dogs, but they didn't bark. They sniffed at him. They followed; he had to kick them off without drawing too much attention to himself. It was raining, but not as heavy, a fine rain but the kind that could soak you through without your noticing. Still, it justified wearing the hood up. When he slipped out on to the main road he looked back up at Stirling's house and saw the police car was still there, although they must have seen him get picked up for work. So they were watching everyone. Just in case.

He walked into town, thinking all the way about what to do and what not to do. *The Magnificent Seven.* They issued parking tickets and drank beers and watched ice hockey and drove steamboats on the great Niagara. They could not storm and destroy. If there was something to be done, he should do it alone. Get to the Old Cripple's mansion first, find Lelewala, get her out of there, cause something to happen that would make it impossible for the conventioneers to escape or prosper.

Something.

He knocked on the door of the women's refuge. A big woman in a wedding dress answered. 'Things must be looking up,' Corrigan said and the woman burst into tears and ran away up the stairs.

Annie Spitz came out of a back room, tutting, and pointed Corrigan towards her office. He sat and looked at the pictures of the bruised women on the wall for five minutes until she returned, all apologies. 'She was supposed to be getting married today. He arrived drunk at her house and kicked her down the stairs.'

'Why?'

'Since when did you need a reason?'

'You tar us all with the same brush.'

'Yes.'

They looked at each other. 'I came to see Aimie. And to borrow some things.'

'She's out back. She would sleep on that swing if she could. She heard about her mum on the radio.'

'Shit.'

'Shit indeed. I had to explain about bad men and her mommy going to a big hotel in the sky.'

'What'd she say?'

'She inquired about getting a room in that hotel.'

'Shit.'

'Shit indeed. What do you want to borrow? We don't have much, Corrigan, and you're welcome to none of it.'

'Thanks.'

She gave him a weak smile. 'Sorry. OK, what are you after?'

'Of all the places I've visited in this town, you have the best-equipped arsenal of any. Better than the gun club, even.'

'You want to borrow a gun?'

'No. I want to borrow several guns.'

'Why? Why several?'

'There are things I have to do. And none of them are legal. I need your help.'

'Does it involve the people who killed Nicola?'

Corrigan nodded.

She drummed her fingers on the table for several moments. She lit a cigarette and offered him one. He refused.

'Eighty per cent of battered women smoke,' he said.

She gave a wan smile and said: 'Ninety. What do you want guns for?'

'Silly question.'

'I know. Nevertheless. I can't just go giving out guns. I'd be an accessory to a crime.'

'As far as I'm concerned it won't be a crime. Besides, you can say I stole them. I came to see Aimie and sneaked them out. Nobody need ever know.'

'Corrigan, I hardly know you, but I really don't want your death on my conscience.'

'Who said anything about *me* dying?'

'You or anyone else. Corrigan, give yourself up.'

'It's gone beyond that.'

He stood up. 'I'm going to see Aimie. I'd appreciate if you'd leave the door to the gun room open.'

He left the room. Annie sat on, smoking and staring at the wall.

Aimie was sitting on the swing, but not swinging. 'I saw you through the window,' she said.

'I saw you too, sweetheart.'

'Is Mommy with you?'

'No, love, she's not.'

He began to push the swing gently.

'She's still at the hotel?'

'She's still at the hotel. I think she's going to stay there.'

'Must be a great hotel.'

'It certainly is.'

'Do you think they have cable?'

'Absolutely.'

'What about *Nickelodeon*?'

'I don't think so, honey, I don't think they have children's TV. Only for grown-ups.'

'Oh. They'll have swings though, Daddy?'

'No, love, they don't have anything for kids at all.'

'Aw.'

'I know. It's not fair. Tell you what, you stay here for a little while longer, then Daddy'll come and get you and we'll go somewhere that has *Nickelodeon* and swings too, OK?'

'Promise?'

'I promise.'

'Daddy?'

'Mmmm?'

'Who shot Mommy?'

He swallowed. 'A bad man.'

Aimie nodded thoughtfully. 'Was it that fat bastard?'

He almost laughed, but held on to it, then thought for a moment. 'Yes, love, it was. But he's dead too now.'

'Is he at the hotel with Mommy?'

'No, love, there's no fat bastards allowed in that hotel.'

*　　*　　*

When he went inside the door to the gun room was lying open and Annie was nowhere to be found. When he opened the front door the fat woman in the wedding dress was standing there with her arms around a tiny guy in a morning suit.

47

The rain continued to follow him, his own personal black cloud. He should have just called a cab and taken Aimie with him and sneaked across the border and started all over again. He'd done it before, escaped from Ireland and rebuilt his life. Maybe he was fated to have his life shattered, maybe he was fated to walk with evil.

Lelewala had come back to fight evil.

Not that she existed.

She was a myth.

She was a psycho.

She was a prostitute.

She was a prisoner.

She was devastatingly attractive and would suck your cock for seventy bucks.

And if none of this was true and she really was that good an actress, then she deserved to go to Hollywood and find fame and fortune with David Hasslefree.

His head was buzzing. He wondered if the brain was as much like a computer as people said. If it got so overloaded with information that eventually MEMORY FULL flashed up on your eyeballs and then it closed down. Or self-destructed. You could buy a new computer or upgrade its memory. But what could an ordinary or extraordinary man do, short of shooting himself in the head to let a little air in?

He just wanted to: *sit with Aimie and tell her good things.*

Stand by my wife's grave and tell her sorry.

Put my good arm round the mad whore Lelewala.

And now he was walking through the rain with a gun in each pocket and one in his sock, just in case.

He arrived at the Skylon Brock hotel and entered through the car park. He got hold of one of the valet parkers and said he was looking for an Irish guy who was attending the horticultural convention but couldn't remember his name. He slipped the valet twenty bucks and told him to go and find out. He reasoned that with Ireland at what passed for peace the gangsters there would have nothing better to do with their time than peddle drugs, so the chances were somebody would be attending the convention claiming Ireland as their territory.

The valet came back ten minutes later. Sure enough, there was an Irish delegation on the fourth floor. Six of them in three rooms. He'd gone to the trouble of writing the names and the room numbers down. Corrigan gave him an extra ten dollars.

'Not a word,' Corrigan said.

'Of course not, Inspector,' the valet said.

Corrigan shook his head and walked to the elevator. He arrived at the fourth floor. He counted the numbers off as he passed each room, then knocked on 467. There was a DO NOT DISTURB sign on the door.

'Mr Adams?' he called.

There was no response.

He knocked and called again.

'Can you not fuckin' read?' an angry voice spat from within. The accent was Northern, and so was the temperament.

'Fire alarm,' Corrigan said.

'I didn't hear a fuckin' alarm.'

'That's where the fire is, the alarm system. Now if you could just . . .'

The door was flung open. A rotund figure in a Skylon bathrobe and a bandito moustache, his face snarled up, stared out. Behind him Corrigan could see a black girl reclining naked on the bed. She was pretty rotund herself.

It only took the Irish guy a second to realize. 'You're not . . .'

'No,' Corrigan said, raising a gun to his face, 'I'm not.'

He forced Adams back into the room. The girl on the bed didn't seem particularly bothered. She began to gather her clothes. 'Mrs Adams, I presume?' Corrigan said.

'Huh,' she replied. She lifted some dollars off the bedside table and stuffed them into a small red purse. She zipped herself into a tight black dress and sauntered across to the door. 'Bye, sweetie,' she said, running her hand under Adams's jaw.

'Cheerio,' Adams said weakly.

Corrigan opened the door and she slipped by, smiling. He closed the door after her and looked back at Adams's disbelieving face.

'What are you, RUC or something?'

'You mean I haven't lost the accent?' Corrigan tutted. 'No, I'm not RUC. But I may as well be.'

Adams stood like a bouncer. Chest out, arms slightly bent but hung low as if he was ready to swing a left hook. Or a right one.

Corrigan had no doubt that he had at least one gun. He had no doubt that Niagara Falls was currently the most heavily gunned town on the continent. The convention might be all about billion-dollar drug deals and they might like to dress themselves up as international businessmen, but distrust and betrayal went with the territory, and where they went, guns followed. It was inhuman nature.

He pushed Adams down on to the bed, then searched the room. He turned up some coke, keys to a hire car and a pistol, then a pair of invitations to the Horticultural Convention's closing-night ball at the Old Cripple's mansion. Exactly what he was looking for.

Adams said: 'What's your game, mate?'

'It's not a game,' Corrigan said, 'and I'm not your mate. Actually, while we're on that subject, where's *your* mate?'

The name on the second invitation was Patsy Calhoon.

'He won't be back for . . .'

There was a knock on the door and a Northern accent. 'You finished getting your hole yet, sunshine?'

Corrigan shushed Adams by putting the tip of the pistol against his mouth. 'It's not only in comedy that timing is important,' Corrigan whispered. 'Now tell him to come in.'

'Come on in,' Adams said.

As the door opened, Corrigan was behind it. Patsy Calhoon entered, holding a brown paper package with a McDonald's logo up before him. 'Fillet o' Fish,' he proclaimed, 'just like home!'

Corrigan put one of his pistols to Patsy's head. 'Smith & Wesson,' he said, 'just like home.'

He tied them up. It took longer than it should have because of his shot arm and missing fingers. But he persevered. Patsy and Adams seemed too stunned to question what was happening to them. They just accepted it. As he was securing Patsy's feet Corrigan said: 'How's the football coming along?'

Patsy blinked uncomprehendingly for a moment, then said: 'Sorry? But do I know you?'

Corrigan tapped Patsy's left Adidas sneaker. There was a hole where the big toe was. 'You have a five-a-side-football foot,' Corrigan said. 'It's a common condition among the unemployed of west Belfast. You've nothing else to do all day but play footie at the leisure centre and not enough money to keep yourself in trainers. Which begs the question about how a bunch of cheapskates like youse get an invitation to the convention.'

Adams looked to Patsy, who shrugged. 'We're just here with the boss, mate,' Adams said. 'Security, y'know, except there's been bugger all for us to do. Quiet as fuck till you showed up.'

'So where's your boss now?'

'He's gone on ahead to the party. He still has some business to finish off.'

'And what's he called when he's at home?'

'Tar McAdam.'

Tar McAdam. Corrigan couldn't help a smile. Former head of the IRA, now promoted to drug baron. If there was going to be shooting later on, Corrigan resolved to make sure Tar McAdam caught one. 'Not content with bombing people into submission for twenty years, now he has them shooting up for Ireland as well.'

'We're only along for the ride, y'know?' said Adams.

'You're not gonna shoot us, are ye?' Patsy said.

'It's nothing to do with us,' Adams said.

'We just do what we're told.'

Corrigan shook his head. 'As ever it was.'

He stuffed socks in their mouths, then rolled them on to the floor and pushed them under the beds with his foot. He made sure the DO NOT DISTURB sign was in place then headed back down to the car park to find their car. His friend the valet helped him out. Within a couple of minutes he was gunning out of the car park and heading for the Old Cripple's mansion.

48

Anxiety was etched on Stirling's face like the menu at the Last Supper. He'd told them he was going out on patrol – them, Dunbar and his crew, pacing the station like relatives at the reading of a will, knowing that there was one night of the convention to go and then they could relax into their fat bank accounts – then slipped the car that was following and made it to the Skylon Tower just as darkness started to fall.

The place was still buzzing with tourists. The Falls were illuminated and the view from the revolving restaurant up top was spectacular, if you were in the mood for spectacular views. Stirling was in the mood for hiding, or running away, or both. He had called home and checked with Cindy how the Internal Affairs guys in the boot were doing, speaking all the time in a surreal code in case anyone was listening, and he was sure they were. *How are your grandparents? Are they getting enough exercise? Are they eating enough?* And leaving out *Are they pissing in the boot of my car?* He had a chill feeling that even if this whole crazy misadventure did work out, if they did catch all the bad guys and lived to tell the tale, that he would be the only one arrested for smothering two Internal Affairs guys.

Then Cindy told him about Corrigan leaving. Again, she didn't say it in so many words. He asked if her sore arm was feeling any better and she said sure, the pain just got up and walked out the door.

Stirling hurried down the steps into the closed amusement park, then made his way across to the store room. As he approached he could hear the dull thud of gunshots as the Magnificent whatever practised under Morton's supervision. He opened the door carefully, just in case they were shooting in that direction. Then he nodded around the volunteers: Morton, the seventy-year-old,

Madeline in a neck brace, Bill the cop. That was four. Five including himself. No Corrigan. No Maynard.

Morton told them all to keep shooting and hurried across. The seventy-year-old was smiling from ear to ear. Evidently he had at last managed to hit the outer edges of a target. Madeline was shooting video. Morton looked worried. Stirling matched him, and then some.

'I thought Corrigan would be here,' he said.

'I thought he was at your place.'

'He was. He left.' He tutted. 'Where's Maynard?'

'Didn't show up.'

'Fuck.'

'I know.'

Stirling looked glumly at their diminishing little team. 'This is hopeless. It was hopeless when we had seven. Now we have five. Fuck it.'

'I know.'

'We're going to have to call it off.'

Morton rubbed the toe of his shoe in the dust on the floor. 'We can't just give up. We have to make the best of what we've got.'

'We've got nothing. We've got you and me and Bill, the A team; we've got Madeline in a neck brace and Methuselah there'll have a heart attack as soon as someone says boo to him. Jimmy, we have to call it off, we're not only going to look foolish, we're going to die looking foolish. They'll put it on my grave. Here lies Foolish Mark Stirling. He died Foolishly. You and me both.'

Morton rubbed his other toe in the dust. 'I know you're right. But I can't just walk . . .'

The store-room door burst open.

As Stirling turned three men in army fatigues stepped into the doorway and stared menacingly across at them. They were wearing balaclavas and pointing automatic rifles at the Magnificent Five.

Stirling was rooted to the spot, his mouth suddenly desert-dry. Morton's autumnal look had returned in an instant. The seventy-year-old's gun fell out of his hand and landed on the floor. Madeline slowly dropped the camera away from her face until it hung limply by her side, filming her feet. Even Bill, the only one with his gun still in his hand, looked like he'd forgotten about it.

The three men in fatigues kept their weapons trained, but stepped to either side of the doorway. One gave a hand signal back out into the hallway, and the clatter of heavy boots on the steps followed a moment later.

Stirling tried to swallow, but could not.

A procession of similarly attired soldiers came trooping through the door. Ten, fifteen, twenty, twenty-five. They formed up in two lines, two deep across the back wall.

The only one not carrying a rifle withdrew a pistol from his belt, checked that it was loaded, then stepped up to Stirling.

'We can explain,' Stirling rasped.

'Good,' said the soldier, whipping off his balaclava. 'So can I.'

It was Maynard.

It was *fucking* Maynard.

'I hope you don't mind,' he said, 'but I was able to recruit some help.'

49

Perhaps he had matured. In his previous life he wouldn't have thought twice about killing IRA men. They were terrorists and had every right to expect it. Drugs were just another form of terrorism. He could have shot them and not worried about his conscience, but instead he had put *socks in their mouths*.

Because he was not a killer any more. He had come to Canada to start afresh. He had changed, even if death in its wisdom had followed him.

Now he was driving to the Old Cripple's mansion with no idea other than to save life rather than take it. Save Lelewala. Save the Magnificent Six. Save the world from the poison the drug barons were peddling.

Was he that noble?

Was he doing it because it was right?

Corrigan lit a cigarette and laughed. He had no idea what he was doing. He had an invitation to the ball. He had a hire car and three pistols located about his body. He was driving into the lion's den with no plan other than not to have a plan. To play it by ear.

If you didn't examine him too closely, he was looking pretty dapper. He'd called into a second-hand clothes shop and bought a tux and a dinner suit. The woman behind the counter said they belonged to a dead guy, and he could well believe it. She said she got most of her clothes the same way. Corrigan suggested she change the name of the shop to Dead People's Clothes, but she didn't think that was very funny.

Warm pockets, as if the guy had only recently taken his hands out of them, musty smell.

Corrigan had combed his hair. He was wearing gloves with cotton wool stuffed in to cover the two missing fingers. He reasoned that not bearing a resemblance to either Adams or Patsy would not hinder him greatly. They were all drug dealers and gangsters and international money launderers and they were bound to spend half their lives in disguise. Morton had told him that more drug dealers died on the operating table undergoing plastic surgery, their cocaine-savaged bodies unable to cope with the stress of an operation, than were ever gunned down in true Hollywood fashion. Even with airport security as lax as ever, somebody was going to get recognized: you couldn't have a hundred and fifty of the world's drug players waltzing through without someone checking out the Most Wanted posters. No, disguise was the order of the day. Possession of an invitation was ninety per cent of it. And confidence was the other ten.

As Corrigan approached the mansion he joined a tailback of cars from the front gate. Stretch limos, mostly. Inside them hoods in dinner suits drank wine and ran their fingers up inside the fine dresses of their hired companions. It was a convention, but it wasn't the kind you brought your wife along to. Classical music floated over the perimeter wall. Corrigan lit a cigarette and drummed his fingers lightly on the steering wheel. When his turn came he wound down the window and smiled familiarly at the closest of the six burly security guards and handed the invitation to him. He was asked to step out of the car while a metal detector was run over his body. It buzzed. The security guard said: 'Can you remove any metal objects, please?'

Corrigan removed two of the pistols.

The guard nodded appreciatively. 'I'll just check these with the armoury; you can collect them when you're leaving.'

Corrigan grunted, then got back into the car. He still had one gun in his sock. And he presumed everyone else did as well. He lit another cigarette, then drove up towards the mansion.

It was some place. His first view of it, emerging floodlit through the overhanging trees, was almost overwhelming, and he slowed the car to allow him to take in some of the finer details. He noted the splendid doric columns, then the rows and rows of white-slatted windows, nearly seventy of them. Off to the left he could see the bandstand, complete with band, and beyond that a glimpse of umbrellas flapping in the breeze around a swimming pool. He saw white doves hunting for worms on the immaculate lawn, then followed their flight back to a splendid white-painted loft on the right, bigger and probably more luxurious than his own apartment. He was impressed. And depressed. All over the world impressive houses had memorable names like Tara or Checkers. There was no brass plate here that he could see, but if there was a name for this place it would be Den of Iniquity. Or the House that Coke Built. To the right, beyond dove control, five helicopters sat in the full glare of the floodlights. There were half a dozen tour buses, about twenty limos. Guards patrolled the forecourt.

Corrigan parked. Then, as he approached the front door, a short girl in a short skirt greeted him and looked at his invitation then pointed him towards a large hall from which emanated the sounds of cutlery and chatter. He lifted a glass of white wine then surveyed the scene within for several moments. Everywhere, drug barons at leisure. It was a buffet affair. They milled and queued and gossiped while holding on to expensive-looking china plates and jabbed their forks in the air to make their points. A tingle went up Corrigan's spine. So normal, so fucking normal, yet they'd killed hundreds of thousands of people between them, directly or indirectly. He knew from home that monsters weren't monsters all the time. They ate bread, they drank milk, they haggled over the price of furniture. They bought underpants and died of cancer. But they were still monsters.

He drained his glass of wine, set it on a waitress's tray as she passed, then joined the queue for the buffet table. It seemed to be about half a mile long. The queue *and* the table. He made small talk. The weather. The ice hockey. He presumed it would be bad form to bring up the hell of heroin addiction. When he reached the food, the quality and quantity of it did not surprise him. He lifted a tray and began to spoon chilli into a small china bowl. He turned, looking for bread, and jolted the arm of a square-jawed mountain of a man dressed in a suit sharp enough to slice pepperoni. A suit with a fresh chilli stain, which matched the one on Corrigan's own.

'You spill my chilli,' said the Italian, with the intonation others reserved for 'You raped my sister.'

They glared at each other, and as they did silence fell around them. There was no backing down. The house was big, but the egos were bigger.

'You stained my jacket,' the Italian said.

Corrigan had no way of knowing if this was the first confrontation of the evening or if they came along every five minutes, but one thing was certain. Whoever he was, he had friends. He could feel their eyes bearing down on him, their hands groping for guns, real or imaginary. Five or six of them had just been standing nonchalantly in his general vicinity, but at the first hint of trouble had become a tight little phalanx of loyal bodyguards.

The idea had not been to draw attention to himself. But nevertheless, it was not the time to back down. It was about *respect*.

'Fuck off or I'll kill you,' Corrigan said.

The Italian's bronzed cheeks coloured. His bottom lip quivered. Then his top.

'Or alternatively,' Corrigan said, 'send me the dry-cleaning bill. Here,' he said, picking up a napkin, 'let me have a go at it first.'

He reached forward to dab at the stain. The Italian's brow furrowed, he glanced at his bodyguards, then he boomed suddenly into laughter, great shotgun guffaws. All around, the distribution and consumption of food recommenced.

'Naw,' said the Italian, fending off Corrigan's help, 'that's OK, my fault too. What about that stain on your . . . can I . . . ?'

'Naw,' said Corrigan, 'that's OK. No damage done.' He flicked at it with his hand, then smiled at the Italian again. He lifted his tray and walked on, heart thumping.

There were no completely free tables. He asked a black guy with flaky skin and curiously Caucasian features if it was OK to sit down. He looked Corrigan up and down and nodded warily. Corrigan sat, took a spoonful of chilli, then said: 'So, what line are you in?'

The guy started to answer, but Corrigan wasn't listening. From somewhere, somewhere near, but also frustratingly far away, there came the sound of an electric guitar, and over it, around it, permeating it, a light, earthy, rhythmic voice that he recognized immediately as Pongo's: but it wasn't the music, or the singing, it was the words, their very meaninglessness, that got to him. Repetitive, like drums, rhythmic like dancing, powerful, like a once great Indian nation . . . *hum, hum, hum, hum, hum-hum-hum-hum* . . .

50

Corrigan followed the humming trail to a large hall where waiters with cotton wool in their ears were busy setting tables for the closing ceremony and trying to ignore Pongo's soundcheck. Corrigan passed between the tables then mounted the half-dozen steps on to the stage. For several moments Pongo, lost in the music, didn't notice him. He came to the end of what could loosely be described as a tune, stopped, stroked his guitar as if it was a prelude to masturbation, which it might well have been, then suddenly looked up as the power died. He went pale as he saw Corrigan standing by his guitar amp. Then he snapped: 'What the fuck are you doing here?' and his eyes flitted warily about the hall.

'Music Police,' Corrigan said.

There was no reaction; he just said bluntly, 'I thought we had a deal.'

'No, I believe you had a deal with Lelewala.'

'Same difference.'

'I've come to get her back.'

'That'll be the day.'

'Good song, ever think of writing one yourself?'

Corrigan moved a little closer. Pongo strummed a little acoustic riff. 'That'll Be The Day'. Corrigan put his hand across the bridge, killing the sound. 'Take me to her.'

Pongo shrugged him off. 'Are you fucking crazy?' he hissed. 'I just have to click my fingers and you're dead. You had your chance. You're not even a fucking cop any more.'

Corrigan had his back to the waiters. It might have looked as if he was bending to scratch his ankle. But he removed his gun and put half the barrel of it in Pongo's mouth. 'In thirty minutes,' Corrigan hissed and lied, 'my people will be here to bust this fucking joint; now take me to Lelewala.'

Pongo took him to Lelewala.

They walked along empty corridors hung with platinum discs and framed photographs of Pongo with President Keneally and Oprah Winfrey. 'Are you serious about *your people?*' Pongo asked.

'Partly,' said Corrigan.

'Because if you are, I've a favour to ask.'

Corrigan snorted.

It took them about five minutes to reach Pongo's private quarters. It was one big fucking house. He unlocked the door and pushed it open, inviting Corrigan to enter before him. Corrigan entered sideways. The possibility of Pongo clunking him over the head with the guitar he still carried was not lost on him. Pongo looked at him innocently, but did not comment.

Inside, Lelewala was lying on a bed. She was fully clothed. Her hair was matted and she was shivering. She looked weakly up at him through the tangled strands of hair that hung over her eyes.

Pongo smiled sympathetically at her. 'How're you doing?' he said softly.

'OK,' Lelewala whispered, but she wasn't.

'What the fuck's going on?' Corrigan said, looking at her, but talking to Pongo.

'You tell me. I get her back here, we start working on some songs, then she goes all freaking freaky on me.'

Corrigan knelt and pushed the hair out of her eyes. Her brow was cold and clammy.

'One minute she was up for it, then she's all floppy.' Pongo shook his head. 'Doctor took a look at her, couldn't find nothing. We gotta big show and she's not going to make it.'

'I'll make it,' Lelewala said. 'I promised.'

'You're going to *sing?*' Corrigan asked.

'*I'm* going to sing,' Pongo said, '*she's* doing backing vocals.'

Corrigan looked from one to the other. 'Are you *both* on the fucking coke now?'

Pongo laughed. 'Don't knock it, man.' He'd crossed to the far end of the room and disappeared through an open doorway. Corrigan could see guitars and amps and the corner of a mixing desk.

He turned back to Lelewala. 'You're not well,' he said.

She nodded hesitantly. 'The evil ... *Corrigan* ... I don't *understand* ...' She gave a little cry. 'I don't feel so good.'

He looked helplessly at her. If Lelewala had come back to fight evil, she'd finally come to the right place.

'Did he hurt you?'

She shook her head. 'He just wants to make music.'

Pongo reappeared in the doorway with a cassette tape in his hand and a ghetto blaster tucked under his arm. 'I've written a song for Lelewala; we're going to sing it on stage tonight. Do you want to hear it now, sneak preview?'

'She's in no condition to sing.'

'She *has* to.'

Corrigan shook his head. There was a curious innocence about Pongo. That despite the fact that he was a cokehead child killer and that there were a hundred and fifty monsters having a party down the hall, he was more interested in getting a positive reaction to his new song.

'There are some songs,' Pongo said, 'that change the way people think. You ever hear Johnny Cash sing "San Quentin"? Bob Dylan's "Hurricane"? Band Aid singing "Feed the World"? I always wanted to write a song like that. Never could. Not until Lelewala came along. Lyrics, melody, everything just gelled, didn't they?' He smiled at Lelewala, who shivered in response and turned hopeful eyes on Corrigan.

Corrigan had supposed he would have to shoot Pongo to get her away from him. And after hearing his soundcheck it seemed the only humane thing to do. But this Pongo was different. He wanted to make a deal.

'What kind of a deal?'

'Let me do the gig, then she's yours.'

Corrigan glanced across at Lelewala. She was starting to drift. Her eyes were becoming unfocused.

'Did you give her something?'

'No way, man, not before a gig.'

Corrigan knelt beside her again. He rubbed her arm. She said something, but it was incoherent. She shivered and snuggled back into the blankets.

'Let her sleep,' Pongo said, 'a rest, she'll be fine. Listen to me . . .' He pulled at Corrigan's shoulder. 'If I tape this song live, and get out of here with it before your people arrive, I'll make ten million from it. Twenty. It's my "San Quentin". The biggest drug raid in history, plus you can dance to it. They're talking about cancelling my contract, but with this I can write my own. I can go on the road. Play the clubs. Get back to basics. Rock'n'roll, man, rock'n'roll.'

He laughed. There was an accompanying laugh from the doorway behind them.

'Rock'n'roll, man, rock'n'roll,' a familiar voice repeated.

Corrigan turned. It was Thomas Vincenzi, the Barracuda, and six hoods in suits.

51

The guard who escorted him along hallways and up stairs was more Neanderthal than Praetorian, and didn't have the sense to search him for hidden weapons. The Barracuda marched regally ahead, his only conversation a breezy 'I knew you'd turn up,' followed swiftly by 'I believe your finger is upstairs.'

'I hope it's in a fridge,' Corrigan said dryly, taking comfort from the fact that he still had a pistol in his sock and some cotton wool in his gloves in case the gunfire got really loud.

The longer they walked, the better and richer the decor became. These were parts of the mansion the conventioneers evidently did not have access to. Maybe the Old Cripple was worried about them stealing the Old Masters. When they reached the third floor Corrigan began to notice wheelmarks cutting deep into the luxurious carpet. He thought it reasonable to assume that if they originated with the Old Cripple he was using a wheelchair to move about rather than a hostess trolley.

Where the wheelmarks came to a final halt, so did they. The Barracuda knocked perfunctorily on the door, then pushed it open. Corrigan was ushered inside, the guardsmen still gathered about him. The Barracuda entered last, closing the door behind them.

There was a man sitting by the window, although he was hardly a man at all. He was bald, but not out of choice. One side of his face was hideously burnt; the other side wasn't much better. One arm was black and withered; both legs were in strict metal calipers. He wore a dressing gown that hung open to display folded yellowed flesh and a clouded plastic colostomy bag. He was a crushed shell of a creature, yet when he turned his eyes on Corrigan they burned intensely.

He did not speak. Perhaps he could not. The Barracuda stood, bemused, as Corrigan stepped forward. 'If I'm going to arrest you,' Corrigan said, 'I'll need your full name.'

He was cracked from behind by one of the hoods and he fell to his knees. When he gathered himself up, his eyes were level with a coffee table on which a small glass dome sat over a plate, on which sat his severed finger, going black like a banana.

The Old Cripple looked where he looked and broke into a smile, although it could just as easily have been a shrapnel wound, revealing as it did bloody gums and shards of heavily filled teeth. The wound opened a little further and 'Inspector,' he said, his voice a harrowing croak, 'you are welcome to my humble abode.'

Corrigan felt the insurance policy of his pistol press against his ankle. He took a deep breath, resisted the temptation to go for his gun and finish it there and then. He was interested. 'Sorry,' he said, 'it's not my style. Although I believe your people have had a look round my place. Made rather a tasty offer.'

From the window came the sound of white doves cooing ungratefully, their fan tails showing above the frame with the suggestion that they were shitting on the sill. The Old Cripple pulled a gnarled hand across his burnt face. The wound narrowed slightly. 'Yes, of course,' he said, 'the indirect approach. We ... *evaluate* people, Inspector, decide how best to take control of them. Some are more amenable to a direct offer. Your good Chief of Police, for example. I think with you, we decided that a more subtle approach was necessary. You would not be easily bought.'

'No,' Corrigan said, easing back to his feet, 'and refusal can often offend.'

'You have ...' the Old Cripple began, then paused, and looked at the Barracuda. 'How do you say?'

'Attitude,' said the Barracuda.

'*Attitude*,' the Old Cripple repeated carefully. 'Yes. Very good. *Attitude*. It is no bad thing, although in certain situations it might be regarded as unfortunate. Perhaps even reckless. After all, we do, surely, hold all of the shots?'

Less six, Corrigan thought, but he nodded grimly.

'How old are you, Inspector?' the Old Cripple asked.

'Thirty-two,' Corrigan said.

The Old Cripple nodded. 'You have met my son Pongo. I have another. He lives, I believe, in Ireland. I have not seen him, I do not wish for him to see me like this.'

'I see your point,' Corrigan said.

'*Attitude,*' the Old Cripple purred. 'My name, Inspector, is Mohammed Salameh. Does that mean anything to you?'

Corrigan shook his head.

'I was once what you might call a terrorist. The finest of my generation, some said, until the Americans came and bombed our camp in the desert and left me for dead . . .' There was a smile again, but different, sharper, like an axe in a dying tree, as he looked at his pathetic body. 'Today I am a finally tuned athlete compared to what I was then. But I swore, I swore on the life of my wife who died in that attack, that I would avenge her death, that I would destroy America.'

There was a deep chill in his voice suddenly, and for several moments his eyes seemed lost in memory.

'And did you?' Corrigan asked.

The old man pulled his hand slowly across his face. When it dropped to the side of his chair he had half closed his eyes. 'When I was young,' he said, 'I was an idealist. I wanted to change the world. I would lend support to any cause I thought worthy. And I was very good. I trained half of the world's freedom fighters. Destroying America did not seem all that big a deal. I would return to the devil's mouth and wage a war such as they had never dreamed of. I thought, how can a country of this size, of this diversity, have survived without terrorism so long? Hundreds and hundreds of ethnic groups all physically and mentally abused, denied employment, kept in ghettos, used as cannon fodder in any imperial conflict the president could dream up. America had, as far as I could see, no redeeming features.'

'You obviously haven't seen *Frasier.*'

There was a flash of impatience in the Old Cripple's eyes. 'Why do you jest all the time?'

'All I'm saying, America isn't that bad. And we're in Canada, just in case you . . .'

'As you grow older, *Inspector,* you will become less flippant. You will be wondering why I'm telling you all of this . . .'

He was. It was becoming a bit like *Jackanory.* 'I'm worried about you missing your party.'

'Yes, indeed. The party to end all parties.' He cleared his throat. It sounded like a cappuccino machine. 'I have thrown this party because my plans for America changed. As you grow older . . . well, things become clearer. Religion. Nationalism. The folly of it all. I came to this country to nurture revolution. But in the end it did not work, because for all their protest, for all their professed nationalism, the people I met all actually loved America. And in their own way, they are happy. Who was I to interfere with that?' He gave a painful little shrug. 'Perhaps I have just mellowed with age.'

'Mellowed into a drug dealer.'

'I'm not a drug dealer, Inspector.'

'You do a pretty good impression of one.'

'I remain a revolutionary. I use drugs to achieve my aims.'

Corrigan smiled incredulously round at the Barracuda, who maintained his bemused expression. The hoods in suits were using up all their mental faculties just to maintain their mean look. He looked back to the Old Cripple. 'Destroying the insidious evil that is America by dealing drugs?' He waved his good hand about the room, but meaning more than just the room. 'And all this, is drug money.'

'Yes, it is. But you have to understand, I'm not in this for profit. What money comes back to me is reinvested in the war.'

'*What* war?'

'The war against drugs.'

'*What* war against drugs?'

The Old Cripple raised his withered hand about the room, but meaning the same epic expanse of house and garden as Corrigan had. 'I could not make the kind of deals I do, I could not meet and entertain the kind of people I have to, if I could not compete on their level of . . .' he took a deep, rattled breath, '. . . ostentatiousness. White doves, Inspector? Do you think that I am really that kind of a man?'

The Old Cripple shook his head slowly. His eyes narrowed. His voice was cold as an ancient rock at the bottom of an icy pool. 'Do you really think that I have put all of this convention together in order to facilitate *drug dealers*?'

'It would seem like a reasonable assumption, seeeing as how they all seem to be in your front room.'

'My *life*, Inspector, has been about giving the oppressed the means with which to fight back. Training them, inspiring them, leading them. For that I have been called a terrorist and hounded to the ends of the earth. I have fought for forty years. I have had many enemies. America. Russia. The British. I have fought them all. But there is one enemy that is bigger than America, bigger than Russia, one enemy that has grown like a cancer, that has destroyed more lives, oppressed more people than any mere government or dictator. Do you know what that enemy is, Inspector?'

Corrigan nodded. It was suddenly quite obvious. 'Drugs,' he said.

The Old Cripple dropped his fist into his lap. 'It has taken me many years of delicate manoeuvring to get into this position. I had to become a drug dealer. I had to win their trust and then their friendship. Eventually I rose to such a position of respect that when I suggested the concept of the convention, they saw that there was good reason behind it, that it wasn't an attempt to dominate or to steal or to kill. Then I had to bide my time until it was my turn to act as host, and all that time people were dying. Hundreds of thousands, all over the world.'

'Think of it,' said the Barracuda. 'Every major drug baron on the face of the earth is here tonight. Every one of them responsible for misery and murder and corruption and poverty and . . .'

Corrigan looked from one to the other, incredulously. 'You mean, you're the good guys?'

The Barracuda smiled. 'That's one way of looking at it.'

Corrigan desperately tried to feel relieved. But he couldn't. His brow furrowed and the gun in his sock sat hard against his ankle. 'So you have the movers and shakers all in one place. You want me to arrest them? Is that it?'

The Old Cripple shook his head.

'What are you going to do then, give them a lecture on the evils of narcotics?'

'Actually,' said the Barracuda, 'he is.'

'And then,' added the Old Cripple, 'we're going to blow them all to kingdom come.'

52

Stirling was in work, as usual. He was trying to remain calm and composed, but his knee was shooting up and down under his desk with excitement. He tried to stop glancing at the clock on the wall, just to get on with his report, keep his head down, busy, but it was nearly impossible. The heavily swollen Magnificent Seven were ready for action and for the first time he felt quietly confident.

Dunbar had come in earlier, checked with his officers, then emerged from his office wearing a dinner suit. Somebody, trying to brown-nose, asked him what the occasion was and he said he'd been invited to the Horticultural Convention's closing-night dance. He wasn't looking forward to it, but it was expected of him.

Uhuh.

Stirling kept his head down. He was supposed to be preparing a departmental Christmas rota on his computer, but every few minutes, when he was sure no one was watching, he switched to a different file, the one in which he'd been keeping his account of the events of the past few days. It had started out as a purely factual police-statement kind of thing, but now he busied himself dividing what he had already written into handy chapters. He was sure the eventual publisher would appreciate it.

It was all down to Maynard.

Maynard had been out for lunch with his crew when they'd come across Madeline getting chopped down by the Big Circle Boys and waded in to rescue her, then looked on in dismay as the police had turned up and threatened to arrest *them* for fighting in the street. Maynard had just been able to stop his crew from having a go at the police. Once he'd got them back to the *Maid of the Mist* he'd been able to quell their anger by telling them about the Magnificent Seven and the convention.

He'd taken a chance.

On his friends, his crewmen, and their loyalty and their sense of fair play and patriotism.

And a rare chance to dress up and shoot at bad guys.

They were all keen to help out; not only that, but they took the *Maid* across the river to the American side and recruited *their* crew as well. And not only that, but one of the Americans was a National Guardsman and he reckoned he could get access to some uniforms and some weaponry to really make a show of it.

So they did.

And Stirling was more than happy.

He looked up from his desk as a figure appeared in the doorway, closing the computer file as he did so. 'Mmmm?' he said.

Bill stood there, bug-eyed, nervous. 'Mark, there are some Internal Affairs guys downstairs want to see you.'

'OK,' Stirling said. They would be new ones, looking for the old ones, still secure but stiff and smelling of urine in his garage. He stood up, pulled on his jacket. 'We go out the back way. You all set, Bill?'

'As I ever will be,' Bill said. He stood aside as Stirling came through the door, then hurried after him down the back steps to Bill's patrol car.

As they sped off the Internal Affairs guys came rushing down the front steps of the station shouting after them.

When they reached Skylon Tower, the team was waiting. Guns and guns and guns and fear and loathing in Niagara Falls. Bill steered his police car to the front of a line of five vehicles: three pick-up trucks, an Oldsmobile, and a Volkswagen. Madeline stood at the front, ready to video their departure and with her fingers crossed that they'd stop and wait for her to catch up once she had what she wanted.

'Well?' Stirling said, as Maynard strode up to the car. 'How many?'

'Thirty-five,' said Maynard. 'We got a couple of extra National Guardsmen.'

'Well done.' Stirling took a deep breath. He checked his guns. He had a Llama 8 automatic pistol, a .38 heavy-duty outdated police weapon, hard-hitting and accurate with a nine-shot magazine. He also had an Eagle Apache Carbine, a semi-automatic recoil rifle with a thirty-shot magazine. It weighed only about nine pounds. He had had both guns for ten years. Oiled and ready to fire at any time, but never fired in anger yet.

Morton was standing off to one side, his fingers checking his own pistol, but his eyes turned up to the sky.

'You OK, Jimmy?' Stirling called across.

For a second it seemed that he didn't hear. Then he turned slowly and nodded. He had a faraway look on his face. Stirling presumed he was thinking about the Empire State Building or his dead wife and children.

Then Morton shook his head, as if he was getting bathwater out of his ears, and hurried across. He leaned into the car and said: 'Sorry, lost in space.'

'You've been down this road before,' Stirling said.

'Different road. But just as dangerous.'

'You remember the plan?'

'There's not much to remember. Smash down the front gate and arrest everybody.'

'That's about it.'

They looked at each other for several moments, then shook hands.

Madeline, videoing it, said: 'Aw, that's cute.'

'Fuck off,' Stirling said.

And then they set off. With tourists looking on and clapping as if it was a parade just for them; in a way, Stirling supposed, it was.

53

At first Corrigan struggled, then he relaxed. Struggling would only make the knots tighter.

Tied up. He had spent most of the past few days tied up. It had become extremely fashionable. There was a gun in his sock, but he couldn't quite reach it. Downstairs the Old Cripple was about to address drug central and preparing to explode a bomb that would kill everyone. Not just drug dealers. But waiters and waitresses and confused Indian princesses.

Then Corrigan struggled again because there was no point just waiting to be blown to kingdom come. He strained. He stretched. From far off he could hear the sound of music. But not *The Sound of Music*. The sound of Pongo. He threw himself to one side. He toppled over. He thumped his head on the carpet and lay there dazed for several minutes. Then he lay there fully conscious but no nearer freedom. The gun dug into his ankle. He shook his leg, trying to shift it; and then he thought suddenly: *what if?*

The chances were he would blow his foot off, but if he angled it just right there was a possibility. What was there to lose but his toes? What was another digit or two? Take the chance ... live a little, before you die a lot. He banged his leg down on the floor with all the force he could muster. Once. Twice. *Crack!* The bullet shot out of his trousers, took the toe-cap off his shoe but left his toes unharmed, if shaken. The window shattered.

There was no one to hear it. They were all too busy enjoying themselves. Corrigan heaved himself across the floor, centimetre by centimetre, lugging the chair with him. In a minute he was lying among the jagged shards of glass.

He ground the rope down into them, felt his skin split, felt the warmth of his blood, but also, also the snap of twine, the steady snap, snap as he pushed into the glass. Then suddenly: snap, snap, snap and his hands were free and in a second he had squeezed out of the remaining knots. Blood was streaming down his arms, but the cuts didn't seem too serious, not to a man who had two fingers missing and a bullet hole to boast about.

He looked out of the shattered window, at the guards distantly patrolling the grounds, their faces turned to the house, thinking they heard something above the musical din from within, tracing the windows but seeing nothing untoward. Corrigan hurried to the door. He peeked out. The corridor was empty. He trotted along, dusting himself down. He hit the stairs. In moments he was just a face in a crowd of hoods schmoozing towards a party that would end with a bang.

The place was humming. There were handshakes and bearhugs and bows. There had been murders and maimings outside, but the convention itself had passed off without incident. The Old Cripple had done well. Deals had been done. Alliances forged. Territories assigned and feuds forgotten. If it had been a movie it would have secured top marks for generating the feelgood factor.

Corrigan slipped into the auditorium unchallenged and stood in the shadows at the rear, watching as the conventioneers sauntered confidently past, drinks in hand. He did not know what he was doing.

He was a policeman. If there was a bomb his first duty was to shout: 'There's a bomb!' and make sure everyone got out in an orderly fashion.

Except he was no longer a policeman and these were among the most evil people on earth. Nobody would thank him for saving them, not even them.

But there were innocents there and they had to be warned. But if he started shouting he would be clubbed to death and that would benefit nobody. He had to find the bomb.

As he stepped out of the shadows he bumped into Tar McAdam. The leader of the Provisional IRA. Another time, Corrigan would have plugged him and thought about the lives he had saved, but this time he apologized. Not that it mattered. Tar was out of it. Staggering. Zonked. He might have wangled an invitation to the convention on the strength of the untapped Irish drugs market, but others would exploit it. Corrigan caught the looks of disdain, the sideways steps of other guests trying to get out of Tar's way, and the embarrassed hellos of those he shouted disturbed greetings to. There was a time and a place for doing drugs, and the end-of-convention knees-up wasn't it. They all knew it except Tar. All the deals they'd worked out would be worth nothing if the drugs led to a careless word or a bump at the bar or a vomit on the table.

Corrigan pressed on, looking, but trying not to look as if he was looking. He had no idea where to look.

The feelgood factor. Life as a movie. Except life lasts a little longer and everyone dies in the end.

Dying is easy, comedy is hard.

Comedy is easy, toffee is hard.

A hundred and fifty drug barons with assorted hired ladies, enjoying the best catering drug money could buy. There had been speeches of thanks outside, speeches of thanks for the thanks, and speeches of thanks for the thanks for the thanks. They were going home tomorrow. They were rich already, but they would be even richer in the days and months to come. And better people too. Travel did that. Broadened the mind and widened the nostrils. Now for the show.

Behind the curtained stage Pongo completed the final check on his equipment. He ran from monitor to monitor, screen to screen, he checked tapes and loops and drum machines, he checked the synths and guitars and the backdrop and the video screen. He gave a little blast of dry ice and then checked the trapdoor through which Lelewala would suddenly appear to hum the vital part of the *Legend of Lelewala*. She was down there. Beneath the stage. Underneath the convention. And she shivered. Worse. She had not yet encountered any of the guests. Pongo had kept her well away from them, but she could feel them. She could feel their evil. Something was building within her.

She closed her eyes. She tried to think of Hollywood and David Hasselhoff. One performance and she would be free. On the road. She would never have to have sex again. She could be a normal human being again. She could think about plumbing and mortgages and acting and the love of a good man who wouldn't have to leave money by the bed every morning unless he had something specific he wanted her to buy with it, like root vegetables. She could even start taking her medication again. She wouldn't have to think about Lelewala. She wouldn't have to be Lelewala. She could close that part of her mind for good. Nail down the trapdoor. She looked up.

The door opened: 'Any time now,' Pongo said. She nodded. Nodded at his red eyes and flared nostrils and rouged face. *Any time now.*

Pongo turned to find the Barracuda and his father. 'Like the make-up,' the Barracuda said.

Pongo grinned. It wasn't make-up. It was coke. He had intended to be clean for this, his greatest ever performance, his defining moment, but he was nervous, very nervous, he needed a little something just to calm him down. So he'd buried his head in the emergency nosebag he wore around his neck. *Now* he was ready. He had his guitar in hand. There was no backing band. There was no need for one. He controlled everything. This was his coming out. His rebirth. His moment.

'Knock 'em dead,' the Barracuda said. Beside him the Old Cripple looked out through a chink in the curtains. They were having a ball. But not for long. He turned to look at his son. It seemed a pity that he would have to die too, but there was no other way. The bomb would destroy the mansion and everything in it. Even the Barracuda, though he didn't know it yet. He was devoted to the Old Cripple, devoted by way of the huge amount of money he was paid and the huge amount he was promised in the will, and he was reconciled to the bomb and happy that he had a three-minute window in which to exit the building and make his way to his own palatial mansion and plead ignorance about it all or some of it, but maybe write a book if the right contract came along. The Old Cripple liked him. He had been a good and faithful servant all these years. It was only fitting that he should die with him. As would have happened in Ancient Egypt. The Old Cripple ran his fingers over the tiny controller he held in his left hand. So small, yet one little switch and they were all gone.

He was quite relaxed about it all. Twenty years of excruciating pain would come to an end. At last he would be at peace. He would be whole again. He would be able to walk and talk and run as he had not been able to since the Marines had destroyed his life.

'I'm going on now, Father,' Pongo said.

Pongo began to turn away, then stopped and bent down to him. He kissed him on the cheek. His father was genuinely touched. They had never been close. He had always kept the playful boy at a distance for fear he would dislodge a feeding tube or accidentally crush a fragile bone. 'Good luck, my son,' the Old Cripple said and clasped Pongo's hand to his chest.

The lights snapped off. There was an anxious buzz from the surprised audience; they'd been primed about Pongo, but not about the lights. The tape of Pongo's greatest hits finished abruptly and then they were plunged suddenly into darkness. It was an anxious few seconds. Groups of Italians and Chinese and Thais and Colombians formed little protective circles, scared of a stabbing in the night, then relaxed as the curtains silently swished back and a green light began to emanate across the hall. At first they could make little out: just shapes. Then images, moving images on a giant screen: the flowing Niagara, a serpent in the grass, a beautiful Indian rowing over the edge of the Falls. Then a single drumbeat. Loud. They didn't know what to make of it. They had expected something easygoing. Pongo does the Bee Gees. Pongo sings Songs from the Shows. Even Pongo does Pongo. But something to appeal to a broad international audience not known for having its finger on the pulse, unless it was a dying one. But this was something different entirely, and if they didn't recognize it, they didn't like it.

The green light was joined now by a white one, shining centre stage. And suddenly stepping into it a diminutive figure in a white jumpsuit with a powdered white face and a guitar slung around his hips.

Still the *drum, drum, drum drum.*

Pongo raised his fist into the air, poised to unleash the cataclysmic creative force that united *his* lyrics with *his* music in a pioneering moment of musical history. His heart was pounding, the blood was racing; this was it, this was his moment, the tape was rolling, the video was zooming in. His time. His moment. His birth.

'Lelewala!' he sang.
Drum. Drum. Drum.
'Lelewala!' he sang.
Drum. Drum. Drum.
'Lelewala!' he sang.
Drum. Drum. Drum.
'I freed her!'
Drum. Drum. Drum.

'I freed her!'

The drumming continued, but it was joined by a humming.

Hum, hum-hum-hum, hum, hum-hum-hum, hum, hum-hum-hum . . .

'Lelewala!'

Drum. Drum. Drum.

Hum, hum-hum-hum, hum, hum-hum-hum.

'I saved her!'

He hit his guitar. There was a howl of feedback followed by the guitar equivalent of *hum, hum-hum-hum, hum, hum-hum-hum* ricocheting around the hall. Several conventioneers ducked. Corrigan, searching under the stage, put his hands to his ears.

Drum. Drum. Drum.

Hum, hum-hum-hum, hum, hum-hum-hum.

Pongo stepped away from the mike, grinning, and pressed a button on the floor with his black winklepicker boot. There was a sudden flood of dry ice.

Down below, Lelewala, humming into a radio mike, began to move.

She closed her eyes as she was slowly raised towards the trapdoor.

All she had to do was hum. Hum along. Quietly. He'd tested her voice. She did sound like a seagull. But she had to be there. She was Lelewala. She was the inspiration. She would thank him in the years to come.

But she didn't feel right. Sitting in the darkness, the *evil* had grown on her. There was something out there. Something formless. Something terrible. And now she was moving towards it. She was drowning in sweat. Her breath would not come. All she had to do was hum.

Hum, hum-hum-hum, hum, hum-hum-hum . . .

Somewhere up ahead she could hear Pongo: 'I did it! I freed her!'

Without warning her head cracked off the trapdoor and her eyes rolled back in her head. The door flew upwards and the spring under the platform propelled her dazed and confused on to the stage. There was an explosion of lights above her and sparklers below and she was blinded. She fell forward. Pongo caught her, guided her forward.

Hum, he went, *hum-hum-hum.*

She grabbed his mike stand, held on to it for dear life . . . the *something* had become . . . *solid.* She looked into the darkness that was the audience. She could not see their well-fed faces. She could not see their bright clothes and expensive jewellery. All she could see was their cold, callous, black dirty souls and abruptly she knew . . . this was what it was all about. This was why she had returned. The monster was here before her. The serpent, the sickness, the horror, the hell. It had nearly destroyed her village, and now it was back, threatening the people of Niagara . . .

'Hum,' Pongo prompted, 'hum-hum-hum.'

Drum, drum, drum . . .

The evil!

Her legs gave way. Pongo caught her, pressed her forward again. There was another whoosh of dry ice and for a moment Corrigan, now at the front of the stage, lost her in it.

She screamed. Long and loud and high-pitched; the conventioneers gripped their ears.

She ran.

This evil could not be allowed to survive.

She had to do it all again.

Sacrifice her life so that others might survive the onslaught of the Devil himself.

She ran. Pongo tried to stop her, but she swerved to one side and found herself even closer to the audience, which was now starting to jeer and throw pieces of food. The evil battered at her head. Tried to burst into her brain. It was trying to weigh her down, make her stop. But she couldn't. She *must* run. She must get to the river. She must save . . .

Corrigan began to clamber up on to the stage, but she was gone again, swallowed up by the dry ice. He stopped, then caught a flash of her charging through a side door. He cursed.

Pongo began to chant again. Nothing could shake him. He'd taken advantage of the dry ice to bury his head in the nosebag again. He was blissfully unaware of the food raining down around him. 'I saved her! Lelewala! I saved her!'

Corrigan battled through the baying conventioneers to the swing doors through which Lelewala had disappeared. As he slammed them open, somebody pushed back the other way. Corrigan cursed, then rammed the door harder. He felt the other guy fall back. He continued on through. On the floor, cursing, wiping at his spilled drink, Chief of Police Dunbar.

It took a moment for Dunbar to realize who it was, but less than a moment for Corrigan to plant his boot under Dunbar's chiselled chin and send him flying back against the wall.

He choked and coughed a 'Corrigan, you . . .' before Corrigan yelled, 'Shut the fuck up,' and picked him up by his expensive lapels. He pulled his face right up close and hissed: 'There's a fucking bomb in there, Dunbar . . . go find . . .' He threw him down, then kicked him in the arse.

He raced on up the corridor. He went through another two sets of twin doors, then saw her about thirty yards ahead, standing, almost dancing at the crossroads of three corridors, trying to decide which way to go.

'Lelewala!' he shouted.

She ignored him. He raced along.

'Gretchin!'

He was just about level with her. Her face was red and her eyes were staring. She turned towards him, but she plainly didn't recognize him. As he reached out to her, she swung up a fist that caught him flush on the chin, and he began to sink to his knees. He retained just enough sense to fling his arms around her as he fell, and she was dragged down with him. But just for a moment. He didn't have the strength to hold her. She squirmed free, kicked back at him as he tried to grab her, then started running again.

'For fuck's sake,' Corrigan wheezed as he pulled himself to his feet again. She was already through the next set of doors. He set off after her, slower now.

The guards on the front door turned as she came tearing across the marbled hallway. Surprised, they started to go for their guns, but then decided she was probably just an upset hooker and started to laugh. Then Corrigan appeared, gasping for breath, and they laughed a little harder, though now they tried to mask it. Not good to upset a guest, but shit, getting breathless over a hooker. Why not just buy another?

'Lela!' he called, but she was down the steps and racing across the grass.

And then he heard a police siren.

A fucking police siren.

Corrigan stopped in his tracks. He looked down the driveway, he could just see the red glare of a police car through the trees. Then came the sound of automatic gunfire.

The guards came running out of the entrance hall behind him, guns drawn, looking where he looked. Then something exploded: way down towards the gate. Flames shot high above the trees.

The magnificent Magnificent Seven.

The guards stood nervously beside him, looking at each other, seeking leadership. All the leaders were inside not enjoying Pongo, the sound of his music so great that they wouldn't have heard the gunfire.

And then the police car was coming up the drive, siren wailing, a mini-van racing up behind it.

'Oh fuck,' said one of the guards beside him and turned to hurry into the house, but a gunshot rang out and he fell before he'd made more than a few yards.

One of the others produced a gun and started shooting at the onrushing police car, but it wasn't done with any great confidence. Corrigan reached down into his sock and removed his gun. He shot the guard in the leg and stepped out of the way as he toppled forward.

The others, shocked, confused, didn't know what the fuck to do. They just stood gormlessly looking at Corrigan.

'Drop your guns,' he said. 'Lie face down, you'll be OK.'

They were just in the act of dropping their guns when someone in the following mini-van began pumping bullets in their direction. They all hit the dirt. Corrigan crawled along the ground trying to get out of the line of fire. As he sprawled in the gravel, he caught a final glimpse of Lelewala running obliviously across the perfect lawn in the direction of the great Niagara.

54

The music, for so long unbearable in terms of quality, was rapidly becoming unbearable in terms of volume. Pongo had overcome the hiccup of his leading lady getting stage fright and was now cruising through the complete Lelewala song cycle. To the untrained ear there wasn't much variation to the basic *drum, drum, drum, hum, hum-hum-hum, hum, hum-hum-hum, I saved Lelewala* – indeed, neither was there to the trained ear – but Pongo knew the subtleties, he knew the little variations. Not for him broad, sweeping musical statements; any fool could do that. His were changes in pitch and intonation, hints of a different light, the slight blurring of an on-screen image. There had to be volume, because that was the nature of rock'n'roll: *he* knew the subtleties, *they* could experience them for themselves later on when they came to buy the CD-rom. All they had to do for now was enjoy the show, get those feet moving.

But dancing continued to be the last thing on their minds. The most upset conventioneers had exhausted their supply of ready ammunition, their plates and potatoes and knives and sweetcorn husks mostly falling short of the stage. A few of them had their guns drawn, but could only wave them about helplessly. Even in such a criminal environment it was considered bad form to murder the host's son. And it wasn't as if they could even leave the auditorium. The Old Cripple himself was due to close the convention, and they had to stay for that, they owed the old gent that much at least. Pongo thrashed away, grinning, towards his and his music's climax.

Corrigan, on his belly, was pulled roughly to his feet. He didn't recognize the face. A late volunteer. *Thank God.* He felt like kissing him.

'Over there,' the guy said, prodding him with a revolver towards where the other guards were gathered, sitting on the grass with their hands above their heads.

'Listen, mate, it's me, *Corrigan* . . .' Corrigan said breathlessly. His eyes scanned the trees, looking for a glimpse of Lelewala, but there was nothing. 'Where's Mark . . . will you take that fucking thing out of my face and get me Stirling?'

The guy whacked the gun into his stomach and Corrigan slumped to his knees. The guy raised his foot and pushed Corrigan down the grass bank. He rolled. He came to a stop beside the other guards.

The police car's driver's door opened, but he couldn't see who got out.

Lelewala was heading for the river.

'Mark – for fuck's sake!'

The guy who'd pushed him looked down the hill at him and raised his gun. 'Shut the fuck up!' he spat.

Corrigan rolled his eyes. 'Will you just . . .'

A bullet spat up grass and soil beside him.

'Jesus fuck,' Corrigan gritted out. 'I need to talk to Mark Stirling . . . there's a bomb . . .'

The guy fired again. This time he was trying to hit him, and he missed by only a fraction.

'Now shut the fuck up,' said the cop.

Corrigan looked to the mansion. He could just see two policemen hurrying up the steps into the reception area. 'Mark!' he shouted. 'There's a fucking . . .' But the other guards dragged him down and shut him up, scared of getting shot themselves.

Pongo thought it had gone well, but he didn't hang about for an encore, even though the crowd had roared as he said goodnight. He ran off stage, his jumpsuit soaked through, his hair dripping, a triumphant smile splitting his face. The reaction had been more than he had dared hope, the anger, the violence, *excellent*. Even Lelewala's exit, with the right editing, could look as if it had been planned, just another dramatic twist to the cycle that was *Lelewala*. The Barracuda was gone. The Old Cripple was still clapping politely. Pongo grinned at him and hurried away to check the tapes. Once he was satisfied that the recording had gone smoothly he would slip out the back way with them and be well away from the mansion before Corrigan's men arrived. Then across the border and ready for the next phase of his career. *Hum, hum-hum-hum, hum, hum-hum-hum.* A classic. But first, the nosebag needed his attention.

The Old Cripple rolled out on to the stage unannounced. For several long moments nobody noticed. But then, gradually, one by one, by nods and whispers and prods, they saw that their host was among them and the angry buzz began to die away. Then the applause started, at first from the front, then gradually building back until the whole convention hall thundered with the sound of their appreciation. Save for a musical misjudgement near the end, they'd had a ball, made their deals, made a fortune and made the world a safer place, at least for themselves. The Old Cripple didn't blink an eyelid. He *couldn't* blink an eyelid, but even if he had been able to, he probably wouldn't have. He was alone now, even with all these people. The Barracuda had slipped away. It was just him and his speech and the device in his hand for setting off the bomb. His sparrow-legged fingers caressed it again.

Gradually their adulation died away. They took their seats again. Then they waited. Waited for the man in the wheelchair and quietly thanked God that at least they had all their faculties. Rumour had it that he was dying. That this was his last public appearance. Shame. *Shame.* But what a triumphant way to go.

The Old Cripple looked at the single sheet of paper in his hands. Five hundred words, each one laboriously and painfully typed with his own burnt and arthritic fingers. With a little grunt he reached up and lowered the microphone from Pongo's singing height to that of his own sitting position. Then he cleared his cappuccino throat and said: 'Ladies and gentlemen, I have come to say farewell.' For a brief moment he studied the pity that had already descended on their faces. 'I think you will all agree that we have had a wonderful few days.'

Cheers and applause.

'That this convention represents a new high-water mark in our campaign for better international co-operation.' His voice was ragged. He coughed, tried to clear it. But no, just a rasp. He should have brought water. He turned slightly, wincing, and looked for the Barracuda to bring him some . . . but no, he was gone. No matter. He forced himself on. 'I am an old man now, I am dying; allow me a little time.' The silence in the auditorium was complete now. His eyes roved across their faces. 'Many years ago,' he began again, 'when I was fit and healthy, I lived in the desert. I fought for what was right. I fought governments and dictatorships and kings and queens. I fought repression and depression and recession, I fought for good against evil. I thought then that the great evil was America. Or Russia. Or China or Christianity. Truly there were many evils for a young man to fight against.'

Laughter.

'But as I grew older I discovered that there was a greater evil, one that knew nothing of national boundaries, that respected no law, followed no politics, had no morals and whose only currency was life and death, but mostly death.'

What's he talking about: satellite television, pollution, AIDS?

'Drugs, my friends, drugs.'

He let it sit for a moment. Some of them were laughing already, even before the punchline.

'And so I had a dream. A wonderful dream. To gather together every major drug dealer and supplier and importer and exporter and manufacturer and wholesaler, every cold exploiter of our fellow man, every killer, like we have here tonight.'

Jeez, what's he . . .

What the fuck does he . . .

'My dream was not to lecture you like this on the evils of drugs. You know them well enough yourself. It was not to try and re-educate you. You are all beyond that. It was not even to try and convert you to religion. For no God would have you. It was, quite simply, to kill you.'

What?

What the fuck?

What's the Old Cripple saying?

Who the freakin' hell he think he is?

Hold on, hold on, he's only joking . . .

The Old Cripple was choking. Gurgling up phlegm and not having the strength to cough it out. The conventioneers shifted uncomfortably. OK, they'd shown respect, but sick jokes like this were pushing it a bit far. It wasn't the old guy that ran the show anyways. It was that Barracuda.

But . . . *but* . . .

The doors at the back of the hall opened, and when they looked round there was a squad of police officers standing there.

It *was* a fucking joke!

Laughter began to ripple around the hall.

The police began to move down the centre aisle. Their guns were drawn.

The old guy sure knows how to put on a show!

One of the Italians jumped into the aisle, sank to his knees and extended his hands, crossed, and squealed: 'Arrest me! Arrest me!'

They stepped round him. Applause began to break out.

The Old Cripple, fighting for breath, was stunned.

Police. That wasn't the idea at all. The police squad fanned out at the bottom of the steps leading to the stage, all save for one who hurried up them and across the stage to the Old Cripple.

He was starting to gag. He needed something to suck out the phlegm. It was the excitement, the drama; if only the Barracuda . . . what were the police . . . he fingered the device in his hand . . .

One flick of a switch and Eternity.

One little flick and peace.

He squinted up at the cop, his face lost for a moment in the dazzle of the stage lights.

There was no harm in killing a few cops for the greater good of mankind. It would not cloud his crowning achievement. He finally found the strength to spit out a cupful.

Triumphant again, he grinned up at the cop.

'Your timing is lousy,' the Old Cripple rasped.

He pulled the . . .

'*Au contraire*, Cripple-features,' said Gavril Popov, and blew the top of Mohammed Salameh's head all over the stage.

55

They were about half a mile from the Old Cripple's mansion, hearts racing, when a Coke lorry pulled out of a gas station a little ahead of them and seemed to stall as it crossed into the opposite lane, blocking the road. Stirling pulled the convoy to a halt and gave a quick blast of his siren. The driver climbed quickly down from his cab and darted away between two houses. Moments later the cab window cracked suddenly and a lick of flame darted out.

Morton, used to explosions, let out a shout and began to wave the Magnificent Thirty-six back. They hit reverse. They'd made only about twenty yards on screeching tyres when the Coke lorry blew.

Had it been a chemicals truck or a gasoline jugger, the whole area would have been devastated. But it was Coke and it just put the fire out itself and added a little life to the surrounding gardens. It also left the shell of a smouldering truck sitting like a burst boil in the middle of the road.

Stirling climbed out of his car to survey the damage as Morton hurried up. 'I think we can take it that they're on to us,' Stirling said.

Morton shrugged helplessly. 'This is the only direct road to the mansion, isn't it?'

Stirling nodded. 'They've been tipped off.'

Behind him Madeline scrambled down off the pick-up truck to film the scene of soft-drink devastation.

'It means if we go ahead with this, it's one big step closer to being a suicide mission.'

Stirling rubbed at his brow. Morton was right. But it was too late to back down now. It couldn't just fizzle out with a fire bomb in a Coke lorry. It would be like orbiting the Moon, but not landing.

'Mark, listen . . .'

'I know what you're saying, but we can't just . . .'

'No ... Mark, *listen* ...'

Morton touched his ear. Stirling turned towards the steaming vehicle. 'I don't ...'

'Shhhhh,' said Morton.

And then he heard it.

The unmistakable sound of gunfire.

'Hey, Mr Policeman, how much you reckon, two million, three million; good night's work yeah?'

Gavril Popov stood at the entrance to the mansion while his *faux* police officers hurried out with bin bags full of cash and jewellery. Then came the women. Beautifully attired hookers clip-clipping down the steps in single file with military precision. Corrigan, hands on head, nodded despairingly at Popov. He moved his hand down to look at his watch. 10.30. Lelewala was heading for the river. The Falls. She was going over. Of that he was certain.

And he was standing with his hands on his head like an arse, doing nothing.

Hands on his head and a gun in his sock.

Doing nothing.

Shite.

Stirling was his only hope of relief, and he wasn't coming. He'd been arrested. Or he'd been taking the piss the whole time.

A gun in his sock which he had to use *now*, or Lelewala would die.

'Popov,' he said, 'I have to ...'

'Shushshushshush,' said Popov, his golden smile glistening off the floodlights, 'you want to know why I therefore do all this. OK. Not for me drug skuldiggery. Stick up the hands and give me your money. As the brothers of my profession have done for all time. Gentlemen bandits, my friend. I suspect Old Cripple not one to trust banks, I suspect right. The others, plenty cash to pay for my women ... Jesus yes, I got that franchise too. All my girls.' He patted one of them in passing and she smiled lovingly back.

'Except one,' Corrigan said, 'your wife.' He stepped forward. A guard stepped forward with him, with a gun. Popov shook his head. Corrigan got spit-close. 'Please let me save her. She's going to throw herself in the river.'

Popov's eyes met his. Corrigan searched for some sign of

sympathy or regret. But there was none. 'So,' Popov said, 'it getting to be a habit. I think she likes it.'

'Popov – please, I have to go after her.'

'I think no way.'

He reached out for Popov's lapels, but the guard struck him on the side of the head with the butt of his pistol and Corrigan rocked to one side. A little trickle of blood raced down his cheek.

He staggered back. 'C'mon! Look, for Jesus . . . look, look . . . if I tell you something really important . . .'

Popov's eyes twinkled. 'I know what you say. Your men are coming here. Me, I'm not so bad, in the world order of big rankings, no way. We lock the doors, wait for your boys to come, put these men's asses in stir long time . . .'

'No . . . Jesus, no . . . there's a bomb, a fucking bomb in there . . . the Old Cripple was going to blow the whole fucking place up . . .'

'Yeah yeah, sure, like I think that doesn't make sense.'

One of his cops locked the mansion doors, then hurried down the steps and handed a key to Popov. Popov held it in his hand for several moments, then tossed it up in the air and caught it. 'Here is the key to the front door. I sure there are a hundred other ways out, but right now they're all scared as shit in there and won't move a goddamn mollusc. I give you the choice of waiting here with them and stealing all the credit for it, or running after silly-head the wife. Up to you, good cop.' He handed Corrigan the key. 'It up to you,' he said.

He nodded once, then signalled for his men to follow him. They had already reversed and readied a convoy of stolen limousines, and now the hookers were busy jamming themselves into the vehicles. Popov strode across the pink gravelled pathway and climbed into his police car, a car Corrigan now saw was one of his own, stolen several months before, but never recovered.

One of Popov's stragglers came running across the drive, signalling frantically. Corrigan turned and saw the reason for his panic. Coming out of the trees that lay along the perimeter wall and fanning out across the immaculate lawns were soldiers. Soldiers with guns. There seemed to be hundreds of them, but there might only have been thirty. They were advancing slowly, professionally, or as professional soldiers might have during the Franco-Prussian wars, with scant regard for cover or camouflage. And running in front of them a lunatic lady with a video camera, and coming behind two cops and a seventy-year-old head-the-ball struggling to keep up and dropping his rifle every few yards.

Stirling.

The Magnificent Seven plus.

Popov, unfazed, took a moment to appreciate the spectacle, then winked back at Corrigan. Then, with a fancy hand signal, like he was leading the Seventh Cavalry into battle, his vastly expanded convoy started to move down the twisting driveway and away from the Old Cripple's mansion.

Lelewala.

She had a ten-minute start. At least.

How far could a barefoot deranged woman run in ten minutes?

Did she have the homing instinct of a pigeon, or would she have to stop and ask directions?

And would she ask them in Tuscorora or Georgian?

A watery grave or David Hasselhoff?

Corrigan raced across the car park. They had not taken all of the vehicles. There was a Porsche. With the keys in the ignition, of course, because the Old Cripple's mansion was the safest place in the world. He roared it into life and down the driveway, through the trees, past the smoking guardhouse by the shattered gates, and sped out on to the road leading to Niagara Falls.

56

It was a huge river, but there was only one place she would go. Above the Falls, immediately above the Falls. Eyes turned as he raced through the town; he hammered the horn for extra results, chasing the night's last straggling tourists off the road. Past the House of Frankenstein, down Clifton Hill, on to the Parkway, ahead of him the Falls.

The lights were out. The night's entertainment was over. The *Maid of the Mist* was tied up. There was only the roar of the great Niagara.

Now, in the darkness, he could see what the Indians had feared. The white foam like a poisonous serpent bite, the body of the mighty snake twisting behind, the cacophony of the water more ominous than any massed tribal drumming.

He was drawing level with the Falls. Up ahead, above them, he could see a figure perched on a wall. Standing, *leaning*. The long hair. It was Lelewala. He . . .

There was a sudden bang and the vehicle swerved violently to one side. Corrigan fought to control it, but he was going too fast, he was up the kerb and flying. The car smashed into the wall that ran along the edge of the Niagara. The wheels buckled beneath him. Corrigan's head cracked off the window and he didn't know where the hell he was for a moment. He held his head and tried to still everything. Then he fumbled for the door handle and pushed; it fell open with a loud screech.

Corrigan rolled out on to the sidewalk. He got to his knees. He looked at the ruined front of the car. Then at the tyres. Flat. With two arrows sticking out of each of them.

Corrigan turned. In a line across the road, between him and Lelewala, the False Faces. With bows drawn and pointed at him. And at the front the man who needed no False Face, Tarriha.

Corrigan got shakily to his feet. There was blood streaming out of a gash in his brow. Barely twenty yards away, Lelewala stood above the Niagara, staring into its blackness.

'She must do this,' Tarriha said.

'Don't be daft,' Corrigan gasped.

'She must! It is the only way the great evil will be destroyed.'

'What evil? For Christsake, Tarriha, you can't just let her . . .'

'The *evil*. The drugs.'

'It's over, Tarriha! The Old Cripple is dead. They're all under arrest. Now come on . . .'

Corrigan lurched forward. There was a stretching of bows. He stopped. 'Tarriha . . . please . . .'

'Arrests? What good are arrests? *If* they go to prison they will be out in a few years. You don't send evil to prison, you destroy it . . .'

'Oh for Jesus's sake . . .' He looked desperately up the wall to Lelewala. She was edging even closer. 'Stand back!' Corrigan yelled. 'Lela! Please! Gretchin! Please! It's just a nightmare!' If she heard, she did not respond. Corrigan turned despairingly to Tarriha. 'What good is this going to do? She's going to die, for nothing! Don't let her waste her life on some crazy superstition. Please! Just let me talk to her!'

'She must die, so that others might live. It is written.'

'Where's it written?' Corrigan yelled. 'In a big fucking fairy book? C'mon!'

'It is written.'

'Well fuck you! I'm going to talk to her.'

He brushed past Tarriha and pushed his way through the line of False Faces. She was on the edge, leaning out. He hurried towards . . .

An arrow skittered off the ground beside him. He did not stop.

Then an arrow ploughed into his leg. He fell silently to one knee.

The Falls thundered.

Then, slowly, he began to rise. He stood for a moment, then continued his walk towards Lelewala, dragging his arrowed leg after him.

The False Faces drew back their bows, ready to finish him. For a second there was only the roar of the Niagara and the beat of his heart; he did not look back, did not see the old Indian's hand rise, did not see the bows drop.

He limped on.

'Lelewala!' he called.

There was no response. The river was too loud. He wanted to dive at her, wrap his arms around her and pull her back from the precipice. But it wouldn't work. She would go over. He had to talk to her. He had to snap her out of it.

'Lelewala!' He was right beside her now. He sat on the wall. She was above him. Wincing at his pierced leg, he clambered up on to the wall beside her. She turned confused eyes to him.

'Sahonwadi . . .' she said half-dreamily.

'No . . . no! Frank . . . Frank Corrigan . . . c'mon . . . Gretchin . . . it's Gretchin . . . just come to me . . . please just come back from the . . .'

She wiped at her face. The spit of the Niagara, the tears of her confused mind.

'Corrigan . . .' she said vaguely, 'I must . . .'

'No! You mustn't! There is no evil! It is gone . . .'

She shook her head. 'It isn't gone, it will only go if I . . .' She leaned forward.

'No!'

He put out his hand. 'Gretchin . . . please . . . don't . . . you're going to Hollywood . . . you're going to make movies . . . David Hasselhoff . . .'

The slightest smile stroked her face. Her head moved to one side. There was a sudden clarity in her eyes. For a second she held his gaze.

Then she jumped.

She was gone.

Swallowed.

'Noooooo!'

Corrigan stood for the briefest of moments. He glanced back at Tarriha. The old Indian's hand was raised in salute. Corrigan nodded. He was a policeman. It was what policemen did.

He jumped after her.

Jimmy Morton hurried down the steps outside the mansion. Elation glowed like radioactivity on his face. 'Like a prisoner-of-war camp in there, Mark.' He rubbed his hands together. 'I knew we could do it.'

'Yeah,' said Stirling. He was sitting on the top step. They'd been inside for a preliminary look. A look at the disbelieving faces. They were fighting among themselves. They'd hardly flinched at the Old Cripple losing his head, but they had not taken well to surrendering their wallets and their expensive jewellery to Popov's men, and they had certainly not taken well to real cops arriving and treating them like the dirt they were.

Now they were locked in. There was no way out. Stirling was going to let them sweat for a while, especially Chief of Police Dunbar, grovelling and threatening in the same mouthful. Madeline had it all on tape. She was about to conduct an interview with Stirling with the mansion in the background. Then he would call in reinforcements from St Catharines. Hell, from Toronto as well. The *Maid of the Mist* crewmen were swaggering about the car park, giving high-fives and complicated masonic handshakes, firing bullets into the air. It had gone like a dream. Nobody injured, nobody killed. Sure, some had escaped, bouncers in smart suits scampering across the grounds like frightened rabbits, and sure, they hadn't searched half the building yet, but that could wait. They were in control.

They were heroes.

Even the seventy-year-old, coming up to him now with a grin so wide his false teeth threatened to slip out. 'Wasn't it great!'

Stirling nodded. Morton nodded. They didn't know what to say to him.

Yes, they were heroes.

But there was a feeling of . . .

'Anti-climax?' Maynard said, pulling off his balaclava.

Stirling shrugged. 'We expected a gun battle. To get shot, or die. But they were locked up waiting for us.'

'So what?' Morton said. 'We have them. We *have them*. We got the bad guys.'

Stirling smiled. 'I suppose it makes a change for you.'

Behind them Stirling's police radio crackled. 'All cars, report of a suicide attempt at Niagara Falls. One woman, one man, man identified as suspect Frank Corrigan.'

'Jesus Christ,' said Stirling. He turned and raced across to his car.

'Jesus Christ,' said Maynard, and raced after him.

'Do you want me to wait . . .' Morton began, and Stirling and Maynard shouted back together, 'Yes!'

In moments the police car was spitting up gravel.

Morton shook his head. Beside him the seventy-year-old said: 'Maybe I should have gone along with them. I gotta taste for this now.'

Morton smiled. The old guy was juggling something in his hand. Batteries for his pacemaker, maybe. 'What you got there?' Morton asked. 'Souvenir?'

'Aw, shit,' the old guy said sheepishly, 'hope you don't mind.' He opened his hand, raised it up. A small black rectangular box sat in his palm. There was a switch on top. 'It was up on the stage, beside the dead feller. I think it has something to do with all that musical equipment, y'know? My grandson, he's into Pongo and all that shit; I thought . . .'

Morton took the box out of his hand. He turned it over, examined the blank underside, then flipped it back. 'Looks harmless enough,' he said. 'Wonder what it does?'

He flicked the switch.

The great Niagara roared.

The False Faces stood along the wall, peering into the dark waters.

Suddenly there was a sound that for a brief moment eclipsed that of the Falls. They turned and looked to the skies above the town and saw a finger of fire shooting up into the starry night.

'It is done,' Tarriha said.

EPILOGUE

Frank Corrigan stood among the ruins of the mansion. The snow that had prevented them coming out here for most of the morning had now tailed off. He stood with his head bent back, looking at the grey clouds peeking through the holes in the ceiling. He shook his head slowly. Then he took out a cigarette and lit it, cupping his hands around the match, drawing the poison in slowly.

'Now look a little to the left,' Madeline called.

He looked to the left. At the remains of the auditorium where Mohammed Salameh had hosted the convention, and where he had been murdered.

'Now pan round to the right,' Madeline shouted.

He turned slowly, trying not to look at the camera. He took in the ploughed-up lawn, covered in snow but speckled by spikes of burned and broken furniture.

'Now, slowly, Frank, look down ... you notice something ... you bend to retrieve it ...'

He bent, he lifted it, he wiped the dirt and ash from it, the dirt and ash the crew had applied not fifteen minutes before. It was one of Pongo's platinum discs. Not the *Lelewala Cycle*, of course. Where was that now? Number one in a dozen countries.

Poor Pongo. Only his tapes had survived, packed away in metal containers and loaded into a limo ready for his escape. Pongo had been found in the front seat, cut to pieces by flying glass. The tapes had been given a dance mix by a top New York producer and a suitably morbid video of Pongo had been put together, and the combination had sent the single and album straight to number one. If he hadn't been dead, Pongo would have been ecstatic.

Corrigan dropped the disc back into the rubble.

'OK,' Madeline called, 'that'll do us here.'

The cameraman dropped his equipment from his shoulder.

Madeline hurried across the debris and hooked her arm through Corrigan's. 'You all right?'

Corrigan nodded.

'OK,' she said, 'just a few more shots down by the Falls, and that's us, OK?'

'OK,' he said. She unhooked her arm. He pulled at the sleeve of his uniform. 'I shouldn't even be in this,' he said.

'Hey, relax, they're not going to arrest you.'

He smiled. They *had* arrested him. They were going to throw the book at him, the biggest book they could find, a hardback with studs in the cover. But the public outcry had been too great. He was released. He was given a medal. And then they asked him, quietly, to leave. Yes, he was a hero, but they had no place for heroes.

And he did. He had no choice, really. There was a book deal, there were the calls from Hollywood. He'd flown out. The movie was being made. He'd tried to ask for script approval, but he'd already signed the contract, and that was that. He had no idea how it would turn out. It didn't much matter. He had enough money now. Internal Affairs was still making a claim on the money that had been paid into his bank account for the house, but it wasn't his fault if somebody wanted to pay over the odds and then disappear off the face of the earth. He'd hold on to it until somebody came forward. Internal Affairs were just pissed off because in all the excitement two of their top officers had been left languishing in a car boot for three days *after* the explosion at the Old Cripple's mansion and had needed emergency hospital treatment.

He missed work. He still called by the station the odd time, but he knew it made everyone feel uncomfortable, especially Stirling. He ran the place, and he ran it different. He was a stickler for paperwork and doing things by the book, even though he wouldn't have been where he was now if Corrigan had been a stickler for the same things.

Madeline drove them along the Parkway. There weren't so many tourists about in the winter season, but to his eyes the Falls looked even more beautiful at this time of year. Cold and austere and frightening, like a governess in an old novel. They parked the car and he stood by the wall while Madeline discussed what was required with the cameraman. The documentary was due to air on her station the following week. Discussions were ongoing with one of the big networks across the border. Madeline was expecting big things from it. She was pretty and petite and charming, yet bolshie too. He liked that. They'd gone out for dinner a few times in the six months since he'd been dragged out of the Niagara, more dead than alive, but there'd been no spark. She was bound for bigger things and he couldn't see himself leaving Niagara. It was home. He had enough money now, but he'd probably start looking around for a job soon. Something in security, maybe. Something at the casino.

'OK, Frank, if you can just look out over the Falls for us,' Madeline said. 'Just look lost in thought. Not *that* lost. You look like you're going to fall asleep. Open those eyes a bit, think of Lelewala.'

He thought of Lelewala.

She was down there.

Why he had survived and she hadn't, he would never know.

Luck.

Her body had not yet surfaced.

It might never.

Some fish might be using it for a bungalow.

He didn't like to think about it, but always would.

He felt a tear coming to his eye.

There was a sharp intake of breath from Madeline. She'd seen it. She let the camera hold on him for a moment, then said *Cut*. She turned immediately to check if they'd captured the tear clearly.

She came to him, smiling. 'That was great, Frank, really great.' She reached up and wiped it from his eye.

He smiled and turned away. The old Indian, Tarriha, had said she would never be found, because she had been claimed back by the spirits. Corrigan thought that was pish, and told him so. Tarriha was taking part in the documentary too, although he was still haggling over a price. He had faded a lot in the past few months and the perceived wisdom of the elders of the Tuscorora Iroquois was that it wouldn't be too long before he too was claimed back by the spirits.

When they were certain they had everything, Madeline and her cameraman climbed into their car. He turned down a lift. She wound down the window and smiled at him and promised to call him about going out for another drink or a meal, but he knew that she wouldn't, and he didn't mind. He stood with his arms folded in front of him, leaning on the wall, watching them drive away.

A tourist stopped and asked if he could take a photograph. Corrigan straightened, pulled his shoulders back and tried to look heroic.

'No,' the tourist said, 'will you take one of me against the Falls?'

Corrigan grinned stupidly and reached for the camera. He took the snap and wished the tourist a happy vacation.

A child's voice turned him back towards the town. Little Aimie was running towards him through the snow. She was screaming and laughing. He smiled widely, bent and opened his arms to her. She put a snowball in his mouth, with some considerable force. He started to cough, he slumped to his knees, and then rolled over. Aimie thumped him in the stomach and he coughed and jumped to his feet and picked her up and nearly threw her into the Falls.

'Easy now,' the woman said.

Corrigan put his daughter down and ruffled her hair. Annie Spitz stood smiling before him. Here there *was* a spark. Quite a big one. They'd got to know one another quite well since he'd been visiting the women's refuge to see Aimie. The court still hadn't granted him custody. Annie didn't mind how much he visited.

She took his arm and they began to walk beside the wall back towards town.

'She still gets to you, doesn't she? Lelewala.'

Corrigan shrugged. 'Her heart was in the right place. But her brain wasn't.'

'Could I be tempted to say the same about you, Frank?'

Corrigan smiled. He guided Aimie across the road. He had tried to dress up her mother's death as best he could, all that stuff about going on vacation to meet God and having such a swell time that it would be mean to make her come home, but she'd just muttered something about *not what I heard on the radio* and then asked if she could go and see the grave. So they went, and they cried.

As they reached the foot of Clifton Hill, Aimie ran ahead of them into one of the souvenir stores and began picking through the racks of Lelewala t-shirts. Annie went in after her. Corrigan remained outside, finishing his cigarette. Across the road a police car came to a sudden halt and two cops he didn't recognize jumped out and pounced on a young guy. In a moment they had him face down in the snow. They had him cuffed and were reading him his rights before Corrigan could negotiate the traffic. When he did make it across he said: 'What's up, son?'

The cop looked up, ready to bark, then recognized the face. 'You're . . .'

Corrigan nodded. 'What'd the kid do?'

'Aw, the usual, sir. Drugs, man, just gets worse all the time.'

Corrigan nodded and turned back to the souvenir shop.